WEDDINGS AND WITCHCRAFT

MIXING UP MAGIC, BOOK 3

ROSIE PEASE

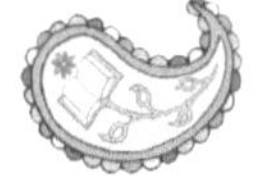

Editor: Paisley Press Books
Proofreader: Jasmine Bryner
Cover Designer: Melony Paradise, Paradise Cover Design

PAISLEY PRESS BOOKS
WEST WARWICK, RHODE ISLAND

For Mom.
Lynb nb n b :-) <3

About This Book

**Wedding bells are ready to ring in Heartwood Hollow...
maybe.**

When a bride-to-be asks me for help with her haunted
"something old," I'm is thrust into a bitter family dispute. The
key to solving the decades-old mystery behind it is helping
the trapped ghost. If only she could remember who
killed her.

The more I dig, the more it becomes evident that not
everyone is happy about the upcoming union. There are those
who don't want the truth revealed, and they aren't afraid to go
after my bakery to keep it hidden.

With my livelihood threatened, the couple's impending
nuptials on the rocks, and a possible murderer on the loose, I
must decide if I can be a baker and a witch or if it's time to
hang up one of my hats.

Weddings and Witchcraft is the third full novel in the Mixing
Up Magic series. It is best enjoyed after reading *Scones and
Spells*.

AUTHOR'S NOTE

Dear Reader,

Thank you so much for picking *Weddings and Witchcraft* as your next read. This is my favorite book out of the series so far, and I hope your dive into the world of Heartwood Hollow is an enjoyable one.

I love hearing from readers. If you'd like to reach out to me, you can do so across social media @WriteRosiePease.

Happy reading!

Cheers,

Rosie

<h1 style="text-align:center">CHAPTER 1</h1>

Early summer in Heartwood Hollow was one of my favorite times of the year. Everything was in bloom, the weather was finally warm day and night, and the kids were out of school. This, in addition to the influx of tourists, made Main Street a much busier place than it was at other times. I loved it.

However, it also proved problematic when trying to figure out where to hold meetings in town for paranormal residents who didn't want everyone to know what they were.

For the first meeting, we'd met at Leafs and Grounds in the back room. Gary, a dryad, let us use the space because he could ensure some privacy from his customers there thanks to a heavy curtain he used to block off the space during open mic nights. Although we'd picked a slow night and there were no incidents with non-paranormal customers, not everyone had felt comfortable in the small, shared space.

When he heard about our predicament, Lily's human boyfriend, John Singer, offered the use of his business. Situated off Main Street, once Singer Furniture was closed for the day, the location was private, and there was no need to come up with an excuse for why we were booking a place.

John's business would make for a good temporary location, but we'd have to find a real meeting space eventually. I'd already been thinking about the town's need for an event space for receptions and showers, but the PSG meetings cemented the need all the more.

Steph let out a happy sigh as we walked out of the Singer Furniture showroom with Lily, Alex, and Chelsea. "That was a great turnout."

Lily turned away from us to lock the door. "It really was," she said when she faced our direction once more. "It was good to see more than the dryads this time."

Chelsea furrowed her brow. "Hey, I was there last month. But I was, what, one of three who couldn't turn into a tree, Joanie and my mom included. I'm glad I convinced some more of my family to come."

Steph nodded. "The wording of the ad was better this time too. I had more time to think about what I wanted to write."

Lily hmmed her agreement. "I thought it was clever."

We reached the parking lot and stopped at Steph's car to say our goodbyes to her and Alex. Lily's car was next. Then Chelsea's.

Chelsea opened the driver's side door of her car. "I'll see you at the party this weekend, right?" She asked in her light lilting accent.

"I'll be there to drop off the cake."

Chelsea slid into her seat. "Great. See you then."

Chelsea moved a few things on the table so I could put down the boxes of cookies, cake pops, and brownies I was carrying.

We said a quick hello, then I hurried back out the door of her parents' house. I still had to get the cake for Chelsea's niece out of my station wagon.

"Joanie, this looks amazing. Annabel is going to love it," Chelsea said when I returned.

"I'm so glad, but I have to admit I was surprised she was going with a mermaid theme since your wedding is coming up soon and is similarly themed."

"Well, they are a little different. Ours is more mature than the cartoony depictions that you'll see here, but Annabel has been obsessed since learning that she's a merrow."

"A merrow? That's like a mermaid, right? Can you tell me what the difference is?" I'd recently learned that Heartwood Hollow was home to more than just the several ghosts who lived there, and me, a reluctant witch who could see them all. It all started with learning that dryads, tree people, were real, but it didn't end there. Fairies, naiads, trolls—all of them were real, and many lived in town. I was beginning to wonder how many actual humans we had here after the attendance at the second paranormal support group meeting had doubled the size of the first one. And I knew there were still more. Many who had told me they were paranormal in the days surrounding the Love a Tree Day Festival had yet to come to a meeting.

"Yes, very similar, although we have ties to Ireland, and mermaids do not."

"And that would explain the accent your family has."

"It does. And why there's a lot of green in my wedding too, not just the blues you'd expect in an underwater cele-bration."

"Wait, it's not actually underwater, is it? I'll need to rethink everything if—"

Chelsea burst into laughter. "No, no. But it will feel like it in the hall we rented down in Snowhaven. Have you seen it?"

I nodded. Since Heartwood Hollow didn't have its own event hall, I was familiar with the city's various event spaces. "I've been several times. Never once is it the same."

A child's squeal from behind us interrupted our conversation. "I love it!"

The young girl wearing a long bright-red wig and a fish tail over her party dress came running up to me. "Thank you, thank you, thank you!"

Her friends soon followed, all admiring the cake. Some reached out for the purple and teal starfish-shaped cookies Lily had cut out and decorated earlier that morning.

Chelsea called out over the giggling, "Not yet, girls, we haven't even had our lunch yet!"

Annabel ran from the room into the kitchen and out the back door. "Follow me!"

All but one of her friends did.

"Hi, Joanie!"

I looked down to see Ivy smiling up at me, decked out in a long blond wig, a pink fish tail over her khaki shorts, floral top, and a fake shell bra over that.

"Hey, Ivy! Are you having fun?"

She nodded big and slow. "But I'm really looking forward to the cookies."

"I bet. Okay, go have fun. You don't want to miss out on any of the games they have going on."

That sent her off after her friends.

"Bye, Joanie!" she chirped over her shoulder.

Chelsea turned to me. "You are staying, aren't you? My family would love to have you here. Mom's taken a liking to you through her interactions with you in the PSG."

I let out a slight chuckle. "Yes, I am. I'm doubling as Ivy's adult to save Ken from all of this. Sam and Sarah are running the shop this afternoon, so I have a few hours to hang out with you all."

"Oh good, because I want to talk to you after about something. It's wedding related."

"Is everything okay? It's nothing with the cake, right?

"Oh, no. no. The cake is perfect."

"Okay, good. There's still some time to change things. If you need to, just let me know. You're still a few weeks away until the big day."

She smiled. "Thanks, Joanie, but no, that won't be necessary."

Chelsea's mom, Pam, clapped her hands to get everyone's attention in the living room and kitchen. "Lunch is ready in the backyard. Please come join us."

A small group of women got up and passed Chelsea, giving her what I'd call major side-eye. If I knew who they were or had even seen them before, I would have assumed the look was for me. Four plus years in Heartwood Hollow and many in town thought I was a witch.

Of course, I'd recently admitted that to myself and anyone else going to the PSG meetings that I actually was a witch. I was still getting used to the knowledge that I could put spells into my baked goods and had been doing it all along without realizing it. Good luck muffins for test takers at the high school, cookies for confidence before job interviews, motion sickness scones for pregnancy symptoms. I could do all of that and more.

Somehow, my being a witch still left me as an oddity within the paranormal community. I was the only witch, the only one who could see ghosts, and the only matchmaker in the town. No one else could do any one of those things, let alone all three together. No one I knew of, anyway.

I turned back to Chelsea, half of one of my first matched couples that I'd made upon coming to Heartwood Hollow over four years ago. The ladies had nearly made it halfway through the kitchen, so I felt safe asking, "Who are they?"

She sighed hard. "Some of David's extended family."

"They didn't seem very happy to see you."

"Probably because they aren't. They don't like me very much."

That surprised me. "Don't like you? How could anyone not like you?"

She shrugged. "Well, perhaps they would if they gave me a chance, but they won't because I'm a merrow."

"How do they even know if they aren't from here?"

"They used to be. All of them. They grew up with my great-aunt, who they had been friends with until she broke up with their brother. They blame her for his death, though I have no idea why. From what I heard, he wasn't even here when it happened." Chelsea shrugged. "Then she was killed two days after his funeral."

I placed my hand to my chest. "Oh my goodness, I'm so sorry."

She shrugged, but I knew it bothered her. "It happened decades ago, but from the stories I've heard, I think I would have loved her."

"I'm sure you would have." Chelsea was one of the kindest and most accepting people in Heartwood Hollow. I was so glad to see her show up at the first PSG meeting. It was part of what made her and David go so well together. He was affable and caring, especially toward animals.

"So why did you invite them if they don't like you?"

"They're all invited to the wedding. They're his family.

Mom was hoping to make this kind of like a peace offering or a warming-up session." The door banged shut, and Chelsea looked toward it. "We should head outside, but let's talk when the party is over, okay?"

I nodded and followed her to the backyard.

Two hours later, the party was winding down. We'd had a lovely spread of finger sandwiches and tea, provided by Libby from Riverview Inn. The kids had played mermaids in the pool, run around, and then gorged themselves on sea-salt caramel cookies, brownies, and a birthday cake fit for a mermaid princess. Upon eating the cookies, Chelsea's dad, Anthony, told me to add them to the order for the wedding. They'd become additional favors for all the guests.

Parents were starting to leave with their kids when Ken arrived to pick up Ivy.

"Thank you," he said with a quick kiss on the cheek. We'd been a strong unit since coming together to help the north woods and the dryads who had once called it home.

Knowing he'd not want to hang around with all the moms who probably still called him "hot doc"—I doubted he'd ever lose the nickname despite not being a doctor—I'd offered to hang out at the party to keep an eye on Ivy. She'd come a long way from the girl who had been so nervous about her first sleepover that she'd made herself sick and couldn't go. She had lots of friends, and now that it was summer, she was always at someone's house or sleeping over somewhere on the weekend.

He looked at me with a hopeful expression. "Are you coming with us?"

"I'll meet up with you in a bit. I'm going to check in at the bakery, but I'll see you both tonight."

"Sounds good." He kissed me again before turning to his daughter several feet away. "Ready, kiddo?"

"Okay, Daddy." She skipped over to him after waving bye to Annabel and a few other kids who hadn't left yet. "Bye, Joanie!"

Turning around, I caught sight of Chelsea. She made eye contact with me and ticked her head up to the back door.

CHAPTER 2

Inside the house, Chelsea presented me with a tiara. The sides were lined with pearls and spiraled shells except for the teeth at each end that stuck into one's hair to secure it in place. The central decorative portion was encrusted with scallop shells, sea stars, and small jewels. At the center was a sand dollar from which three tube-like things were attached to the back, poking out from the top.

"Oh, this is lovely," I said as I admired the piece. I pointed to the tube-like things. "What are these?"

"Those are sea urchin quills, bleached in the sun. This particular kind would normally be a dark-brown color."

I gently ran my finger over one of them and down to the sand dollar. That's all it took for me to figure out why Chelsea had wished to speak with me.

"It's haunted by my great-aunt," she continued, confirming what I already knew. "The one I mentioned earlier. Is there anything you can do? I would love to wear this for the wedding, but I don't think I want her in there when I do. What if some of his family can sense her? I don't want anything to go wrong that day, and if they didn't like her then, I don't want it to affect now."

I knew all too well how a haunted object affected the present. This was the third time I'd come across something like this in as many months. This was becoming a pattern and a much bigger issue than I had previously thought.

"How could you tell it was haunted?"

"Oh, I can't, but that's what I've been told. Ever since my great-aunt died, it has a way of turning up for family events, so Mom wasn't surprised when it made an appearance the day I went shopping for my wedding dress." She sighed dreamily. "And it goes so perfectly with the dress I found, and I didn't even see the tiara until after I'd picked it out. Don't you see? It was meant to be."

Chelsea placed her hand on the ornate tiara, firmly pressing it into my hands, which were already holding it. Her anxiety about the situation was almost palpable.

"Do you think you can help?" she asked. "Please say yes. You're the only one who I think can. Is there a witchy spell you can cast or something?" She bit her lower lip as she looked at me, her eyebrows pinched with concern.

I smiled at her as the tiara's energy coursed through me. That was a new sensation. "I will do my best." From her comment about casting a witchy spell, I assumed she hadn't heard that I'd done this twice already. And although there had been two meetings of the paranormal support group already, I hadn't revealed my abilities included seeing ghosts. One thing at a time.

She clasped her hands together. "Thank you so much. You have no idea what this means to me."

At that moment, David walked through the front door. His face lit up upon seeing Chelsea.

"Excuse me." She rushed over to him and then threw her arms around him.

He nodded over her shoulder at me as I gave him a small wave before turning to give them some privacy.

At that moment, Pam walked inside carrying a few trays of food.

"Can I help with the cleanup?" I asked.

"Oh sure, sure. That would be lovely. And you're just the person to tell me how to best wrap all this up so it's still good tomorrow." Pam set the trays down on the kitchen counter. Then she glanced down and saw the tiara in my hand. "She got you to agree to help, I take it?"

"She did. I'll do what I can." Then I sent Pam off for some plastic containers.

"Thank you for that," David said from behind me. "Anything to help the day go by smoother with my family."

Pam returned with several containers, so I set the tiara down on the table and began gathering up the remaining cookies. David stepped forward to help.

"Are they all against you two marrying one another?"

"Not all of them. My parents have come around over the years, my grandma too, but everyone else? They're doing what they can to break us up."

"Why? Chelsea's great."

"I agree. I'm sure she's told you that they don't approve of her being a merrow."

Pam handed me a container, now matched to a lid that was underneath it.

I placed the cookies into it. "Well, she can hardly change what she is. She told me about her great-aunt too."

"Yes, there is that, which I think most of this stems from. We're all from the sea. We're supposed to get along, but ever since the incident, most of my family think mermaids of all kinds are bad. But merrows are the worst."

"Of the sea? You mean you're a . . . merman?" He hadn't come to either of the paranormal support group meetings.

He laughed, throwing his head back. "No, I'm not. I'm a selkie."

"That's the seal, right?"

"Yes. Can't you tell?" He poked at the non-existent pudge of his stomach. "I'm a seal when I wear my skin in the water."

Chelsea handed him a slice of cake from one of the trays. "Leftovers. You have to try it."

"And if you keep feeding me like this, I really will be a seal on dry land," he joked as he dipped his fork into the cake.

Conversation paused as David took a bite, Chelsea seeming anxious to see his reaction.

"Oh, wow," he said. "Can we add this to our flavors? How had we missed this before?"

"I certainly can." I passed another container, this time of cake pops, to Pam. "You only chose two out of your three flavors."

David shoved another forkful of cake into his mouth. "So good."

Pam waved me over to the remaining section of cake, and I showed her how to use plastic wrap draped on top and pressed into the cut portion to keep it fresh.

"Genius!" she said. "I've been leaving the cut ends exposed for years under there. Thank you for everything today. For this and for helping Chelsea. It means so much to her."

"It's no problem, really, and I'm sure it will be a big help to your mom, too, when it's all over. I hope you don't mind, but could I stop by sometime to learn more about your aunt and see some photos?"

"Absolutely. Mom will have most of them. She's already left, but I'll give her a call later and get back to you."

"Perfect."

CHAPTER 3

I pushed open the front door to Suncraft Bakery and stepped inside. My business for over four years, I'd rarely used the front door, usually opting to come in through the kitchen, especially first thing in the morning when I arrived with my team to do the baking for the day. I stood at the entrance, taking the sight of the bakery in.

The yellow interior with pink and purple decorations was cheery, and I'd recently added a few new elements to the shop —a couple of tables and chairs for customers to stay and eat. In addition, they could bring their own drinks here to enjoy with their treats. Most came with to-go cups from the coffee shop. Although I could boil water and make tea, nothing I could do would be able to compete with what they made over at Leafs and Grounds. They were the masters at all the fancy beverages. Even if I was good at making those sorts of drinks, I wouldn't want to step on Gary's toes. But maybe I could talk to Libby about offering tea here on occasion. Once I attended one of her teas at the inn again first, that is.

Sam looked up from the pastry cabinet where he was consolidating the unsold items onto a single tray so the rest could be washed and made ready for tomorrow's baked goods. "Hi, Joanie. How was the party?"

"It was good, thanks."

Before I could say anything else, Sarah stepped in from the kitchen, a broom and dustpan in hand, ready for the end-of-day cleaning routine. "You didn't need to come in. We've got this." Her confident smile assured me of this fact.

"I know, but I wanted to say hi and to thank you both again for covering for me this afternoon. Besides, I had to return the cake stand." I held up the tote bag in my hand, then turned back to Sam. "A lot of the little girls loved the graham cracker sand you applied to the bottom layer and mixed in with the icing between layers."

He beamed and deservedly so. I was proud of him for the idea. Sam was working for me full time this summer, splitting his time between the bakery's kitchen and shop. His time here was winding down, and I wanted him to get as much experience before he left. In a little over two months, he'd be at culinary school. I had no doubt he'd do well there.

"Thanks! I can't take all the credit, though. I saw it on a TV show," he admitted.

"But you applied it well and made your customers happy, so be proud of your accomplishments." I crossed the room toward the kitchen door, practically trading places with Sarah as she walked toward the entrance to start sweeping.

Sam nodded, then placed another tray on top of the stack. He scooted down to consolidate the few cookies and cupcakes that were left in that case. All the scones were gone and likely had been since lunchtime. Even though I couldn't sell the pineapple and bacon scones that I'd sold at the Love a Tree Day Festival, my other scones had become the most popular baked goods in the shop.

I entered the kitchen, letting the door swing closed behind

me, as I pulled the cake stand out of the tote bag I'd been holding. I set it with the other things that needed to be washed in the sink, then stowed my bag in the closet before returning to the dishwasher to load up a rack to send through.

A few minutes later, Sarah stepped back in with the dustpan to empty. I stood at the sink, lathering the cake stand with suds, staring at the wall in front of me thinking about what Chelsea had asked me to do.

"Everything okay?" she asked me.

I glanced over at her and tilted my head in question.

"I've been in here twice already, and this is the first time you've noticed me. The floor's done."

Had I been that caught up in my thoughts that I'd tuned out everything around me?

"Thinking about one of my couples," I replied.

"Uh-oh," Sarah started. "It's not Lily and John, or else we'd all know it, and it's not Ashley and Rich. Everything is good between them from what I've heard. Ashley just moved in with him . . . although this would be the time when they'd have problems. It's a totally different animal when you live together as you have to get used to new habits. Take Jill and me for example. We were best friends throughout school, but we almost killed each other a few months into living with one another. We have different ideas of what cleaning up after a meal entails, much of that thanks to you." She gave me a pointed look.

That got a chuckle from me. "No, no. It's nothing to do with them, but I'm glad to hear they're doing well." With school out for the summer, I didn't see them as often as I had been.

She walked over to the trashcan and dumped the dustpan's contents into it. She turned toward the closet where we kept the broom. "So who is it? Have you found a new match?"

I shook my head. "It's Chelsea and David."

Sarah froze in her tracks, leg still in the air. She slowly put it down before cocking her head to the side as she looked at me. "But they're already together. They're getting married in a few weeks."

"I know, but here we are. There's some long-standing grudge between the older generations of their families."

"Oh, I've heard about that." As one of the town's biggest gossips, I didn't doubt that. "But there's something more to it than that. It's something witchy, isn't it?"

I hadn't told Sarah outright that I was a witch, but I'd stopped denying it when she brought the topic up, especially since the paranormal support group started. She'd long believed the rumors about me. Turns out she'd been right the whole time.

"Something like that." I rinsed the cake stand and set it to the side. I'd put it away in the morning once it was dry.

She finally put the broom away. "Well, good luck."

"This one shouldn't be too bad. Although it involves an old murder."

Sarah threw her hands up into the air, stopping me from saying that the case had been solved. "See? I told you. But that's awful. Who?"

"Chelsea's great-aunt."

"Do you know who did it?"

"I didn't want to ask at a kid's birthday party," I said, rinsing the sink clean, and Sarah nodded, "but I'm meeting with Sandra's sister, Nancy, soon to talk a little more about her. I'm sure I'll find out then if not before."

Sarah walked over to me and put her hand on my back between my shoulders. "Well, solved or not, if I've learned anything with your last two couples, it's never as easy as you think it's going to be." She reached under the sink I was standing at, then pulled out the glass cleaner. "I thought I wouldn't have to tell you this after the knife incident, but be careful. This is serious stuff."

"I will."

Sam poked his head into the kitchen. "You get lost back here?"

"Coming!" Sarah scooted back out into the shop, and the door swung closed, leaving me alone with my thoughts once more.

CHAPTER 4

If anyone in town was going to remember what caused the rift between the merrows and the selkies beyond the gossip surrounding Sandra's murder, it was going to be someone at Olde Templeton Diner. Donna Templeton, the owner, made it her business to know everything going on in town, and she and her customers had been immensely helpful with my two other ghostly cases.

After leaving the bakery, I called Ken, offering to pick up burgers for the three of us for tonight. His response was an immediate yes, and he gave me a list of what he and Ivy wanted—two burgers, fries, onion rings, and mozzarella sticks. I had it committed to memory by the time I reached the small stone diner. The building was one of the oldest in town and had been in Donna's family for generations.

"Joanie!" Donna called across the diner as I walked in. "What brings you here? Coffee?"

"Decaf. It's late." Usually by now, I'd be drinking herbal tea so as not to be kept up all night from the black and green teas I drank during the earlier part of the day.

"Coming right up." She spun around to the two coffee pots

on the counter behind her and grabbed the one with the orange top, then pulled a white ceramic mug from their spot. She set the mug down at a seat on the front counter and poured coffee into it as I finished crossing the diner and slid up onto the open stool. "What brings you here at this time of day?"

"Dinner duty." I placed my takeout order with her, adding my usual to what Ken and Ivy had requested.

"You could've called this in," she said, her back to me as she rang the bell by the kitchen window to tell her nephew, the diner's cook, that a new order had come in. "Would have saved you some time."

"Oh, I know, but I wanted to see you too."

"Aww, you know how to flatter an old lady."

"Pish . . . You are not old."

"Old enough. I started getting those retirement flyers in the mail about two years back."

"You? Retire?" I waved at her, dismissing that statement.

"That's what I said." Donna raised her arms up and to her sides. "I could never leave this place. My nephew is going to have to pry the diner key from my cold dead hands."

From the back, a male voice yelled, "I have a key, Auntie!"

Donna threw her head back in laughter. "He's a good boy. He'll do great." A little louder, she added, "When the time is right."

I'd cut it close by getting here when I did. It was late in the day, and the diner closed at five since they didn't have a dinner service. I was the only customer here and probably would be the last one they'd serve.

With no one else to wait on, Donna came around the counter and sat on the stool next to me. I was quite fond of her and didn't want her to think I only came here for information or to drop off muffins in the morning, so we chitchatted a while before I came around to the topic I was here to talk to her about.

"I have a question for you."

"Sure thing." She eyed me, quiet for a moment. "Is this one of your matchmakery things again? Who is it this time?"

"Yes and no," I answered honestly, but I didn't give her names. It wasn't my place to tell her about David's family making things hard for him and Chelsea. "I'm wondering what you might recall about Sandra O'Grady."

She whistled. "Wow, now that is not a name I've heard in a long time. The poor girl was murdered. I was a young teenager then, so I don't have all the details, but I'll spare you the ones I know because it wasn't pretty."

"Did they catch whoever did it?"

"Oh sure, sure. It's not like we have some killer runnin' round here or anything like that. My goodness! Why don't you stop in and wait for Walter and Paul in the morning? They should remember more than I do. They've been getting those retirement flyers I mentioned a lot longer than I have." Her lips curled into a sly grin.

The bell at the kitchen window dinged, and Donna slid off her stool. She bounded between the counters to grab the large brown paper bag.

"There you go. Enjoy." She plopped it in front of me.

"Thanks, Donna. We will. I'll see you in the morning." Taking hold of the bag, I hopped off the stool.

As I walked outside, it dawned on me that I had left my car at the party. That's what I got for stepping out of my usual delivery routine. I was so used to dropping everything off and heading back to the bakery immediately. Staying at an event was out of the ordinary and had thrown me off without me realizing it. Oh well. The station wagon was fine where it was. I'd go get it on the way back home from Ken's.

I headed down Main Street, which was had quieted down now that most of the shops had closed. Aside from Old Templeton, most of the restaurants were still open, but the first wave of diners was already eating, so few people were on the street. I tilted my head back and soaked in the late-afternoon sun, careful to keep walking in a straight line so I wouldn't hit any of the planters leaning up against the storefronts or the occasional mailboxes on the other side of the sidewalk closest to the road.

"Excuse me," a male voice called as I passed my bakery across the street, causing me to stop and look around. A man, slightly older than I was with dark-brown hair, stepped down from the bakery entrance and waved at me.

"Hello, I shouted across the street. Can I help you?"

He looked both ways before jaywalking across the street. "Are you Joanie Sunevall, the owner of the bakery?"

The question felt a little odd considering I wasn't even at the bakery, as if he knew the answer before he asked. I didn't recognize him, but that didn't prevent him from knowing who I was. Since the tree festival and the planting the week after that, I'd experienced several return out-of-towners addressing me by name when they came into the bakery.

"I am," I answered, trying to hide the bit of apprehension in my voice. "Is there something I can help you with? Although if the answer is you're looking for some baked goods, you'll have to come back in the morning when the bakery is open. We closed about a half hour ago, and I'm on my way to go have dinner." I held up the brown paper bag for emphasis.

"Oh, no, I've already had several of your baked goods today." He patted his stomach, which wasn't at all pudgy. "They're delicious. I found myself in town today—I live over in Astoria—and when I stopped in and tried your cookie, I thought you had something special going on. When I had the palmier, I *knew* you had something special. Lunch was a whoopie pie, and that sealed the deal."

I transferred the bag to my other hand. Without handles, it was a bit awkward to hold. "Sealed the deal for what?"

"Sorry, I should have introduced myself. Name's Nelson James. I'm an investor for local businesses throughout Brambleberry Bay and beyond."

"I see. But how does this concern me?"

"I'd love to talk to you about that at your earliest convenience. You have vast potential for expansion here and elsewhere."

I quirked an eyebrow. "What sort of expansion are you talking about?" How weird that only today I was thinking about offering drinks to my customers who chose to stay and eat their treats at the bakery.

He raised his hand up and over in an arching motion. "The sky's the limit for a business like yours. Bigger location, bigger kitchen, franchising, food trucks. You could have it all."

Franchise the bakery? Who would put the spells in the muffins for the test takers at any other location? Or the confidence in the cookies?

"But there's only one me," I replied, shifting my dinner back into my other hand.

"True, but you could train someone to run a shop like yours."

My thoughts turned to Sam. It would be great to give him a place to land right away after school, if he wanted that, of course. But that was still four years away.

"Now, I see that look," Mr. James said, a grin spreading across his face. "The gears are turning. Let's get a coffee or something when you're able, and we can talk all about your options before you decide."

I took a moment to gather my thoughts. It was only coffee, not a commitment. "Okay, I think I can do that. The shop is closed tomorrow, so stop by Wednesday or any other day and we can figure out a time to meet."

"It's a date. I'll be there. Let me get you my card in case you need to contact me." As he reached into his jacket pocket, I wondered how hot he must have been in it. Today was a warm one for early June. I shouldn't delay getting dinner to Ken and Ivy either. Thankfully Donna had vented the containers so the fries wouldn't get soggy.

I looked the card over once he handed it to me before sliding it into my tote bag for me to fish out later. "Thank you, and if you don't mind, I'd really like to go eat my dinner before it gets cold."

"Oh, sure, sure, enjoy. We'll talk soon."

"Have a good evening."

"You too, Miss Sunevall." He gave me a nod before crossing back across the road and heading down Founder Street.

I shrugged off the somewhat strange encounter and continued to Ken's house for dinner.

CHAPTER 5

I only needed to wait five minutes before Paul and Walter walked into Olde Templeton for breakfast the next morning. It was their ritual. The two old men ordered the same thing every day, including one of my muffins for each of them. Even on Tuesdays when I was closed, Donna made sure they'd have their muffins, saving two from Monday. Not so secretly, those muffins were their favorite. They'd told me the Monday muffins always gave them a pep in their step, and they liked that they got a second dose on Tuesdays.

"Just the two I was looking for," I called as they crossed the tiny diner.

"Us?" they said in unison, each of them pointing at the other.

"What did they do now?" Donna asked.

"That's what I'd like to know." Walter turned to his friend. "Are you up to no good again?"

Paul shook his head. "Are you?"

The two laughed as they sat down on their usual stools. I swore Donna would stop someone else from taking those spots if they ever tried to sit there before the two men in the morning.

I blew on my cup of coffee before taking a small sip. "Do you two remember a Sandra O'Grady?"

Walter's face took on a somber expression. "Oh, the poor girl. You know she was murdered, right?"

I nodded. "But so far no one has told me who did it or anything."

"That was a long time ago," Paul commented. "Why the interest?"

Trying my best to look innocent, I said, "Oh, you know me. Can't keep out of people's business lately."

"Say no more," Walter answered. Paul sat nodding beside him.

The two men understood what I was getting at. It wasn't the first time I'd come to them with questions. They had helped me immensely in my last two ghostly mysteries.

"To use a term you kids use these days, there was so much drama surrounding her death," Walter continued. "She'd been found, no, I won't go there. My brother was on the force back then, and he saw her. It wasn't pretty."

Paul picked up the story. "But there was a mystery surrounding who she was dating, a potential cheating scandal, and let's not forget her ex-boyfriend had recently died. His funeral was two days before she disappeared."

"So who did it?" That was my biggest question right now.

"Well, a lot of people thought it was her boyfriend at the time. Greg, I think his name was," Paul said. "Rumor had it she was cheating on him with Marvin Strong, one of the young black men in the neighborhood."

"I'm sure we don't need to tell you what many in town thought about that back then," Walter added.

He didn't. I'd learned plenty when I helped out Kate and

Daniel. They'd loved each other, but Kate's family had forbidden her from dating Daniel just because he was black. They'd spent the rest of their lives loving one another from afar, marrying other people, having children, and later grandchildren. Life was funny sometimes, and now Kate's granddaughter and Daniel's grandson were dating. And I was dating Kate's grandson. As for Kate and Daniel? They were together now.

"But Greg didn't do it?" I asked.

"Nope, it was Marvin," Paul said.

"Why would Marvin do it?" I took a long sip of my coffee.

Walter shrugged. "Why does anyone do that sort of thing?"

"And that's if he even did it," Paul added. "I always thought it might have been Bruce Malloy."

"Mmm . . ." Walter nodded large and slow. "That's a good possibility."

I set the cup back on the counter. "Who's Bruce?"

"The brother of Sandra's ex, Brad."

"So you think there's a chance Marvin didn't do it?"

Walter shrugged again. "I hate to say it, but I think he was an easy target. You know how it was."

I nodded, not needing to hear more. Plus, I had to get back to the bakery.

At that moment, Donna placed their plates in front of them, then returned to the kitchen. It was as good a way to end a conversation as any.

"Well, thank you both for your time. This has been very helpful." I smiled warmly at the two men.

"Glad we could help," Paul said through a mouthful of muffin.

"Enjoy your breakfasts." I took one last sip of my coffee

before putting it down, then slid off the stool. "Thanks for the coffee, Donna!"

"See you tomorrow," she called from inside the kitchen.

Talking with Walter and Paul had been helpful, but I was still left with numerous questions. I could only hope I'd get more answers soon.

At the end of the day, I walked up Main Street and down Cooper Court over to the tattoo parlor where David was one of the artists. I hoped he could put me in touch with his family in a way that wouldn't make it seem like I was doing favors for Chelsea or her family. Although they had been the ones to ask for help, I needed to remain neutral about what had happened all those years ago. Casting my feelings into what was happening now could fuel the strong emotions that David's family had toward Chelsea, and I didn't want that.

The door chimed as I opened it and stepped inside. I'd never been in a tattoo shop before, so I had little to compare it to, but the parlor was clean, and the art on the walls was impressive. Most were tattoos blown up onto canvases, but several others showcased nautical scenes. Did the others who worked in the shop like the theme or were they selkies like David?

David stepped through saloon-like doors at the rear of the shop and approached the glass counter in the center of the room. "Hey, Joanie. What's up?"

I walked toward him. Inside the counter were all sorts of jewelry one would use for pierced ears, belly buttons, eyebrows, and more. My mom had never let me get my ears pierced when I was little. Just as well since I hated needles. "Hi, David. I was hoping you could help me."

"I can certainly try. What do you need?"

Over the next few minutes, I filled him in on how Chelsea's request had me looking into Sandra's murder. "If anything, I'm hoping to at least make Chelsea feel better. At best, I want to help your family realize how great she is. Then you two can have the wedding you've always dreamed of without worrying if your family is going to do or say something."

His ever-present smile brightened. "That would be amazing. Chels has been so upset over this whole thing. I mean, it wasn't easy at the start of our relationship either, but after my parents came around, I figured we were good. I never expected this with my other relatives. Let me call my mom. I'm sure she'll be happy to take you over to my grandma's. She's the glue of our family. Knows everything and keeps everything. If you have questions, she'll have answers and the photographs to prove it."

"Thank you so much."

He picked up the shop's landline. "Hey, Ma. Yeah, everything's fine."

I wandered over to some art on the wall as David talked and stopped at a drawing of a woman, who looked vaguely familiar, on a beach draped in seaweed. The next piece was of a three-masted ship with tentacles wrapped around it. A kraken if I recalled correctly. After all I'd learned about Heartwood Hollow and the supposedly mythological beings who called it home, could that thing be real?

"That's a kraken," David said from right behind me, confirming my thought.

I jumped. "Are they real?"

He shrugged. "Once upon a time, but I don't know of any live ones. Bet my grandma could tell you a few stories, though. Speaking of, Ma says she can take you on Tuesday. That's your day off, right?"

I nodded. "That would be wonderful. Saves me from having to ask anyone to cover for me too, especially since I did that for Annabel's party yesterday."

He handed me a phone number. "That's my ma's. Said to call her tomorrow so you can make plans."

"Great I'll do that. Thank you." I swooped my arm around the room. "This is beautiful work, by the way. I particularly like this one." I pointed back at the woman with the seaweed.

"Thanks. That's one of mine."

"You drew this?"

"Yep, and my cousin Dylan put it on me." He lifted the sleeve of his shirt to reveal a tattoo of the beautiful woman.

"Wow."

"It's Chelsea if you can't tell."

I looked closer at the drawing on the wall and nodded. "I thought she looked familiar."

"Drew it after one of our beach vacations."

"It really is lovely. Well, I should let you get back to whatever you were doing and head home. Saffy is going to be wondering where I am if I'm late with dinner."

David laughed. "I know how cats can be. And we can't have that. Good luck."

Hopefully I wouldn't need it.

CHAPTER 6

At eleven sharp on Tuesday morning, I met with David's mother, Celia, at her stepmother's house, a box of muffins and scones in my hand. I'd baked them this morning at home with the hope of smoothing things over to allow me a chance to learn about Sandra and what had happened all those years ago.

Celia brightened when she saw the box. "Any chance you have more of those sea-salt caramel cookies in there?"

"No cookies, but I made some scones in that flavor. Muffins too, though they aren't the same flavor."

"Wonderful. I'm sure my ma will have milk or tea or what have you to go with them." She fiddled with her keyring before finding the right key, then slid it into the lock on the door. "Ma? I'm here, and I brought Joanie with me."

"Come in, come in," a voice that sounded vaguely familiar called from somewhere in the house. "Kettle is on the stove, already hot. I'll be down in a minute."

Celia waved me inside, then followed me into the living room. "You can set those on the coffee table. Can I interest you in tea? She has all kinds."

"Tea would be lovely. Something with caffeine preferably. It's early still."

She nodded and then ducked out of the room, returning moments later with three mugs on a proper tea tray with honey, a creamer pitcher, and a sugar bowl. "I wasn't sure how you take your tea, so I brought a bit of everything. Like I said, Ma has it all. Careful, the cups might be hot from the water."

I hadn't even met David's grandmother, but I liked her already. Hopefully, this was a good sign for the start of my investigation.

Celia took a small wood box off the tray and opened it for me, revealing several flavors of bagged tea.

"I know I had said something with caffeine, but I'm so intrigued by this blueberry aloe variety, that I must try it." I pulled out the bag, then set it in my cup of hot water.

"It's one of my favorites," the familiar voice said from just beyond the doorway.

I looked up as an older woman stepped into the room and had to stop myself from letting my mouth fall open in surprise. "Greta? You're David's grandmother?"

"Sure am. Now, dear, don't look so surprised."

"But aren't you a troll?"

"Sure am." She smiled. "You weren't expecting that?"

"I can't say that I was. I don't mean to sound rude, but when David said his family wasn't happy with Chelsea being a merrow, I was expecting you all to be selkies."

Greta laughed as she plopped onto the sofa with me, leaving the middle cushion open. "Well, to tell you the truth, I'm only his step-grandmother, but I've known that boy since the day he was born. He's my grandson through and through."

"I didn't see you at Annabel's party, though."

As she prepped her tea, Greta said, "I was down in Saltair Shores. The senior center had sponsored a day trip down there to see a matinee. Got my ticket months ago and wasn't going to pass up on the trip especially when I'll see everyone again in a few weeks. I paid over a hundred dollars for that ticket, and well, that's quite a bit of money."

I picked up my mug. "So you have no issues with Chelsea being a merrow?"

"Goodness, no."

Celia also shook her head as she sat down on the recliner situated across the coffee table from us.

"Matter of fact," Greta began, "I understand a bit of what she's going through. Think I had it easier since I didn't come into this family until after all the kids were born. They're all selkies."

"Is there a problem with selkies being with non-selkies?" I blew on the tea, eager to try it. "Forgive me, I'm not sure how this all works. When two paranormal beings get together, do they have hybrid children like in the stories?"

Celia nearly spat out her tea. "No, nothing like that. There won't be any half-merrow, half-selkie children around here . . . not that I'd have a problem with that. We don't exactly know how it works, but somehow the children take on the paranormal being of either the mother or the father. It seems random. It's not like girls will be what the mom is or boys will be whatever the dad is."

"Interesting," I said, trying to think of the right thing to ask next. "So if that's not an issue, why is your family so against Chelsea and her family?"

"I adore Chelsea," Celia stated, "but it took a while. I've grown up believing selkies and merrows—any type of mermaid, for that matter—don't mix. They just don't. We can be friends, but we can't be more. Unfortunately, not everyone in my family has shifted away from that mindset."

"So it has nothing to do with Chelsea's great-aunt?"

"Well . . ." Greta said, letting the word hang for a moment. "That doesn't help her any."

"David said you could help because you know everything that happened back then. But you weren't a part of the family then, were you?"

Greta chuckled. "Oh, I've been around a long time. No, I wasn't married into this family yet, but David's grandfather and I had always been close, even after he got married. We'd been neighbors growing up and good friends all those years. I loved his first wife like a sister. It was so sad when she died. Especially with the kids so young, but within a few years, he and I were together. So I can absolutely still help you. Let me go get you some photographs that might help."

Greta stood up and walked over to a closet, where she dug out a large shoebox. She returned with it and then set it down on the coffee table next to the tea tray. "I've had these photos for years. I scrapbooked many, but these are either the duplicates or ones that don't belong in the scrapbook for whatever reason."

She sat back on the couch, then lifted the lid and drew out a handful of photos. She shuffled through a few before handing one over to me. In the old black-and-white photograph, ten young adults formed a human pyramid. Four as the base, three on top of them, then two, and finally one.

"Everyone looks so happy here," I said, studying the faces. "Is it a party?"

"Uh-huh. High school graduation. That's me there." Greta pointed to the woman in the row of three. Then she pointed to the man at one corner of the pyramid and let her finger linger. "That there is David's grandpa. His first wife is above me, although they weren't married yet. That was another year or so away. Up top was Sandra."

"Oh wow, so you were all friends?"

"Uh-huh. Remember, there were no rules on who you could be friends with, just who you could be with if you get what I'm saying." She traced her finger along the photograph, stopping at the man next to her in the pyramid. "This here was Sandra's boyfriend at the time, and next to him was his brother, Bruce. Bruce was best friends with my husband."

"So what happened? How do we go from this photo to Brad dying and Sandra being murdered?"

Greta sighed, picked up her tea, and drew a long sip. I did the same with my cup, politely waiting for her to tell me.

"Oh my, that does look like a fun time," someone new said from close by. But only I had heard her.

Where there had once been an empty cushion between Greta and me, now sat a ghost. She appeared only slightly older than she did in the photograph. Her red hair hung in loose waves to her shoulders, and her dress was green with gray polka dots. Her shoes were t-strap sandals with kitten heels. If she hadn't just appeared in the living room, she could have passed for any of the summer tourists here in town ready for a semi-fancy dinner at one of the restaurants or high tea at the inn.

The ghost gasped. "Wait. That's me!"

If I had been able to react to Sandra's presence, I was pretty sure my mouth would have dropped open from the shock of her ability to speak. Two of the ghosts I had recently helped were unable to do so until almost the very end. Here, Sandra seemed to have no trouble. Maybe this case wouldn't be as difficult as the others after all. I'd simply ask her who killed her and be done with it.

I waited, hoping either she or Greta would speak.

"And that's hmm . . . no. That's, nope, can't remember either. Huh, that's funny. You'd think I'd be able to remember because they were all with me," Sandra said, scratching her head.

"What can you tell me about that day?" I asked Greta, hoping her answers would spark something in Sandra's memory. Why couldn't she remember?

"That was such a fun day. We'd been to the beach, all of us. A secret spot where we were free to let our fins hang out, or shift into seals, or in my case"—she lifted her legs to show me what Gram would call sensible shoes—"let my hairy feet soak in the hot summer sand."

"Oh yes! That's her right here." Sandra leaned in and tapped the photo. "The beach was lovely. We'd go there because . . . I forgot again." She grew quiet but didn't seem too upset even though Greta had just told us about the picture.

"Well, that whole summer was a blast," Greta began.

"It really was," Sandra added. "That was the summer I . . ." Again, her words trailed off. She turned toward Greta to listen.

"We were at the beach at least every few days. There was a great drive-in between here and Knoll's Grove, and we went there nearly every weekend. Had to take two cars, of course, to fit us all, but we'd park next to each other so close we could climb from one car to the other. It was the last summer we'd all be together before adult life took over. Brad was going to school out of state come the fall. Doris, here, was already engaged to our friend Miles." She pointed to the corner of the triangle opposite David's grandfather.

"Brad, that's it. That was his name!" Sandra clapped with excitement at remembering. I doubted she would have without Greta's mentioning him.

Greta placed the photo of the human pyramid on the

stack of photos she'd already gone through and flipped to another one. It was a smaller group shot, but Sandra was still there.

"I should know these people," Sandra said, quieter than she had anything else. "But I don't. Why?"

I wished I had an answer for her.

"Then the week before he left for college, Sandra dumped Brad. It was a shock to everyone. If you ask me, I had expected them to get married once he was back from school, despite the rules. Bruce said it really tore his brother up. Brad never would have admitted such a thing."

"What happened then?"

She sighed. "Well, Bruce couldn't stand to do anything with Sandra because of what she'd done to his brother. Plus, with all of us taking on full-time work, pairing off, or continuing with school, we all sort of fell away from the group, though some of us stayed closer than others. Sandra ended up seeing someone new, another merrow, but there were rumors she was seeing someone else behind his back."

She must have meant the rumor about Marvin.

"We'd see her in passing," Greta continued, "but it was never the same. Even a whole year later, the friendship hadn't recovered. And how could it once we'd picked sides?"

I understood what she'd meant. I'd seen it happen all too often with friends in high school and college. But everyone I had matched back then had stayed together. My record was perfect. I hoped it would remain that way.

"Then a week after Christmas, Bruce's family got the phone call that Brad had been killed in a car accident. Slid off the road during a snowstorm. Bruce was heartbroken, understandably, but livid too. Brad had been avoiding Heartwood Hollow as much as possible to not run into Sandra. He'd stay for holidays the least amount of time possible and rarely left the house when he was here. I don't think he ever got over the breakup, not really. And Bruce never forgot either. If you ask me, he blamed Sandra for his death. Brad wouldn't have been up at school at the time if he hadn't gone back early to avoid her. Then two days after Brad's funeral, Sandra was reported missing and found murdered later that evening."

"That's awful."

"How horrible," Sandra echoed beside me as if the story weren't about her.

Greta nodded. "It was a tough time for the whole town, to lose two young people so close together like that. Everyone was torn up about it. Brad had such a bright future, and Sandra was a dear. The only person happy to see her go was Bruce, but he was already grieving so much no one gave much thought to it."

So no one had looked into Bruce as a possible suspect in Sandra's murder? To me, he sounded as likely to be the killer —and perhaps even more so—than Marvin. But I wouldn't admit that to Greta and Celia.

"Wow. That's a whole lot to think about." I stuck out my bottom lip and blew out a stream of hot air so strong it moved a wisp of hair across my forehead. "So let me get this straight. Your family dislikes the idea of merrows and selkies being together because they are different, but you have no problem with them on the whole as long as they aren't together."

"It certainly was the case back then."

"But your family dislikes Sandra, and by extension Chelsea because they are related, for something Sandra did to your husband's best friend's brother?"

"Also correct. Now I don't personally blame Sandra for what happened, but again, at the time, I wasn't a part of this family. I'm sure you understand how the emotions surrounding a tragedy don't make for the most rational of decisions. Once the idea is there, it's set. Even after all these years, for them, that belief isn't going to go away." She sighed again, then had a sip of tea. "Like I said, sides were chosen, and over the years, the dislike of Sandra morphed into one of disliking all merrows."

No wonder Chelsea had been worried when she came to me for help. Chelsea and David's wedding was going to be full of merrows and selkies who didn't like one another. I was sure helping free Sandra from the tiara would help. But after talking with Greta, the question now was, would it be enough to make things go smoothly on the big day?

CHAPTER 7

Somewhere along the walk from Greta's, I lost Sandra. I shouldn't say lost exactly. I knew where she was the last time I saw her, and the fortunate thing about ghosts like Sandra was that they'd reappear eventually.

She and I had been walking next to one another, talking, but then she'd dart off to check something out. She'd catch back up, and we'd chat some more. Then she would take her time looking around at everything, even mid-conversation as I tried to jostle a memory free from her.

The most I ever got was, "I know I'm supposed to remember all of this. It's familiar."

She waved me on ahead at the corner of Founder and Main, almost right outside of my shop, before darting past me and heading to the Riverview Park at the end of the street. Hungry, and knowing I couldn't keep up with a ghost who could blink in and out of visibility at will, I took her suggestion and continued my walk home, wondering when she'd show back up.

My calico cat lifted her head to watch me come into the

living room but remained on top of the couch in front of the window.

"Hey, Saffy. I'm home for lunch."

All it took was for me to say *lunch* before Saffy was up and sprinting toward the kitchen as if I hadn't fed her in days, never mind hours. Silly cat.

I cracked open the refrigerator to take out leftovers from last night's dinner. My elderly neighbor, Matt, had come over again, and I'd made a delicious chicken casserole with several sides. He'd taken a majority of it home, of course. I couldn't let him go hungry—or really couldn't let him stick to his microwave meals for long—but I'd kept enough to have for today's lunch and dinner, or perhaps tomorrow's lunch depending on where the day took me.

My first stop after lunch would be to Marvin Strong's family. I knew of the Strong family, but I didn't know where they lived since I'd never made a delivery there. I hoped they'd be willing to speak with me about what had happened, but this had to be a sensitive topic and I would have to respect their wishes if they chose not to say anything.

Saffy reached her paws up the lower cupboards as I prepared my chicken casserole leftovers, eager to get any of the chicken she could get her hands on.

"None of this is for you, I'm afraid, but I'll make it up to you before I leave." She couldn't have most of the spices in the stuffing portion of the casserole.

She thumped back down on her behind, then ambled over to her bowl.

"I know, I know. Let me throw this into the oven and I'll take care of you."

She tapped her bowl impatiently.

"One more minute." I put half of the casserole into a small baking dish and then slid it into the oven before turning it on. Doing it this way allowed for more even cooking of a single portion instead of having overdone outsides and a cold interior. No one wanted that.

I placed the remaining leftovers back into the fridge and grabbed out a small container, then set that on the counter. Saffy only had breakfast and dinner on days I worked, so she didn't need this midday meal, but she'd never let me skip feeding her lunch when I was home. I got out her food from the lower cupboard as well as an extra cat dish and scooped a half portion for her. Then I popped the lid on the container from the fridge and pulled out a few broken-up pieces of plain chicken to put on top of her food as an extra special treat.

"There you go, Saf," I said, taking away the empty bowl she'd been tapping and placing the new one in front of her. I set the dirty one in the sink as Saffy stuck her head into her food, her bum wiggling. She let out a *purt*, a strange noise I'd only heard her make when she was excited to eat, a cross between a purr and a chirp. With that sign of satisfaction, I brewed myself a cup of white tea as I waited for my food to reheat.

Thirty minutes later, half of my tea was gone, Saffy was back on her spot by the couch, and I was pulling my lunch out of the oven. I cut into the center, allowing the steam to rise out of it. Perfect. Now all I had to do was eat, then it would be off to find out where the Strongs lived.

Another thirty minutes later, I was done with lunch and ready to leave. Sandra had yet to reappear, but I still wasn't worried. She had more energy than any of the other ghosts I'd encountered recently, and there was no doubt in my mind she'd pop back up if I needed her.

I headed back toward Main Street, this time to Town Hall.

If anyone could tell me where the Strongs lived, it would be my best friend Courtney, assistant to the mayor.

"Be with you in a minute," Courtney said as I stood at her office door without looking up.

"Take your time."

That got her attention, and a smile spread across her face as we made eye contact. "Joanie! What are you doing here?"

"I need to find out where someone in town lives."

"And you didn't think to look it up on your phone?" Jill, Courtney's assistant, asked from her desk to my right.

"I never even thought of that." My phone didn't work inside my house, and there was no need for it while at the bakery, so although I had a cell, I rarely used it. More often than not, I forgot I even had one.

Jill shook her head, looking down, but said nothing. I was likely the least tech-savvy twenty-something in town.

"Who do you need to find?" Courtney asked, drawing my attention back to her.

"The Strongs."

"First name?"

"Mrs.?"

Next to me, Jill sighed.

Courtney dragged her mouse around and clicked a few things before typing in something short. "We have several Strongs in town."

"Any way you can tell me who's oldest?" I asked.

"You probably would want William. Says he's sixty-seven." She reached into her desk and pulled out a pad of paper and a pen, then scribbled something down. She ripped the sheet of paper off the pad and held it out to me. "Here."

I walked over and grabbed it, narrowing my eyes at her slightly. "You're really forthcoming with the information today. Last time I came looking for help, you wouldn't say anything. What changed?"

"All I'm doing is looking in the online phone book." She turned her screen around, then shrugged with a slight chuckle. "It's not anything you couldn't find for yourself."

Back across the room, Jill stifled what sounded like a snort of laughter with a cough.

"Thanks, I owe you one, but right now, I have to go." I held up the paper between my index and middle fingers.

"Call me later," she said as I turned and headed out the office.

"I will," I said over my shoulder, already out of eyeline with Courtney. Stepping out onto the porch of Town Hall, I looked at the address of my next destination. I knew exactly where I had to go.

CHAPTER 8

It was almost like déjà vu, heading to the row of houses across from the grocery store. I'd been here two months ago to talk with Rich and his mom, Beverly, about Rich's grandfather. Daniel had been following his grandson around and interfering with Rich's blossoming relationship with Ashley. Beverly had mentioned that there were only three Black families in town back then, so I didn't find it surprising that the families would live near one another. Some of the various family members had intermarried, sisters of one marrying the brothers of another. It must have made for a large tight-knit family unit.

I found myself wondering what that would have felt like. Throughout my childhood, it had been me, Mom, Gram—who lived a few blocks away—and my aunt and cousin, who lived fifteen minutes in the opposite direction from Gram. We were close to one another, still were, but we were small with many noticeable absences: my father, my uncle, and my grandfather. My grandfather had died when I was young enough to have no memories of him, but my father and uncle had both left by their choice. I wouldn't have known someone was my father if I passed him on the street.

I shook my head clear of thoughts about my family as I approached the two-story yellow Italianate house.

"Sandra, are you there?" I asked quietly.

She popped up beside me. "Hey there, sugar." She'd changed since I last saw her. Her red hair was now in braided pigtails, and her dress was a harvest yellow with large roses all over it.

I wondered then if she remembered who I was with her memory troubles. "My name is Joanie. I'm the baker here in town—"

"I know that, silly." She nudged my shoulder with her hand. Solid, like most ghosts were when they appeared. "Why else would I call you *sugar*? Those sweets I saw earlier looked mighty tasty."

"Thank you." I'd never been complimented by a ghost on my baking before. "In addition to that, though, I can see ghosts, and lately, I try to help them."

"And you want to help me? Why?" She seemed genuinely curious.

"Your great-niece, Chelsea, is a friend of mine, and she asked me to."

"She's a great girl."

"So you know who she is?"

"Why wouldn't I? She's my great-niece."

Continuing past the Strong house so it wouldn't look like I was having a conversation with myself on the front lawn before knocking on the door, I said, "I wasn't sure since you don't seem to remember much from before."

She sighed. "Yeah. All that is rather hazy. But everything from now, I know. So what did you need me for?"

"I'm hoping to find out more about the man they say killed you."

"Killed me? Oh, dear." She seemed to take her having been murdered well. "You will be safe, right?"

"Yes, I'll be fine. I'm going to talk with his family and was hoping you'd come along. Maybe something can jog your memory."

She nodded firmly. "All right. Whatever I can do to help."

I turned back around and walked up the flagstone path to the house. As I was about to knock on the door, it opened, and Beverly jumped back, holding her chest.

"My word, Joanie. What in heaven's name are you doing here?" She took a deep calming breath.

"Hi, Bev. Sorry to startle you. I was hoping to speak with William Strong."

She squinted at me before calling, "Uncle Willie! There's someone here to see you." She looked back at me. "No treats? Uncle Willie loves your stuffed peanut butter cookies."

"I'll make note of it for next time. As for what I'm doing here, I'm trying to help my friend Chelsea. Her wedding is coming up, and her fiancé's family doesn't like hers that much because of something related to her great-aunt—"

"Sandra O'Grady. If you're poking around because you think my Uncle Marvin did it, you can head on home."

"I don't think that at all," I said, the words coming out in a rush. "I want to get the whole story. It's the only way to help."

She sighed. "Well, you were able to help my Rich and Ashley, so who am I to argue if you want to hear what happened from our side of things? Let me call my aunties over, too, if you don't mind. They have a lot to say on that matter and live right here in town."

I nodded. "Please do." The more the merrier as far as I was concerned. Who knew what would get said that could be the key to unlocking Sandra's memory or provide that piece of evidence that had been overlooked for years?

"Come on in." She held the door open for me, and I stepped inside. Sandra hurried in behind before the door closed, not that she would have hit it. She would have walked right through it. Perhaps she'd forgotten that fact.

Beverly directed me through the living room into the large kitchen. It had been updated over time with new appliances and curtains, but its 1950s pale-yellow tile still covered the lower two-thirds of the walls, capped by a thinner black row of tiles.

"Sit at the table if you don't mind," Bev said, picking up the landline from its cradle.

I pulled out a chair and sat at the six-person rectangular table at the side of the room.

Sandra poked her head into the room, looking carefully at everything. "I feel like I've been here before."

This was the most promising development she'd made since first appearing. Maybe all she had needed was more exposure to things she knew.

Bev hung up the phone at the same time an elderly Black man shuffled down the stairs. He walked with a cane, but in the other hand, he held a wooden box. He set it on the table in front of the chair. Although his body was old, the spark in his eyes told me he was still as sharp as ever. "Sorry to keep you waiting, but I overheard what you wanted to talk about, and I thought you'd like to see some photos of how we remember our Marvin."

"My aunties are coming," Bev told him. "They'll be here in a few minutes."

"Oh, lordy." He turned to me, his grin growing mischievous. "I hope you don't have anything planned for the rest of the day. They'll talk your ear off."

"I'm willing to stay for as long as you want to talk." I gave him a conciliatory smile. "It's not the easiest subject."

"No, it isn't," he agreed. He told Bev to get us lemonade as we waited for her aunts to arrive. She'd just brought over the pitcher and set it on the table when they burst into the kitchen through the side door.

Sandra had hopped up on the counter, seemingly wanting to listen to what everyone had to say. As she saw them, her eyes lit up. "I think I know them."

This had to be a good sign.

Bev and Willie introduced me to Gloria and Deborah, both of whom I already knew from their visits to the bakery. They regularly came in on Sundays after church.

We spent the first half hour drinking lemonade, looking at photographs, and talking about Marvin as a child. His family was adamant that he'd never hurt a fly and was the type to rescue a bug from the house instead of kill it. He was a friendly boy who loved all the neighborhood animals and regularly took them in if he didn't know who they belonged to.

Marvin certainly didn't seem like a person who would turn into a murderer based on all those true crime shows one of my college roommates watched whenever she had a spare moment. Still, I guessed it would have been possible to snap in the heat of the moment. That made me wonder about the rumored relationship between him and Sandra, but before I jumped to that particular topic, I asked, "How did he meet Sandra? Was it through school or . . ."

"They were in the same grade, but it wasn't until fourth or fifth that they became friends," Willie started. "Sandra had a pet cat that had gotten lost, and she walked around putting up flyers. He saw her and offered to help, taking half the stack. Turns out, the cat had gotten stuck up a tree, and he found it while walking around the neighborhood with those signs. He climbed up the tree himself and coaxed the cat back down."

"After that," Gloria said, "Sandra always made sure to include him in social things all through school, and they regularly played together outside of it. She was here a lot after church and loved our mama's Sunday biscuits and gravy." She took a sip of her lemonade. "Mm-mm! They were the best. I've been making them for the family these last fifteen years since Mama passed. They're good, but I can't get them to be just like hers. A little too dense if you ask me."

Deborah waved her off. "She's not here to talk about your biscuits."

"She's a baker," Gloria replied, the word *baker* stressed so hard it sounded more like two words. "Maybe she can help."

"Quit it, the both of you," Willie said. He turned to me. "See, I told you they could talk your ear off if you let them."

"All right, fine," Gloria said, sounding a bit flustered. "Where was I?"

"You were talking about them being friends outside of school," I answered, hoping to get the conversation back on track even though I probably could help with her biscuit troubles.

She raised her hand and brought it down just as quickly, saying, "Ah, yes. They had their separate friends too. As you probably know, not everyone liked the idea of white girls being friends with Black boys back then, but Sandra's family wasn't like that. They were newer to the area, and her father had a thick Irish accent. Her mom not as thick, but it was there."

"They experienced a bit of, what is it that you call it now?" Willie cut in, then thought a moment. "Othering, that's it. They were othered, too, if I remember correctly."

Seemed like Heartwood Hollow had always been a bit wary of newcomers. Perhaps I'd been lucky when I came here. The most I'd experienced were curious stares and rumors about my being a witch. What would it have been like here decades ago with rumors about me like there were now?

The time had come to ask one of the main questions I had. "Now, I've heard that the two may have been involved romantically?"

"Oh, that." Deborah rolled her eyes. "We would only be so lucky. She was a great girl, and I think he may have had a crush on her."

"How could he not?" Willie asked. "I did. She was always so nice to him and sweet to everyone."

"But no, they weren't together," Gloria confirmed. "That's just what the cops said to give their case—if you can even call it that—extra weight."

"Our brother was devastated when he heard what happened to her. He wept right here at the table," Willie said, pointing and pressing the table with his index finger repeatedly.

"When they came for him, it was a shock to all of us," Deborah said. "He didn't put up a fight, didn't say anything. He knew what fighting would do. Sadly, they only saw his cooperation as complacency and a resignation to his guilt, remorse."

"Was there an investigation?" There had to have been something. "A trial?"

"*Pfft!* An investigation?" Willie barked out a cynical laugh. "They thought they'd caught their guy. What more was there for them to do?"

"They certainly didn't listen to us," Gloria said. "Never did. Didn't care that he had a good job at the car dealership—"

"One my daddy helped him get," Bev added. She'd been so quiet I'd almost forgotten she was here.

"Or that there was no evidence that he did it other than the fact he occasionally went down to the beach by himself to fish." Gloria poured herself some more lemonade.

"That's where it happened?"

"Mm-hmm, a private beach only a few locals knew about. Sandra told him about it. Said she'd seen a lot of fish there close to the dock." Gloria sighed. "Probably why there was no evidence either. The rock got tossed back into the water."

Given the location of her murder, I wondered if this had more to do with *what* Sandra was than *who* she was. Could someone have seen her transform and killed her out of fear or misunderstanding? And if she had been hit with a rock, was that why she didn't remember much of anything?

"We had a glimmer of hope that they'd release him when another girl was found dead about a year and a half later, and again when another went missing the year after that," Deborah started.

"And the year after that," Willie added, "but they determined those incidents were unrelated to what happened to poor Sandra.

"And it's possible they were," Deborah continued, her sigh sounding nearly identical to her sister's. "We jumped at anything that we thought could help our brother, but either way, our hopes were dashed—"

"And our Marvin stayed in prison." Gloria took a long sip of her lemonade, then leaned in and pointed at me. "So what do *you* think now that you've heard *our* story?"

Although I believed there was a rush to judgment and that Marvin was likely innocent, I didn't know what admitting it would do at this point. The Strongs were mad this had happened to them, to Marvin, and that he'd died in jail. I would have been too. It wasn't fair.

Instead, I asked another question that had been on my mind. "I'm curious to know, who do you think did it?"

They grew quiet and all looked between one another. In a combined voice, they said, "Bruce Malloy."

"He was so angry after his brother died," Deborah said.

"Why he took it out on Sandra, I'll never understand," Gloria added.

"He knew she liked to go down there no matter the time of year, even in the early winter like it was," Willie said. "It was her place."

"And they never looked into him at all?" Walter and Paul had told me as much, but I wanted it confirmed.

Deborah shook her head. "Nope. He got a big ole pass because of what happened to Brad."

"Plus, they already had their sights set on our brother," Willie quipped.

I nodded slowly, taking it all in. "Thank you all for talking with me." I glanced over their shoulders at Sandra, who was staring at photographs of the family on the fridge.

She walked back over to the table to look at the photos Bev's family had spread across the table. She tapped at a yellowed black-and-white photo.

I leaned in slightly to see around her hand. It was a picture of the Strong family. I recognized Gloria, Deborah, and Willie, all much younger than they were now. Sandra's finger rested on Marvin.

"Him. I know him." She was momentarily ecstatic over remembering something, jumping around in a tight circle, then sobered. "At least I think I do."

"We thank you for listening," Willie said. "It's not often we get to talk about Marvin with people outside the family."

"You be sure to stop on by if you need any more information," Bev said. "We hope it helps you with Chelsea. It's not fair to her what's going on, and if you can get that family she's marrying into to see some sense in everything that happened back then, all the better."

Gloria rolled up her short sleeve to expose a tattoo of several symbols I didn't recognize on her upper arm. "Her fiancé did this for me. Took a couple hours. I really liked talking with him. He's a nice boy, but some of his relatives? Nuh-uh."

"You've got this, though," Bev said with a reassuring smile. "Rich told me all about your matchmaking, and if you got these two together, then they'll stay together."

I sure hoped she was right. Chelsea and David were meant to be. I knew that every time I saw them with one another when the butterflies swarmed my system. However, I also knew their match—as strong as it was—wouldn't be completely fulfilled until I could resolve the problems and start to heal the wounds of the past that were affecting the present.

But time was ticking away. Would I be able to get it all done before the wedding?

CHAPTER 9

I stepped into the bakery the next morning. The light on the answering machine blinked with three messages. Although most orders came during working hours, it wasn't unusual to have one message every few days, but three? Even with our being closed yesterday, like any other Tuesday, having three messages was unheard of.

As the rest of the team got to work on the start of their morning preparations, I pressed play on the machine.

The first message was from one of the moms who had gone to Annabel's birthday party and wanted to place an order for three dozen cookies to pick up tomorrow morning for a coworker's birthday. No problem. We'd be able to do those first thing tomorrow.

The second order was for another three dozen cookies that the caller hoped to pick up this afternoon before her family returned home out of town. At least a dozen had to be the salted caramel. Easy enough. We'd fit them in between my two deliveries.

The third wanted two dozen cupcakes for her husband's birthday and wanted to pick them up this afternoon as well, shortly before we closed. The flavor? Salted caramel, which was one of the flavors I'd served at Annabel's party. Although the woman who'd called hadn't gotten one while she was there with her daughter, her daughter had raved about them. Okay, I'd have my team work on these when I made my second round of deliveries.

My pineapple bacon scones had been a hit last month as a result of the Love a Tree Day Festival, but one of my treats hadn't been this popular since I introduced my maple cream cheese whoopie pies as a March special two years ago. But even so, I didn't think I'd gotten such big orders for them all at one time. I'd need to put these on the regular rotation for sure at this rate.

"What did you put in those cookies?" Gina asked once I updated the team.

"Are you sure it was salt you sprinkled on top?" Bryan joked.

I laughed. "Positive. It was just sea salt." However, Gina's question had me wondering if I'd somehow done this to myself. I hadn't intended to put anything extra in the cookies, but I'd recently been experimenting with intentional thought as I made my treats as part of my training as a kitchen witch. There'd been the scones I'd hoped would have the town's residents entrust me with what paranormal being they were, and they lined up to admit they were mermaids, trolls, dryads, and more. Since then, I'd helped one guy get the confidence to ask out his girlfriend—not someone I'd matched, but I wished them all the best—helped someone else ask for a raise only for them to end up with a promotion, and helped the baseball team at their state tournament by sending a basket of treats with them on the bus for all their away games.

All along, things like this had been happening, but until last month, I hadn't realized I was actually responsible for any of it. Instead, I'd chalked it up as the power of suggestion mixed with the rumors of me being a witch. Good luck muffins before tests, confidence cookies before job interviews, scones to help with pregnancy symptoms. Now I accepted I was a witch and had put spells in all their baked goods whether I'd intended to or not.

Lily looked at me, an eyebrow arched in skepticism. She knew I could put a little something extra into the baked goods without adding calories. The others didn't, although they probably had their suspicions by now.

"Are you sure?" my green-haired baker asked me. Now that most of the trees had stopped blossoming, the dryad's hair had transitioned to a green shade from the yellowy-pink it had been a few weeks ago.

I shrugged, truly at a loss for this one. "I didn't do anything. Perhaps they liked the ratio of salt to caramel. Speaking of, Gina, can you get started on making some? Bryan, can start muffins and work on those until you are done with the first batch then hop to scones." I put Sam and Lily on cupcakes and pastries at least until the caramel was done. Then someone would start doing cookies with me until I had to leave.

Gina was hanging up the phone as I walked back through the kitchen door after returning from delivering muffins to Double Aitch and Olde Templeton.

"What's up?" I asked, watching her release a long sigh as she stared at the wall.

She turned and looked at me, wide-eyed. "You are not going to believe this. We just had an order come in for lunchtime."

"Okay . . ." That wasn't anything unheard of.

"Joanie, it's five dozen cupcakes and another five dozen cookies."

"All sea-salt caramel?" I quickly did the calculations in my head to see if I even had enough supplies for all of that.

"Not all of it, although at least half of each should be. The rest can be an assortment."

"All right." I took a deep breath. "Okay. I'm going downstairs to come up with a game plan. You all keep working on what we need to get the shop stocked for the day."

I bounded into the basement where we stored all our bulk dry goods and kept a freezer and another fridge for perishables. Every day I had a near-perfect estimate for what I would need. I didn't keep an abundance of goods, preferring to get everything fresh whenever possible. These orders had been completely unexpected, though, and I wasn't prepared. After seeing what we had for sure, I estimated we'd have enough flour and sugar for the influx of orders today, but then I wouldn't have enough for tomorrow. And never mind enough salt. It was a staple in the bakery, too, but not in the quantities I needed for all the caramel.

I'd have to send someone to the store. Sam. He could take my car. It would give him good experience in how many supplies to buy based on what the orders were. It was a skill I hadn't learned until my second trimester of school. I didn't feel right going myself. This day was already too weird.

I came back upstairs holding a large basket full of goods. I plopped it onto my station and then began to unload it all. "Bryan, go downstairs and grab our sacks of flour and sugar. Sam, I'm going to need you to go to the grocery store. You're getting a crash course in buying enough supplies for a large order. If they don't have what we need, you're going to have to drive to Knoll's Grove to check their grocery store. I don't think we have time right now for the restaurant supply store in Snowhaven. I'll have to do that after work sometime this week. Probably tonight depending on how things go."

Sam nodded. "You can count on me." He ran over to the phone to grab the order slip pad and a pen.

I got him started on what he'd have to buy but had him do the calculations for how much we would need of it all after subtracting what we had on hand.

After a few minutes, Sam proudly proclaimed, "Got it. I'm ready to go."

I fished my keys out of my pants pocket and then tossed them to him. He snatched them out of the air as the phone rang. Again.

We all stopped what we were doing.

"Suncraft Bakery, Lily speaking. How can I help you?" She paused to listen to the person on the other side of the line. "Okay . . . Okay . . . Sure, we can do that . . . Okay. That's fine . . . We'll see you then. Thank you. Have a great day." She hung the phone back up on the receiver.

"Sam, don't go anywhere just yet," I said over my shoulder before turning back to Lily. "How bad is it?"

"You are not going to believe this," she replied. "Two dozen chocolate salted-caramel cookies, two dozen chocolate chip cookies, and two dozen lemon drop cookies."

I liked the twist they'd put on the caramel cookies by asking for them to have a chocolate base, but this day was growing busier by the minute.

Behind me, Sam sighed. "Do we have enough chocolate chips and cocoa? What about lemon curd?"

"Grab whatever we'll need to make this order. It's going to be easier for us in the long run if we don't dip into tomorrow's supplies for it."

He quickly did the calculations on the order slip he had.

"Now go before we get any more orders."

"Call me if you need anything else."

"I will."

We made it ten minutes before I had to call Sam. He'd made it into the store and was going down the first aisle with the carriage. I told him to grab more cinnamon, as well as some pecans, mini marshmallows, oats, and peanut butter.

"That's quite the assortment, and I think I have an idea of what you're making. Can you tell me so I can find out if I'm right?"

"Two dozen cowboy cookies."

Sam laughed. "That's what you call them?"

"Yeah. Why?"

"I think that's what we call kitchen sink cookies. A little bit of everything."

"Oh, I like that better."

"But what's the cinnamon for? Because it isn't for those."

"Snickerdoodles."

"Got it. I'll get all of that too."

I hung up with Sam, and the rest of the team and I continued baking until Sarah arrived.

"What in the world is going on?" she asked after I filled her in on the orders. She grabbed the first tray of goods for the shop.

"I have no idea. It's never been like this. Even on our busiest days, I've always been able to anticipate exactly what we needed plus a few extras for the day-old shelf." I wiped my hands on my pink apron and went to grab a tray from the cooling rack so I could help her in the shop.

"Nuh-uh, I got this." Sarah pushed the door between the kitchen and the bakeshop open with her foot. "You're needed back here a wicked lot more than out there. It'll take me a few extra minutes solo, but it's nothing I can't manage."

I hurried back to my station. "Thanks."

The next hour was a welcome quiet—minus a phone call from Sam to say he head to Knoll's Grove to see what they had for sugar—as we prepared everything for my lunchtime deliveries. It was cheat day at the yoga studio, then I had to make it to the inn to deliver scones and cookies for Libby's tea service, and then there was a first birthday cake smash at the photography studio.

"I'm putting a moratorium on orders until I get back and can assess where we are with everything," I stated as I boxed up the three orders. Thank goodness it was a nice day out or else I'd have been kicking myself over my car not being here for the deliveries.

Once I loaded up the orders into the bike trailer, I ran across the parking lot to the yoga studio's back door with my first delivery.

Kim opened it for me without my needing to knock. "Everything okay?"

"Just a really busy day. Unexpected." I panted slightly.

"Here. Let me take those. You do what you need to do. I'll bring the check over a little later."

I thrust the box into her waiting hands, perhaps a bit too forcefully, and spun on my heels. It was a hundred and fifty feet to my bike. I made a run for it and tripped when I was halfway there. Lunging forward, I caught myself on one of the yoga practitioner's cars rather than hitting the pavement. That would have made this already chaotic day turn sour. If I wasn't careful, something like this could easily happen again.

Standing, I took a deep breath, then turned toward the sun. I centered myself, placing my palms together and clearing all thoughts from my head. If anyone were to see me, it would look like I was doing yoga by myself, and in a way, I was. This was something Gram had taught my cousin and me when we were little, although I hadn't done it in years. I'd seen Kim end her classes this way, but without the turning toward the sun part.

I drew in another deep breath through my nose and held it.

Five . . .

Four . . .

Three . . .

Two . . .

One . . .

I slowly released the breath through my mouth until there was no air left in my lungs.

Five . . .

Four . . .

Three . . .

Two . . .

One . . .

My next breath was a normal one. The complete process would have included holding my exhale for another five seconds before repeating the whole cycle at least one more time, but I'd done enough to get myself back on track. Feeling better, I power-walked to my bike and hopped on. I quickly dropped off the cake, where the photographer promised me pictures, then I rushed toward the inn. I was cutting it close.

Libby stood waiting for me in the driveway and waved me down. I coasted to a stop as she approached. She reached into my bike trailer and picked up one of the boxes.

I climbed off the bike. "Morning, Libby. Sorry—"

With a wry smile, she said, "Don't worry about it. I know it's cheat day." She started walking toward the kitchen entrance at the side of the building.

I grabbed the two other boxes from the trailer. "Yeah, that too."

She stopped in her tracks and turned back to look at me. "You okay?"

Scurrying up the driveway to catch up with her, I replied,

"Have you ever had one of those days where you expected a slow day because those days are always slow, but instead you ended up with possibly the craziest day you've ever had?"

We continued walking into the kitchen as Libby answered. "There was that one day when the B&B over on Pine Street lost power, thanks to a pine tree of all things, and suddenly we were at capacity and having to turn people away—helping them make other arrangements, of course. I wouldn't let anyone not have a place."

"Well, my day has pretty much been like that." I told her all about the overwhelming amount of orders we'd gotten at the bakery.

Libby set her bakery box on the side table where she kept her tea trays. "That's so strange. And they're all asking for the caramel ones?"

"Uh-huh. So you have some of those, too, because it made things easier." I placed my box next to hers.

"Don't even worry about it. I trust you. And they must be good if every order is asking for them."

"You have a point there."

For fifteen minutes, I helped Libby prep her tea trays, stacking everything just so. It made the day feel almost normal, but I was only delaying the inevitable.

I stepped back from the table, breaking down the bakery box. "As much as I'd love to stay for tea—"

"You need to go. I get it. Scoot."

"But really. I think after today, I'm coming for tea very soon."

Libby waved me off. I'd been telling her I'd come to tea for weeks and hadn't found the time. Annabel's party was the closest I'd come to a tea party.

"See you Friday," I called over my shoulder as I hurried out the door.

I sped back to the bakery.

"Where are we with everything?" I asked as soon as I walked into the kitchen, not stopping until I reached my workstation.

"We are pulling the last of the cookies for the huge order from the oven now. The cupcakes are cooling but still need to be frosted," Gina answered.

"And the afternoon orders?" I hated putting orders on hold if they were coming in, but until I was certain we'd finish what we already had, I couldn't take any more.

"We can handle it," Lily assured me.

"Have we gotten any more calls?"

Bryan snorted. "Several."

"And Sarah popped her head in twice to see if we could take orders from people in person," Gina added.

I'd left Sarah alone in the shop all morning. Was it as crazy there as it had been back here? I'd kick myself for not calling in reinforcements if it was.

Worried, I rushed toward the door separating the kitchen from the shop, then quickly pushed it open. There were only a few customers inside, including a regular who came in at this time every day to get something to go with lunch and a married couple who stopped in occasionally. They looked up, likely startled at my sudden entrance. I greeted them, hoping my frazzled state would be hidden by my smile.

Taking a deep breath to calm my nerves, I sidled up to Sarah as she rang out the couple buying four cupcakes, one of each of our daily flavors so they could split them.

She handed them their change and their small pastry box. "Have a great day," she said as they turned to walk toward the door.

"Everything going okay?" I asked once they'd left, concern obvious in my tone even to myself.

"Minus the two orders people tried to place, it's been a completely normal Wednesday in here."

"You sure? I can see if Lauren can come in."

She raised a hand. "It's all good. You go back and finish those orders. Are we still stopping any incoming ones?"

I sighed, both out of relief and frustration. "No, we can open back up, but we can't take anything that needs to be picked up before the end of the day. No after-school pickups. End of day—that's it."

"Got it."

I returned to the kitchen and updated my team with how we were going to take orders. Sam had returned with plenty of supplies, so we could handle whatever came our way.

As if on cue, the phone rang.

It stopped after one ring. No doubt Sarah had grabbed it so we wouldn't have to stop what we were doing back here.

"I'm really sorry about this, everyone," I continued. "If you absolutely have to leave, I understand. This is longer than I've kept any of you before without prior warning. Or if you need to call anyone to change plans, feel free to do so. I'm waving the no cell phone rule for the moment."

"We're not leaving you," Sam stated as he rolled out cookie dough.

"How would you expect to finish everything if it was just you?" Gina added from the stovetop where she was making more caramel.

Sarah popped back into the kitchen a moment later. "Got an order for a five-p.m. pickup. Three dozen cookies."

I grabbed a mixing bowl from the counter on the way back to my station. "What flavor?"

"Any flavor, although she said she'd had the salted caramel ones at Annabel's party and those were delicious."

"That's easy enough. We're prepping a few dozen of the

sea salt right now, so we'll add in another two dozen and can pick a few from the case to add variety."

Sarah gave me a thumbs-up and turned back into the store.

No more than five minutes had passed before a familiar voice hysterically cried my name in the shop, the wail clear as day through the door separating the rooms. "Joanie!"

Something had to be majorly wrong.

CHAPTER 10

Everyone in the kitchen stopped at the commotion.

Telling everyone to get back to work, I dropped the measuring cup I'd been using into my mixing bowl, then dashed into the shop.

As soon as she saw me, Chelsea flung herself at me and wrapped her arms tightly around me. "It's all ruined," she sobbed.

"What is?"

Another customer walked into the shop, so I pulled Chelsea back into the kitchen with me and then pushed her toward the bathroom to give her as much privacy as she needed. I closed the door behind us. It was snug but manageable.

"My dress is ruined!"

"Your wedding dress? How?"

"David's mom brought a few of her relatives to the house to see the dress, and I showed it to them. In a continued effort to play nice, I invited them to stay for lunch and put the dress back in the downstairs closet. Well, Celia's aunt went upstairs to use the restroom, and all of a sudden, the water is coming down the wall in the kitchen. She flooded the bathroom!"

I pictured the mess, shuddering at the thought. But I was missing something. "I'm not following."

"The other side of the kitchen wall is the closet! It was raining in there! All over my dress." She covered her face with her hands.

Now I understood. "I'm so sorry, Chelsea. Can they do anything about the dress? Take it to the cleaners?"

"Not now. Between the silk and the lace, there's nothing to be done for it. It's ruined."

Part of me found it ironic that a woman who could turn into an underwater being would choose a dress that couldn't get wet, but she didn't need to hear that.

"I'm sure it was an accident," I said and gently patted her upper arm. "All of the houses in town are on the older side. These things happen."

"No way. No one needs that much toilet paper. She wasn't even in there long. It was like she flushed the whole roll. I'm telling you—she did this to sabotage me." She let out a shuttered breath. "What am I supposed to do?

"First, breathe." I drew in a deep breath through my nose and encouraged her to mimic me.

She did.

"There. Now, is anyone still at your house?"

She shook her head.

"Well, call your mom or your maid of honor. Someone supportive who isn't David. Pull the dress out and let it dry. Reevaluate when it is. Maybe not all is lost."

She nodded, a single sob of a hiccup escaping. "Everything is going wrong."

I gave her a quick hug to calm her and hopefully stop her from breaking down again. "Not everything. Even if the dress is ruined, you'll still be marrying a wonderful man in a couple weeks. And that's what matters in the end, doesn't it?"

Chelsea sniffled. "Yeah. I guess you're right." She wiped her eyes and her cheeks, catching the tears that had fallen.

"There, all better," I said once she cracked a smile. "You good to get out of the bathroom?"

She let out a small chuckle. "Yeah."

I reached behind me and opened the door, then stepped backward into the kitchen to give Chelsea enough room to walk out.

"Hey, how's the . . . thing . . . with my great-aunt going?"

"I did some digging yesterday. Talked to David's grandmother and the Strongs." I waved my arm in a displaying motion. "As you can see, things are a bit crazy here right now. I haven't been able to do anything else today, I'm afraid."

She brought her hands up to her mouth. "Oh, my goodness, and here I am dragging you away from your work. I'm so sorry. What's going on that you are so busy?"

She followed me to my station. Someone must have grabbed the batter I'd been working on as it had gone missing. I told Chelsea to stay and then rushed to the cooling racks where several trays of cookies lay waiting for the next step.

"They're ready when you are," Sam called over his shoulder at me.

I grabbed the first tray and brought it back to my worktable, then grabbed a bowl of the salted caramel Gina had finished.

"Oh, are those the same cookies you had at Annabel's party?" Chelsea pointed to the bowl.

I dropped a small spoonful of caramel onto the center of a cookie. "It is, just not starfish shaped."

"Those were delicious!"

Never tired of hearing compliments about our baking, I

smiled. "Thanks. Guess that's why we're making dozens of them today. I had no idea they'd be such a hit after their debut."

Her mouth dropped open. "Dozens? Joanie, how many people have called in orders?"

"Seven? Ten? Almost all wanting at least a dozen of these or more."

"It's the salt," she said under her breath.

"What?"

"The salt." She leaned in and whispered, "We seafolk like our salt. Always add extra to our food, so when we can find a sweet with noticeable salt already in it? Perfection."

So had all these orders come from merrows and selkies?

Chelsea stood back up and crossed her arms. "I think you were set up by my future family."

"What do you mean?"

"If you talked to David's grandmother, word must have gotten out about you wanting to know about my great-aunt. Greta isn't against our relationship, but she doesn't hide that sort of stuff from anyone. She probably told Bruce Malloy, not even thinking twice about how much he hates my family. She's an open book, especially to him. They've known each other most of their lives, and David's grandfather was his best friend. Bruce probably organized the whole thing." Her face darkened. "He's like that. Always doing something to make other people's lives difficult."

"So you think he got other selkies to flood my shop with orders so that I'd be too busy to investigate?" I looked around at the growing boxes of prepared baked goods ready to be picked up. "I hope I didn't bake all of this for nothing."

"If they ordered them, they're going to pay for them. They wouldn't cancel. I don't think they'd be that cruel to someone who isn't me, and I'm sure they want those cookies. Besides, you have their names on their orders, don't you?"

"You have a point. And all the orders have been picked up so far." I placed the final cookie back down and then rushed to swap the tray out for another one. Once the caramel set, the cookies would be ready to be boxed up.

"Well, I'm going to let you get back to work," Chelsea said when I set the next tray onto my station. "I'm sorry they did this, and I'm sorry for taking up your time. I didn't need to bother you over the dress. It's not your problem."

I set down the spoon I'd been using for the caramel, then pulled Chelsea in for a hug. "Don't even worry about it. If this is them, so what? They gave me a bump in profits for the day. Sure, I'm busy, but it won't stop me from helping you or your great-aunt."

"Thanks." She let go of me and saw herself out, leaving me to finish the cookies.

As I returned the next tray to the rack a few minutes later, Sarah popped her head into the kitchen. "Joanie, there's someone here to see you."

Thinking it was Ken here to surprise me, I asked Sarah to have him come back later. I couldn't take any more time out of the day. He'd understand.

"It's not Ken," she replied.

"Then who is it?"

She lifted her hands out in front of her in an exaggerated shrug, her lip drawing down into a frown. "He looks familiar, but I can't be certain I've ever seen him before."

"All right. Be there in a minute."

Who in the world was it?

CHAPTER 11

I rushed to wash my hands to ensure I had no caramel on them when I went out to speak to whoever was in the shop. They'd have to deal with whatever was on my apron, though. I was a baker—random smudges of flour, batter, and frosting came with the territory.

Mr. James's smiling face welcomed me into the shop. I'd almost completely forgotten about his wanting to get together to talk about the possible shop expansion.

"Joanie, wonderful to see you again." He rushed toward me and shook my hand.

"You too, Nelson," I replied, making sure to use his name. Doing so made people feel special that you remembered them. It was something I'd learned in one of the hospitality classes I'd taken as an elective at culinary school.

"I'm back in town and was hoping you'd have the time to chat about what I mentioned the other day."

I looked back at the closed door to the kitchen. "Now?"

My face must have revealed more than my tone because he asked, "Is it not a good time? It will only be a few minutes, coffee at most. I won't take up much of your time."

Something about the way he said it made me believe he'd take up way more than he was saying he would. And after the day I'd been having, I had to wonder if Mr. James's desire to help me expand my business was even legitimate. Chelsea's suggestion that I'd been set up came back to me. I couldn't waste my time on something that wasn't real. Especially today.

"Sarah, would you mind going and boxing up whatever needs it? Someone should be coming in for their order soon. Slips are by the racks."

She nodded, one eyebrow slightly raised. I rarely asked her to step into the kitchen, but I needed my privacy out here. Luckily things were so crazy in there, she wouldn't be able to push a chair up to the window to snoop like she was known to do.

"I can give you five minutes right now," I told Mr. James once the door between the rooms had swung closed. "There's still a lot to do before the end of the day."

"Come on," he said with a too-sweet smile, "let's grab a coffee."

I shook my head. "Here's fine. Really. It will take five minutes to walk over there and order." Never mind waiting for the drinks to be made.

Undeterred, he said, "Wouldn't you like to sit down for a few minutes to discuss this?"

"I have chairs right there." I pointed to the small seating area at the side of the room. "We can talk here."

"But what if one of your customers comes in? You wouldn't want them overhearing and spreading rumors around town about you doing something to the bakery, would you?"

The rumor comment raised the hairs on the back of my

neck. It was as if he knew exactly what buttons to press. But they weren't good ones.

"If a customer walks in, then I will be able to assist them because I am here." I walked toward the table and sat at one of the chairs. Aside from my bike ride to make deliveries, this had been the first time I'd sat down all day. I'd likely regret sitting once I stood back up, but it was too late to worry about it now. I gave Mr. James a pointed look, wondering if he'd slip and give up the ruse. "Is there a problem with talking here? After all, this is my bakery . . . the one you want to help me expand or so you say."

"So I say? Look"—he put up his hands—"I don't know why you won't believe me. I'm an honest guy trying to take a prospective business partner, who just so happens to be a pretty girl, out for coffee."

I crossed my arms. "At a time when I've already said it's not good for me."

Finally, Mr. James joined me at the table, likely realizing he wasn't getting anywhere.

But it was too little too late.

"I have a ton of orders coming in, and all you're doing is trying to distract me from doing them right now. You can go back and tell David's family that I'm not biting this time. They'll have to figure out some other way to keep me busy."

"David? Who's David? I didn't turn up a boyfriend in my research about you."

Research? All he'd told me before was he'd tried some of my baked goods on Monday and wanted to talk. This had to be a setup.

"I am not getting involved with someone who is having issues with her boyfriend and his family," Mr. James continued.

I barked out a laugh. "David is not my boyfriend, and you

know it. Your acting is very good, but I'm not buying it anymore. I won't tell anyone that, though, so you can get your full payment for this gig."

Mr. James popped up from the chair. "My research also never revealed that you are crazy. All I wanted to do was help a local small business reach its full potential. After this, I'm not sorry to say it will not be your bakery." He gave me one strong nod of his head before turning around and storming out the door.

If he had been hired by David's family, then it was a good riddance to have him finally leave. This whole ordeal had taken longer than the five minutes I had been willing to give him. Now I could finally get back to work. On the other hand, if he wasn't hired by them and had been telling me the truth, then I'd blown my first decent chance at expanding the bakery into something more. With everything going on, however, I hadn't had much time to think of it and imagine the possibilities. I could only hope another opportunity would come my way once the time was right.

"That was certainly interesting," Sandra said, popping out of nowhere and sitting down at the seat Mr. James had vacated.

"It was," I replied, hoping she'd take my lack of elaboration as a hint I didn't want to talk about it.

"Do you really think he was hired to bother you?"

I stood. "Anything is possible. Did you hear about Chelsea's dress?"

"I saw the whole thing. Nasty what that woman did." So Chelsea was right. It hadn't been an accident.

As I walked back into the bakery kitchen, Sandra followed me. I hoped she realized I wouldn't be able to talk to her in here like I could when we were alone.

"Everything okay out there?" Sarah looked up at me from

the counter in the middle of the kitchen where we kept our boxing supplies. She kept her finger on a piece of string at the top of the box she was wrapping.

"It's all good. You're okay to head back out there."

"Joanie gave that man a real what for!" Sandra added before looking around the kitchen. "Wow. They ordered all those cookies?"

"Yeah," I answered, not thinking.

"What was that?" Sarah asked as she finished up with the box.

"Just giving myself a little pep talk, that's all. Okay, every-one, you've all done great. A little longer and we'll be done." I clapped my hands, then thrust my fist in the air. "Go team!"

Behind me, Lily laughed, as did Sandra. Sarah shook her head slowly as she walked by me and into the kitchen as if embarrassed for me. The others were all looking down and hadn't seen me and my poor excuse for a cheer routine.

"You're funny," Sandra said from behind me as I returned to my worktable after grabbing another tray of cookies needing caramel. "You remind me of someone. I can't say who though. Are all ghosts like me? Unable to remember?"

I shook my head.

"That's all right. I like being unique. These cookies really do look delicious. It's a shame I can't try one. Chelsea was right when she talked about us loving salt . . ."

Dropping caramel onto the cookies became one of those zen sort of tasks and I tuned everything out as I completed this tray and the next. Then I ran out of caramel, which caused me to tune back in.

Sandra was still talking. About cookies. "I think I also enjoyed peanut butter cookies. You know, the kind with the chocolate piece in the middle? Again, it was the salt from the peanut butter that did it."

Maybe she needed exposure to something that would jog her memory the same way these cookies were helping her recall her favorite kinds. But what?

I gathered up the ingredients I needed to make a smaller batch of caramel, then took it all to the stovetop.

Sarah darted back into the kitchen, grabbed two of the boxes she'd packed, then returned to the shop. Someone must have been picking up their order. I'd have to ask her if they were all from out of town, meaning David's relatives who'd come for the party, or if any of his in-town relatives had placed orders too. After this, I'd have to start instituting our getting last names for the orders. First names had always been good for us before since everyone knew everyone in town.

I whisked the sugar and water together in a saucepan until the sugar dissolved, then added in the butter and brought the heat up under the pan. Although I had to wait about ten minutes until it would be done, I set the timer for seven to ensure the caramel wouldn't burn.

"Did you know that this place used to be a floral shop?" Sandra asked, leaning against the central counter behind me. "There only ever was the one baker when I lived here. There was a candy shop, though. I've noticed we don't have one of those anymore in town."

She followed me back to my station, where I cleaned up while waiting on the caramel.

Next to me, Lily set down her piping bag. "Just need to finish adding a bit more decoration to these and then I think I'm done with what I have. Let me know if any of you will need help in fifteen minutes."

"Great job, Lily. We've almost made it, everyone!"

"Is her hair always green?" Sandra asked. "That seems to be a thing with you young people these days."

Glancing at Sandra, I realized how easy to forget that she wasn't from this time period. She wore jeans, although not the current style, and a short-sleeve button-up with a neckline that had extra ribbon extending from it and tied into a bow. No one in Heartwood Hollow would have batted an eye if they could see her.

"In my day, the most colorful hair around was mine." Sandra floofed her red locks, which were down today. "Well, mine and most of my family's."

When the timer went off, I walked back to the stovetop. I took the pan off the heat, turning off the burner in the process, then added in heavy cream, followed by vanilla and sea salt. As I whisked it all together, Sandra talked more about the flower shop and the florist. It was great she was starting to remember things from before, and it gave me hope she'd remember who killed her . . . eventually.

I set the pan to cool as Lily finished the decorations on her cookies. She moved over to help Gina frost the last of the cupcakes. Bryan and Sam finished up shortly thereafter, adding their treats into the oven. Fortunately, those didn't need to be decorated. I returned to my station to finish cleaning.

When I turned back around, Sam was slumped against the wall. Gina and Lily were leaning against Gina's workstation, and Bryan had turned one of the milk crates Sam had used to carry supplies into the kitchen earlier into a makeshift stool. My team looked the way I felt.

"Why don't you all go home," I suggested to them.

"But the stuff isn't all out of the oven," Sam protested weakly.

"I can take care of it. Load your things into the wash racks if you haven't, and I'll send them through when you all leave."

"You sure?" Lily asked, tilting her head slightly to get a better look at me.

I nodded firmly. "Positive. I've asked enough of you all already. This is way longer than you've had to stay before, and I appreciate it so much, including the staggered lunches. I will make it up to you all."

"With a day off tomorrow?" Bryan half joked.

I laughed. "If only it were Monday. No, but I'll think of something."

"She already bought us lunch," Gina scolded him.

"No, it's okay. You all deserve it," I said, my hand up to stop Gina from trying to refute my statement. "But tomorrow will feel much more like a regular day with so many of our orders today coming from those who were heading out of town."

Sam, usually one of the last to leave whenever he didn't have somewhere to be, was the first to straighten. His area was already clean. He headed for the closet, grabbed his signature beanie that he wore no matter the weather, and walked toward the back door. "See everyone tomorrow."

Gina and Lily were the next to leave, followed by Bryan.

Sandra continued talking as I worked. I wondered if she was this chatty during her life or if she was making up for lost time. Unfortunately, none of what she'd said so far had been useful for figuring out who'd killed her. Then again, with her memory the way it was, she could have remembered but had forgotten to tell me.

I slid a rack of dirty baking supplies into our industrial dishwasher at the corner of the room, then turned to her.

As she paused to take a breath, I asked, "Any luck remembering who killed you?" I hadn't meant to be so blunt, but I was tired and hungry. Although I'd made sure my team had all had lunch, I hadn't taken the time for myself to have anything.

She blinked her eyes twice rapidly as if she hadn't been expecting the question. She thought a moment. "Nope."

"Sorry, it's just that you've been talking about a few things here and there that made me believe you were remembering more, like the florist and the candy shop. I had to ask."

"I really am trying," she said, reaching up and touching the right front side of her head, "but it's not there. And I don't think I could ever forget this town. People change, but overall, this place doesn't."

I hoped the part about the town wasn't true. Having our paranormal support group suggested that it wasn't. If the group had existed back when Sandra was alive, perhaps there wouldn't be the same level of animosity between the selkies and the merrows that there was now. It would have been one less hurdle for Chelsea if being a merrow wasn't also a problem.

I glanced at the oven. There were two minutes left on the timer. "Hold that thought." I darted into the shop. "Can you help with some boxing?"

"Sure." Sarah followed me into the kitchen. "Where is everyone?"

I explained as we each grabbed a tray of cool cookies, and she set to boxing as I pulled the remaining trays out of the oven. Thank goodness they looked perfect or else I would have been scrambling to make new batches.

When she was done boxing, Sarah headed back into the shop with the broom, dustpan, and glass cleaner as I drizzled still-hot caramel onto the cookies. Now they needed to set, but beyond that, we'd survived our crazy day of baking.

With nothing left to do but wait for those cookies, it was time to clean back here. As I went about my routine, Sandra continued talking, this time about swimming in the river versus the sea, the sea being preferable because of the salt content.

I finished at the same time Sarah returned to the kitchen to put the cleaning supplies in the closet. Together we packed up the remaining two trays of cookies then headed into the shop to wait for the last pickup.

The time we'd usually flip the sign from *open* to *closed* came and went, but with the last order still here, we couldn't lock up. I offered to let her go home, but she refused.

Finally, five minutes later—fortunately not longer than that—two women sauntered in. I recognized both of them from Annabel's party. They were two of the women who had sneered at Chelsea as they walked by to go outside while she and I were talking.

"Hello, ladies. We have your orders waiting for you right here." I smiled, still trying to be nice despite my suspicions of what had happened today and doing my best to not let on to how tired this day had made me. Placing my hand on one of the boxes, I let my fingers pivot on top as I walked around the corner to ring them out. "I thank you so much for all your business today. I'm so glad everything was such a hit at the party on Saturday."

"You're being much nicer to them than I would be," Sandra said. She, however, didn't have a business to run. No matter why they had ordered, they were here to pay for that order. It would have been a different story if no one had come for their baked goods.

They said nothing as each woman paid for her order, and Sarah handed them their stack of boxes.

"And those were the ringleaders," I told Sarah after they left.

She cocked her head to the side. "Ringleaders?"

I walked to the door to finally flip the sign to *closed* and lock up for the night. Then as Sarah counted the day's till, I told her of my suspicions regarding today's influx of orders.

"How can people be like that?" Sarah asked, shaking her head as she turned off the shop's lights.

I led her out the back door, Sandra right behind her. "No idea." The words came out as a half scoff. "Now if only that was the last of it, I'd be happy."

"You think there could be more?"

"I really hope not. Today was exhausting." Given my opinion on spreading gossip, I couldn't believe I was about to ask her my next question. "But tell me if you hear anything, okay? I'd like to be prepared if it isn't."

CHAPTER 12

Beyond the three dozen cookies ordered yesterday for this morning, which I doubted were related to the rest of yesterday's orders, nothing new had been called in overnight, much to my relief and that of my entire baking team. I'd brought them all coffee, going so far as to meet Gary at Leafs and Grounds before it officially opened for the day to get it. Although my team was grateful for the coffee and the small pick-me-up the caffeine gave them, they trudged through the morning more than they would have had yesterday been a normal Wednesday. I'd have to figure out something to make it up to them still. Too bad we didn't have any Monday muffins left. That would have done the trick for all of us.

Although I felt some of the lingering effects from yesterday's long day, I wasn't in as bad a shape as the others seemed. Then again, I'd pretty much gone straight to bed after a small dinner and a cup of herbal tea meant to quiet my mind so I would sleep restfully. Saffy hadn't minded and took the extra time to curl up in between my knees in stride. Without my usual dinner, however, I'd woken up ravenous and was especially grateful for Gary having stashed a marsh-mallow rice treat away for me.

After a quiet morning, I let the team all go home early, vowing to take care of the cleaning for everyone with the hope they could all rest before continuing their day. Sam was due back in the shop for a shift, but I even told him to grab a nap and lunch before returning. I had the shop handled by myself until then.

The whole day was slow, almost as if we were being rewarded for surviving yesterday's craziness. Our regulars had come in, but no one else. It gave me time to work with Sam some more to go through the proper cleaning protocol of the shop and cashing out the register at closing time. I hadn't made it to the bank yesterday during its extended business-banking hours with all the chaos at the bakery, but I'd get there today. When I called Rachael at the bank to tell her I was coming right at the end of the day, she promised to stay until I got there.

"It's the least I can do after all you've done for me," she said, referring to my keeping her stocked with baked goods containing ginger to help ease her morning sickness during her pregnancy. Now that she was in her second trimester, the symptoms had lessened, but they weren't gone entirely. Rachael didn't know about my being a witch, and I doubted she would have cared with as much as she'd been helped. But part of me wondered now if it was truly the ginger in the treats that had helped her or the well-wishes I'd been thinking when I baked them—the unintentional spells I'd put into the recipe. Maybe it was both. It probably didn't matter since the treats had worked.

On my way up to the bank, I called Ken. My shoulders relaxed at hearing his voice, and I sighed in relief.

"Joanie, is everything okay? You sound off."

"Yeah, it's just good to talk to you. How are you? What are you up to?"

"Hanging out with Ivy, trying to figure out dinner."

Normalcy. That's what I needed.

I turned into the bank parking lot. "Mind if I join you?"

"Not at all. How far are you?"

"At the bank now to make a deposit."

"Great. Then I'll see you soon."

I pressed *end call* on my cell phone screen and pulled open the door to the bank. Rachael greeted me with a huge grin on her face.

"You look wonderful. Positively glowing," I told her.

"Thank you. I feel so much better. More and more every day."

I plopped my purse onto the counter of the business-banking window and then drew out the deposit envelope, made extra heavy by the coins I had brought with me. "I'm so glad. Let's get a look at you."

She stepped back and pressed her hands to her small but noticeable bump.

"Do you know what you're having yet?"

Shaking her head, she returned to the counter. "We still have a few weeks to go before we find out. We opted not to get one of those genetic tests to find out. But I'm so excited."

"Be sure to let me know, okay?" I pulled out two handfuls of rolled coins and a paper envelope of dollar bills, then passed it all to Rachael.

"Think you want to make a gender reveal cake for us?"

A welcome grin spread across my face. "That would be so much fun! I would love that."

"Great, I'll be sure to drop it off to you in an envelope after my appointment."

"Wait, you don't even want to find out beforehand?"

"No." She ran the bills into a sorter machine to be counted. "I want to be as surprised as everyone else. Mark wants to know early, but he'd never be able to keep it from me. And if that happened, I'd be liable to burst with the news and ruin the surprise for everyone. It's better this way."

"I'm honored to be entrusted with your secret. Thank you." I'd been confided in a lot recently, but this type of secret was one of my favorites.

"And how about some cookies with pink and blue on them to go along with the theme?"

"Of course. I can do whatever you like. Any flavor requests?"

She thought a moment as she stacked the coin rolls. "I'll get back to you on that."

"Sounds good. You have plenty of time."

Rachael keyed a few more things into her computer, and then the little printer next to it lit up, spitting out a small piece of paper after a few moments. She handed me my deposit slip, which I put back into the bank envelope. "Have a great rest of your day, Joanie."

I had every intention of doing just that.

CHAPTER 13

"What are your thoughts on pizza?" Ken asked as he opened the door to let me inside. "That new pizza place opened up finally."

"Sounds good to me." I'd been looking forward to having another pizza place nearby that delivered.

The one on Main Street did enough business that it didn't need to have a delivery service. There was another place right outside of town in Bug's Creek that I liked too, but they didn't deliver either. The new restaurant, Mama à la Pizza, was nestled on a side street, a little off the beaten path with no other stores around except for a small credit union next door. As a result, it would probably do most of its business via delivery.

We perused the menu online before settling on a pepperoni and pineapple pizza, pepperoni on half because Ivy wasn't a fan. She'd gotten more adventurous lately in what she ate, but some things were still a work in progress. By the time we placed the order, garlic knots and cheese fries had also been added to our cart.

Ivy had been playing outside, enjoying the warm

summer evening on her new swing set, since before I got there, leaving Ken and me to wait for dinner. I leaned against him on the couch, drawing my feet up onto the cushion.

He laid his arm behind me, settling his hand on my upper arm. "Long day?"

"Today wasn't bad. Yesterday, however, was a trying day."

"Oh?"

I had yet to tell him about my agreeing to help Chelsea with the tiara her great-aunt was haunting, so I filled him in until the doorbell rang. He answered the door and paid for our pizza, then brought it into the kitchen, me following behind him. After setting the food down on the counter, he called for Ivy in the backyard.

Never one to miss calling dibs on the largest slice of pizza in the box, Ivy came running inside. "Hi Joanie!" she chirped as she skidded to a halt at the table.

"Ready to eat, kiddo?" Ken asked, opening the pizza box.

Ivy bounced with anticipation, and her eyes lit up at the huge slices. They were so big I wouldn't have been surprised if she couldn't finish it given the other sides we'd gotten.

Ken slid the slice of pizza out onto a paper plate, then handed it to Ivy. She marched over to the table and climbed up into her chair, the plate still in her hand. She never put the plate down as Ken handed me a slice and then took one for himself. Ken grabbed the container of garlic knots, I took the cheese fries, and as we joined Ivy at the table, she pushed the pizza slice on the plate until the tip hung over the edge. She took a huge bite.

"It's hot!" She fanned at her mouth.

"Thanks for the warning," I told her, then blew on my slice to cool it down. As delicious as piping-hot pizza was, the last thing I needed was to burn my tongue or mouth on gooey cheese. It would hinder me at my job for a few days if I did that, and I needed my tastebuds in tip-top shape.

Ken folded his pizza slice in half and took a bite. "Hot," he agreed, "but so good."

Ivy nodded exaggeratingly. "Yum, yum, yum," she said, her mouth full of another bite of pizza. The temperature of the first bite must not have bothered her too much.

I blew on my slice once more for good measure before I tried it. "Oh, this is good."

"Good call on the flavor combination," Ken commented, reaching for a garlic knot.

"Well, once you told me Ivy liked pineapples on pizza, I thought it would be good to try. Reminds me of the scones I made last month, only pepperoni instead of bacon and obviously the cheese." I turned to Ivy. "Do you like cherries?"

"Like the kind on ice cream sundaes?"

"Exactly those kind."

"Uh-huh! I always steal Daddy's too." That didn't surprise me one bit, although I was sure it was more "stealing" than actual theft. Ken was so wrapped around her finger, he'd just as easily give them to her if she asked.

"Pretty sure I saw it on the menu as an available topping. We should try it sometime."

"Okay!"

Ken looked at me as if I'd said something crazy, but I wasn't sure if it was more a reaction to my suggestion or her agreeing to it. I laughed.

Ivy set down her plate for the first time since Ken handed it to her. She clasped her hands, interlacing her fingers, and leaned forward. "Joanie, I have a question."

"So serious." I mirrored her position. "What is it?"

"You know how we went to Annabel's party the other day?"

"I do." Now I understood where she was going with this. I took a bite of pizza as a stall tactic, wanting her to say what was on her mind instead of accidentally saying more than I should.

"Are mermaids real the way that dryads and you are real?"

She sat waiting expectantly as I glanced over to Ken.

"She's been going on and on about it since the party," he replied with a shrug.

I swallowed my bite, ready to answer her, but she added, "How am I supposed to be their guardian and help protect them if I don't know if they even exist?"

"Do you want them to?" I asked.

"Uh-huh. That party was so fun! They even let us keep the mermaid tails."

"Well, I have it under good authority that they do exist, and maybe someday you'll get to meet one." I hoped my non-confirmation about any of the party's attendees would satisfy her curiosity. She'd met several people she'd consider mermaids that day, but it wasn't up to me to tell her.

She clapped excitedly. "That would be so cool!"

"Just remember that a lot of people don't believe in these sorts of things, though, and wouldn't even if you told them, so—"

She laid her hands flat on the table. "I haven't told anyone. I promise. That would make me a bad guardian."

"You're doing a great job, kiddo," Ken told her, and I agreed. Keeping a secret like that was difficult for a seven-year-old. It had been hard enough for me as a teen about my seeing ghosts.

Picking apart a garlic knot, I asked, "Is that all you wanted to know?"

"Yep!" She pushed the pizza slice farther over the edge of

her plate so she could eat some more of it then lifted the plate toward her face.

Somehow, Ivy finished two slices of pizza, the second having portions of pepperoni on one edge, a garlic knot, and several fries. Ken was shocked she didn't pick the pepperoni off, but I knew I could get her to try anything, especially after pointing out that if she didn't like it, she'd still have plenty of pizza left to eat. Despite their enormous size, Ken and I finished off the other slices. The pizza was that good.

It was still light out after we ate, so Ivy headed back outside. Ken and I sat back on the couch, resuming our earlier positions. I needed to get him a tea kettle so I could have tea whenever I visited, even if I was the only one who used it. Although I had a feeling that if I did that, Ivy would start. I was younger than her when I'd first had tea, drinking from a child-size mug. Gram had given the mug to me when I visited one time, filling it with one of her friend Miss Susan's herbal blends. I'd been hooked on tea from that day on.

"I can tell something is still weighing heavy on your mind," Ken said. "Care to share?"

In the few months I'd known him, Ken hadn't always supported my dealing with ghostly issues, even after seeing it for himself. And that had been a successful attempt to help a ghost who turned out to be his grandmother, where he gained a previously unknown cousin from it.

We'd broken up over my abilities and insistence to help others when my next case involved a possessed knife that led to its current owner pulling it out—closed—in my shop. Ken had said it was too dangerous for me. He'd come around eventually, though, and right in the nick of time.

Since then, Ken had been keeping more of an open mind about what I could do, but if he thought a closed knife was putting me in danger, then what I was about to tell him would put him to the test.

I took a deep breath. "Sandra, Chelsea's great-aunt, was murdered."

His eyes grew wide as he raised his eyebrows. "Oh . . . wow. That's terrible. How long ago was this? Did they catch the person who did it?"

"Years ago. Before Chelsea's mom was born. Someone went to jail for it, but after talking to some people, I'm not so sure he was the one who killed her." I filled him in on what I'd been told by Greta and the Strong family.

"And you can't ask Sandra?"

I shook my head. "She doesn't remember anything about her death, let alone who did it. Sometimes she remembers nothing at all."

He nodded slowly, taking it all in. "Couldn't get an easy mystery to solve, could you?"

I laughed. "I thought this would be my easy case when she showed up able to talk. So much for that."

"Well, I could ask around at work. We do a lot of volunteer work at the senior center, and some of the seniors volunteer for different things at the hospital. One of them might remember something if I ask." Rubbing the side of his face with his hand, he sighed. "But be careful, okay? If the person who went to jail is innocent, then we don't know if the murderer is still out there."

"You know I will, but you don't have to do that. We don't need people to start spreading rumors around town."

He laughed. "They already do. And I won't say anything about the murder. I could say I'm looking for information on a girl who had been friends with my grandmother. It's a great cover."

"I know all of this makes you uncomfortable. Are you sure?"

"Please. It would make me feel better knowing that I can help in some way. Especially because this is a murder case."

It warmed my heart that he wanted to help. But how could he go poking around without stirring up the rumor mill? Heartwood Hollow had been shaken by the two deaths so close together. Undoubtedly, most of the volunteers he'd talk to would remember when this all happened. After the tizzy last month created by my asking about the north woods, I now expected it would happen again once word got out about "hot doc" asking questions about Sandra.

But we had to try.

"Okay. You can help. But no telling me what I can and can't do. I'll be okay unless I get crushed by an overwhelming pile of boxed cookies."

He belted out a laugh but quickly quieted when he saw I wasn't joking. "Could that really happen? Wait, I take that back. You tripped over a piece of lettuce." His smile returned.

The memory of how I'd met Ken made me smile, but "I did not trip over lettuce. The hairbrush with your grandmother in it jumped out of my bag and made me fall."

"Is that what happened?" He chuckled as I nodded. "So what about these piles and piles of cookie boxes?"

Although he still had a smile on his face, I doubted he'd be entertained by my answer. "I was the subject of some sabotage by extra busyness in my attempts to find out more information about Sandra."

"See? This is what I mean by being careful."

"It was harmless. The busyness was extra business. They paid me. David's family doesn't like Chelsea because they don't like Sandra for what they feel she did to one of their friends. And then he died, and then she died."

"Wait, was he murdered too?" The sudden uptick in worry was evident in his voice.

"No. He died in a car accident while he was out of town."

He seemed to be relieved by my answer and began to play with my hair.

"For all we know, the killer is long gone," I added a bit sleepily thanks to a full belly and the motion of his fingers. "Wouldn't we have heard about more murders?"

"Not if the killer believes they got away with it and never killed again."

I hadn't thought about that possibility. It was plausible, especially if it had happened because a human saw Sandra as a merrow.

"Do you think David's family is hiding the truth about the real murderer?" he asked when I didn't respond.

I shrugged. "Anything is possible, I guess." It was one of my theories, although Ken's suggestion of an accidental murder was quickly taking root in my mind too.

"Well, there's nothing more we can do about it this evening, so how about we sit for a little while longer, and then Ivy and I can walk you home. I know you have to get to bed soon and need tea first. Gotta get up early since those cookies won't bake themselves." He grew quiet a moment. "Or can they?"

Now it was my turn to laugh. "I don't have that type of magic."

CHAPTER 14

Friday proved to be a normal day in the shop, and it left me hopeful that Wednesday's attempt to stall me from looking into Sandra's murder would be the end of it. The wedding was fast approaching, and I had yet to hear an update about Chelsea's dress. For now, I was taking that as a good sign.

On Saturday, Sam and I drove a large order of sugar cookies up to the senior center for a cookie-decorating program along with a vast array of toppings. His grandmother, Trudy, had come up with the idea, and he and I were thrilled to volunteer our time and the supplies to be a part of this event. The orders I'd gotten on Wednesday had more than made up for the cost of today's event, so in a way, the attempted sabotage had been a blessing in disguise.

We rolled our supplies into the center's cafeteria, where all the tables currently stood empty but would soon be full of people.

Ken lit up and waved as I made eye contact with him across the room. He was talking with Liz, one of my customers who had recently gotten a job as an assistant activities coordinator for the nursing home, as well as several other people from town. Although I didn't see nametags or badges designating them as such, I assumed they were volunteers and staff here at the senior center.

"Hi, Joanie!" Ivy called as she ran up to me, a rag in her hand. She stopped a couple feet away. "I wiped the tables so they are really clean. Let me show you where to put all of that."

If she kept this up, I'd have a new high school intern by the time she was old enough.

We followed Ivy to a row of long tables set up along the far wall. Unlike the rest, these didn't have chairs set up in front of them.

"Daddy said to put the cookies over there," she said pointing to one end of the tables, "and all of the decorating stuff after that." She scrunched up her nose.

"What do *you* say?" Asking for her help or opinion had gone a long way in forming our relationship since our misunderstanding over blueberry muffins the first time she came to my house.

"I say you make two piles of cookies. One here"—she pointed to the close end of the table before pointing to the far end—"and one over there. All of the decorating stuff can go in the middle. Then the line won't get too long. Who likes to wait for cookies?"

"I like your thinking. I think we'll do that."

She beamed before running off toward another table, leaving Sam and me to set up.

Soon, we were joined by two of the volunteers Ken had been talking to. They set up bowls for us to put decorations into and trays in front of the piles of cookies. That way participants could put their cookies and decorations they wanted to use on trays, making everything easier to take back with them.

After we were all set up, Sam excused himself, and Ken popped over to say hello, giving me a quick kiss on the cheek.

"This looks great. You went above and beyond with it all."

I surveyed the colorful spread. My team and I had made double the number of cookies that had been requested. The extras were needed. If I knew kids and the elderly like I thought I did, more than a few cookies would go missing before the end of the activity.

"What's in that box?" Ken pointed to the last box on my rolling cart.

"These are pastry bags in case any of the cookies survive the event and don't get eaten before everyone goes home." I'd stayed up stamping the bags with my logo, hoping that the participants' family members would be inspired to stop by to satisfy their own sweet tooths after seeing the treats. Sure, I could have ordered them that way, but as the only sweets baker in town, I never worried about my bags on a normal day. However, there'd be people from outside of town participating today, and getting my name out there would be a benefit to me.

Since Mr. James's visit about expanding—whether he was hired by David's family as another distraction being beside the point—I'd begun to think more about an eventual bakery expansion beyond the table and chairs I had in there now. I didn't know what I was going to do, but little steps now like these bags to help make Suncraft Bakery's name more visible would pay off someday.

Ken kissed my forehead. "That's a great idea."

"I may have stuffed them all with a coupon for a free cookie, too, as an added incentive to check out the shop."

He laughed, then muttered, "piles of cookies," likely

thinking back to my comment the other night about being crushed by full cookie boxes.

"Where can I put these?" I tapped the box on the cart with my foot.

He scanned the room, then pointed. "How about over by the door on that little table there? We can have the kids grab them for anyone at the tables who needs one. That way, the seniors don't need to keep getting up."

"Great." I took one step away from him.

"After the event, there's someone here I think you should talk to about the whole Sandra thing."

I turned back toward him, an eyebrow raised. "Who?"

"His name's Vince McAllister. Used to be the editor for the town's paper. Now he's one of my senior volunteers at the hospital, and he likes to keep everybody informed about what's going on with notices all over the bulletin boards here and at the hospital. He's how we got so many people to sign up. He made sure everyone knew about it. If anyone's going to know anything from that time, it would be him."

"Thanks." I got onto my tiptoes and kissed his cheek. "It means a lot that you would look into this."

"I told you I would."

"Yeah, but you didn't have to."

"And go back on my word? Who would I be then?" He pointed to Ivy over at yet another table, scrubbing away. "Besides, if the guardian ever found out I didn't help you when I could, I'd never hear the end of it."

He had a point. Ivy took her job very seriously. After another quick kiss on his cheek, I turned and wheeled my cart to the table Ken had pointed to. As I plopped the box down on top of it, Sam walked through the door, holding his grandmother by her arm.

"Look who I found," he said, a big smile on his face. "Grama, you remember Joanie, right?"

"Of course I do. I'm old, but my memory is fine. Lovely to see you again, dear." She dropped Sam's arm and extended both of hers toward me.

"You too, Trudy." I walked into the woman's waiting hug. She was comfortable and warm, likely a result of her multiple cardigans despite the weather outside. It wasn't hot in here, but it wasn't cold either. "How have you been?"

She stepped out of our embrace and with a wry smile said, "Well, I'm not getting any younger, but I can't complain."

I smiled back at the old woman, and she patted my hand. Her wrinkled skin felt soft, almost velvety. Although Gram was young for a grandmother, her hands were on their way to becoming like this, and it made me want my Saturday phone call with her all the more. I still needed the wards put back up around my house too. I'd have to convince her to come visit. She'd been saying she was going to, but her coven was restructuring after the death of one of its prime members.

"I'm glad you are doing well. And thank you for coming up with the idea for this event. It's wonderful, and I'm so happy to take part."

She chuckled. "Well, I wanted to do something different than our weekly BINGO night. There's only so many times a month I can do that. And I miss doing things with the young people. They were my favorite part of running the candy shop. Sammy's the youngest, and well, he's no child anymore."

A blush crept onto Sam's cheeks. "Grama . . ."

"Now, you hear me," she started. "It's the truth. Look at you. A wonderful young man if I do say so myself."

"He really is," I agreed.

Just then, a swell of noise reached the room from down

the hall, and moments later, dozens of senior citizens entered the room. My neighbors George and Nathan waved to me as they crossed the room and found seats close to the cookie table. No doubt, George would be trying to sneak a few. He had a huge sweet tooth. Both he and his son did.

"Shall we go find a seat before all the good ones are taken?" Trudy asked Sam.

"Lead the way." To me, he added, "You're sure you don't need me for anything?"

"Go have fun." I shooed him away with my hands, a big grin on my face. He'd been looking forward to this since we put it on our calendar at the shop.

"Come find me when the program is over," Trudy said. "I'd love to talk with someone who knows what it's like to run a store on Main Street."

I nodded, and they turned away off in search of seats.

"Hello, Joanie," a familiar voice said from behind me.

I spun to find my neighbor Matt standing there, his page boy cap in his hand. "Hi Matt, I'm so pleased to see you."

"Signed up as soon as I heard your cookies were going to be involved. Have you seen my little friend anywhere around? I assumed she'd be here since her dad is running today's program."

I scanned the crowd for Ivy but didn't see her. "She was here earlier. She'll be so excited to see you." Since having dinner together that first time, Ivy had developed a real fondness for Matt, and he for her.

"All right everyone," Liz called across the room, his hands positioned around his mouth to act as a megaphone. "I know you're all happy to see one another but remember to leave some room for the kids to sit with you. You're doing this activity together."

As if on cue, a second swell of noise reached the room, this one louder and higher pitched.

Students from the elementary, middle, and senior high schools entered the room in pairs, but the line quickly devolved as the kids spotted loved ones or their friends.

"Mattie!" a voice squealed over the din.

Matt chuckled. "There she is." He braced himself, setting one foot slightly in front of the other as Ivy came bounding toward him. She paused just long enough to curb her momentum before wrapping her arms around his middle, and he pulled her in for a hug.

"How's my best gal?"

"Great, Mattie." She looked up at him. "Will you sit with me?"

"I would sit nowhere else. You go on and pick the seat."

She took him by the hand, and he nodded his farewell to me as she led him to an open spot at a table already occupied by Annabel and another girl I recognized from the birthday party, along with three senior citizens.

When it seemed like everyone had found their seats, Ken and Liz hushed the crowd, thanked everyone for coming, then called me up to explain how the activity would go.

Two hours later, the cookie decorating was over, and everyone had made at least one cookie. The conversation had kept everyone at their seats unless they needed a refill on decorations. It was great to see the different generations interacting so harmoniously, no one caring if the kid over there was a mermaid or that man over there a dryad. If only we could act like this all the time. Maybe Sandra wouldn't have been killed if people had been like this back then.

Until I learned who the killer was, my current belief was that her death was tied to a human seeing her change. Or she was killed because of the supposed blame that had been placed on her for her ex-boyfriend's accidental death. Or because her then-current boyfriend had been jealous of a romantic relationship that probably didn't exist.

I sighed. I was no further to solving her case than I had been when I started. Hopefully the former editor of the paper would have a lead for me.

As people filed out of the room, many stopped to thank me for the program. Some told me to make this a regular activity or to come back at Christmas with holiday decorations. Others told me they were heading to the bakery right now to get more cookies. It warmed my heart to be a part of such a great event.

Once most had left, I quickly stopped to chat with Trudy, but it was easy to see she was tired. When I offered to come visit her at the nursing home in a few days so we could talk then, she agreed, and Sam brought her back to the nursing home. Since it was connected to the senior center, he didn't have far to go and returned a few minutes later to help me with the cleanup.

Ken tapped me on the shoulder as I gathered the remaining supplies at one of the tables. I turned toward him to see he was standing next to an elderly man.

"Joanie, this is Vincent McAllister, who I was telling you about earlier."

Vincent stuck out his hand, and I took it in mine. His handshake was firm, and his hands rough as if he'd worked with them all his life. Not what I'd expected for a newspaper editor.

"Please, call me Vince. Ken told me you have some questions regarding a murder we had back in town decades ago. I'd be happy to tell you what I know." He leaned in. "And what I think." He straightened and gave me a wink.

I liked him and his mischievous nature immediately. "I would appreciate that immensely, thank you."

"There's a small office down the hall that we store supplies in for several of our other activities here at the center. We can talk there."

Where hopefully I would get some answers.

CHAPTER 15

After checking in with Sam, who said he was fine continuing to clean up and could find his way home from here, I followed Vince to the office. Inside was a small desk, two chairs, several storage shelves, and boxes everywhere. I cleared a box off each seat so we could sit while we talked.

"Before we get started, I wanted to say I like what you're doing with the paranormal support group you have going on."

If he knew about it, he had to be paranormal himself. But how had he figured out I was involved with its founding? "Oh, thanks. It's not mine, though."

Pushing his glasses up his nose, he chuckled. "My sources say you were instrumental in getting it started. I'll hope you'll consider having a meeting here at the senior center or in the nursing home. You'd get a whole other group of attendees looking for support who can't get to your current meeting place without drawing suspicion from their nurses or care-takers who might not know what they are. I'm sure you can see how some might need what you're offering."

Before I could open my mouth to say it was a good idea,

he said, "I'll help you set it up in a way that anyone who isn't paranormal won't find out what's going on."

"Thank you."

"But that's not why we are here today, is it?" He shook his head. "No, you're here to find out about the murder of Sandra O'Grady, a merrow. Yes, I know what she was. I make it my business to know everything when I can. Wish I could have helped you with the north woods case you had last month. I never thought those six people up and left town never to be heard from again. Didn't realize they were all dryads, but I had my suspicions about a few of them. You did a great job pulling the town together for that tree planting. Now you're doing it again with the support group and even with decorating cookies."

I shrugged. "They're just cookies."

He dropped his head down and looked at me over his glasses, one eyebrow raised. "I think you and I both know they're more than just cookies. You're only learning what they fully are, though. I look forward to seeing you at full power."

Was that what all this was? Were these things happening with greater frequency because my power was growing?

Vince clapped his hands. "Okay, back to the topic at hand. The murder of Sandra O'Grady."

"I'm trying to help her great-niece, Chelsea. She's marrying David Hamn. His family, well, most of them, hate her and her family."

"Ah, the selkie family."

"Correct, and they don't like her both for being a merrow and for being related to Sandra. I wish they could see how happy she and David are together, but his family blames Sandra for their friend's death. They don't seem bothered at all by the fact Sandra was murdered days later. That's how much they hate her."

Vince nodded slowly. "Right, Brad Malloy. Tragic. But he was miles away. How could she be responsible?"

I told him what I'd heard from Greta about his avoidance of town and his family's belief that he wouldn't have died if he'd been in Heartwood Hollow.

He rolled his eyes. "It was tragic what happened, but that's ridiculous. He wasn't some child with hurt feelings running away to hide. Besides, I have it under good authority he was seeing someone at the time and that's why he wasn't home much."

This was news to me. "Does his family know?"

"Don't imagine they do, but I covered that funeral. A woman was crying far off in the distance, standing even farther from the gravesite than Sandra stood with her current boyfriend. She'd already been told to leave by his brother, but she refused. His family pulled him away after he began yelling at her, begging him not to make the day any harder than it already was." He leaned back in his chair. "My belief about this other woman, however, is that he hadn't introduced her to his family yet. Don't know why. Could be any number of reasons. Never saw her again after that. She certainly wasn't from here."

"So hours after her ex's funeral, Sandra ends up dead. Didn't anyone think to look for a connection?"

"I doubt they looked too hard once Marvin was offered up as a potential suspect."

"Not even at her boyfriend?"

"Nope. Though he readily offered an alibi. The winter carnival over at Knoll's Grove."

That struck me as odd. "He went to a carnival without his

girlfriend? And only a day after a death that rocked the town?"

"That was my first thought too. Turns out he was working for most of the window when the murder had to have happened, but only his shift was corroborated with coworkers. As for the rest of the time . . . just because you say you were in a crowded place, does that mean you were there? Too bad we can't ask him again to see if his story's changed. He's been dead now for several years."

"Okay, so let's say Greg was at the carnival the whole time he said he was. What about Bruce?"

"You'd think they'd have looked into him more after the cemetery confrontation. But investigators chalked it up to his brother dying, and his whole family vouched for his whereabouts during the time of Sandra's murder."

You sound skeptical.

He chuckled. "It's my job to be skeptical. And although I think they should have investigated him more since he wasn't where his family says he was, I don't think he did it."

"You don't?" The Strongs felt otherwise. I had doubts about his innocence myself.

"Nah." He pushed his glasses back up on his nose.

"So who did it then? Her boyfriend?"

Vince shook his head. "My guess? Someone in town completely unrelated to any of what was going on."

What did that mean? "As in a wrong place, wrong time sort of situation? A crime of opportunity? Could it have been because she was a merrow?"

He smiled cryptically. "All good questions. I hope you'll uncover the answers."

"You mean you don't know?" The hope that had been building inside me deflated.

"Sadly, no. Two deaths, even in vastly different ways, in such a short time . . . As you can imagine, it was a lot for this town to handle. I tried to get as much information as I could, leveraging my position as editor and wanting to get the information to the townspeople, but there weren't a lot of leads. It's probably part of why they jumped to close the case as quickly as they did. They wanted justice. If you can call it that. Some think they got it. But I don't. Don't think you do either."

I shook my head. It all felt too convenient.

"I don't think it's anyone anybody had any reason to look at," Vince continued. "Nope, the police had Marvin in their sights and never let go. It's unfortunate. He was a good young man. Bought my daughter a car from him when he first got into the business. Asked for him specifically because it would help him more than some of the others."

He sighed and scrubbed at his face with his hands. "I'd like to say things have changed in this town, and perhaps they have in some ways, but you see the way rumors spread around here. That sort of thing can do a lot of damage. Did for poor Marvin and his family. I'm hoping you're the start of something new around here with your support group. I'm serious about that offer." He stood and held his hand out to me. I gladly took it, and we shook.

"So how do you know all of this?" I asked. "About me and the paranormals in town. I hope you don't mind me being so bold as to ask, but you're the first to mention it without offering it up. You're paranormal, right?"

Nodding, he grinned. "Not going to tell you what, though. As I said earlier, maybe you'll get to find out the answers."

Vince grabbed the door to the office and held it open as he waved me through. I pondered his statement a while. What paranormal being would be best suited to be a newspaper editor? Steph was a dryad, but he wasn't one given what he'd said about the north woods. He didn't come off as a merperson or selkie either. I doubted he would have remained calm through our conversation about Sandra if he was.

Vince followed me out the door and locked it behind him. "You have a good day now, Joanie. It was nice chatting with you."

"You too, Vince, and thank you."

We parted ways, him continuing down the hallway and me returning to the cafeteria. I could hear Ivy's squeals of delight before reaching the room. Ken was chasing her around the tables, rags in each of their hands.

"That looks fun!" I called over the noise.

Ivy and Ken both slid to a halt.

Ken walked toward me, smiling. "You get what you need from Vince?"

"More information, more questions." I shrugged. "You know how it goes."

"Anything I can help with?"

"I could use a sounding board."

"Well, we're all set here. Ivy has a sleepover tonight, so how about we grab dinner and we can talk about it."

"Sounds great." I looked around. No one else was here. "How did Sam get home?"

"He left with a friend from school a few minutes ago."

"So you're sure we're good here?" Without having finished the cleanup, I felt guilty.

Ken picked up a box by the door. "All we have to do is put this in your car."

After some debate about where we were going to eat, we settled on delivery from Mama à la Pizza again. It allowed us to eat and talk without prying ears. The last thing I wanted was for someone to overhear our conversation and start up a new swell of rumors after such a great day of community togetherness.

I filled Ken in on everything Vince had told me.

"Sounds like you're going to have to talk to a lot of people if you ask me," Ken said through a half-mouthful of food, then swallowed.

I took a sip of my water. "Where do I even start?"

"You just spent the afternoon with a few dozen people who were around at that time."

"I swear, the paranormals have good genes."

"Yes, we have a large seventy-plus population." Ken laughed. "Well, if Vince thinks it would be someone who lived nearby, we could start there. Who were Sandra's neighbors? That has to limit it somewhat."

"But how do I find that out?"

"If it were today, I'd say look in an online phonebook. But it looks like you'll be heading back to the library for what you need. Someone there will know." He popped a fried pickle into his mouth.

At this rate, I was going to need a research assistant if everything kept leading me back there.

CHAPTER 16

The library was closed on Sundays during the summer, so I didn't have a chance to go until Monday evening. There, Emily showed me how to do research with a town directory, something similar to an old-fashioned phone book but organized by street instead of by last name. I'd found out from Chelsea where her grandmother and great-aunt had lived and started my search there. As I copied the list of all their neighbors, I recognized several names but only through their younger relatives. And although Ken hadn't lived in town long, I brought the list to him to see if he recognized the names. Aside from the fact his dad grew up here and he'd visited his grandparents here as a kid, Ken's work put him in contact with many seniors through the hospital's volunteer program. It had been enough to introduce me to Vince, but would it help me catch a killer?

The next day, I met Ken at his office. He'd cross-referenced the list with his roster of volunteers. Three names had floated to the top, and two were in today.

The first was cuddling a newborn in the NICU. The parents didn't live in town and had other kids so couldn't always be here. But Wilma was only too happy to spend a few hours sitting in a rocking chair talking with her little friend.

"She doesn't say much," Wilma whispered, "but she's warm and a great listener. And she doesn't mind my singing either."

I almost hated to bother her because of how peaceful she looked.

"Now, what's this you wanted to know about my old neighbor?"

I looked down at the baby sleeping against her.

"Oh, don't mind her. She doesn't understand what you're saying yet, not the words anyway, but she will know your tone, so even though it might not be the best of subjects, if you can talk in a nice soft voice, like this," she cooed, "that would be best."

All right, anything for the baby. "Is this good?" I asked, trying to sound the way Wilma had.

The woman nodded.

"She is such a doll." Just looking at her made me smile. "Anyway, I was wondering what you may recall about your neighborhood around the time of Sandra's death. Any weird things going on?"

The woman tittered a little laugh, and the baby stirred. She shushed her back to sleep, rubbing small circles on her back with two of her fingers. "Weird things? It's Heartwood Hollow, dearie. Weird things happen around here every day. But no, I can't say that I recall anything weird happening that stuck out then or continues to do so today."

"Anybody new move in before it happened who changed the neighborhood dynamic? Someone she didn't like or didn't like her?"

"No, no. Everyone liked Sandra, well, until poor Brad died. But can you blame Bruce for how he felt about her afterward? So grief-stricken. Wasn't thinking straight if you ask me, granted he didn't like her before that thanks to Brad's leaving, but I eventually think they would have made amends if Brad hadn't passed. Then obviously her too. Sometimes it's hard to make peace with someone who isn't there."

In all my years of dealing with ghosts, I had learned that to be true. It was often hard for the ghosts I saw to make amends with others, living or dead. Many times, sadly, that was what was keeping them here. Could Sandra, as Wilma put it, be wanting to make peace with someone? Was that why she was haunting the tiara Chelsea wanted to use for her wedding? If so, who?

As I thought about her, Sandra appeared behind the older woman. "Oh, what a beautiful baby."

"Well, how about people you never saw again shortly thereafter?" I asked Wilma, unable to call attention to Sandra's presence.

"No, no one left either. One of our neighbors down the street was one of the six who disappeared in the north woods. Hawthorne, his name was." She grew quiet. "No, if anyone left, it was because they passed away."

The baby woke up then and seemed to stare at Sandra, who began to hum a song. The baby soon drifted back off to sleep.

"Well, thank you for your time," I whispered. "Enjoy the rest of your day."

"With this one here"—she nodded toward the baby—"my day will be perfect."

Sandra following close behind me as I slipped out of the NICU. "Did you remember the woman I was talking to?" I asked.

"Hmm . . . I feel like I should since she was talking about me"—I glanced back at her and she was holding her head where I assumed she'd been struck—"but no, I don't remember her." She continued to follow me back to Ken's office, where the second volunteer would be working by now.

"Well, hopefully you'll know the next person. He was your next-door neighbor."

That cheered Sandra up, but by the time I entered the office, she was gone. Like the other ghosts, she seemed to appear when called but disappeared after she'd expended her energy. She'd been around for a while during my conversation with Wilma. I shouldn't have been surprised when she left, but I'd hoped she would have been able to stay for my next conversation too.

As he worked, Ken sat chatting from his desk with an elderly man, who was sorting through a stack of papers at a small round table in the corner of the room. Ken glanced up from his computer, and his easy smile grew when we made eye contact. "Ah, Joanie. This is Clayton Pierce. He was a good friend of my grandpa and dad. Now he helps me with grant work for the hospital's efforts to give back to the community. Has already identified a few leads that we've applied for. Haven't heard back on anything yet, but those things take time. Clayton, this is my girlfriend, Joanie Sunevall."

"Nice to meet you," I told Clayton.

He looked up at me, a trace of a smile on his face, but his steel-blue eyes seemed rather dull. "I was telling Ken I don't think I'll be much help, unfortunately."

"Oh, you never know. Really, anything you remember, even if it's small."

He chuckled, but once again the light didn't reach his eyes. "That's the thing. I don't remember any of it. I was in a car accident"—he flipped to the next page in his stack—"about five years after the time you're looking for information on. So, although I lived in the neighborhood, I wouldn't even be able to tell you who lived across the street or next door back then unless I'd been told. And I was. Several times."

I tried not to let my disappointment show, but maybe there was another way to get useful information from him. Instead of asking him about what he remembered, I tried a different approach, hoping he'd tell me something someone had told him. "So were your neighbors helpful when you returned home after your accident? I can't imagine not being able to remember anything of my past."

"It's not all bad. Gave me a fresh start. I remembered the basics of life like walking and talking after some rehab, but I didn't know how to do my job anymore."

"What did you do?"

"I was an accountant, but I've been told I didn't like it. So I guess that worked out that I had to find something else to do."

"Which was . . ."

"I became a grant writer for the hospital here. Medical research, not the community stuff Ken does here, but a lot of the skills cross over. So here I am. My therapists say it's good for me to get out, socialize, and use muscles I might not otherwise use sitting around. Although I'm still sitting here, I have to walk around the hospital to get here and am using other parts of my brain. And I like it."

"That's really great."

"It is. And to get back to your other question, most of my neighbors were great too. The lady across the street cooked for me. Casseroles each week so I would have easy leftovers. One of the local boys cut my lawn because it was hard for me the first few years. Not the next-door neighbors, though."

Sandra's family if the town directories were correct.

"I guess they'd lost a daughter a few years before my accident and kinda kept to themselves after that. Parents down-stairs and their living daughter upstairs with her husband and soon two kids too. Good kids. A little loud sometimes, which was no good for my headaches that I got as a result of the accident, but that's not their fault."

I'd hoped Sandra would appear again with the mention of her family, but nothing. Guess it was time to wrap this conversation up. "Do you still get headaches?"

"Sometimes. Something fierce, that's for sure."

"Aw, that's too bad. Okay, well I'll let you both get back to your work. Good luck on the grants and thank you for talking with me."

"Oh, sure, sure. Have a good day." He dipped his head down once before returning to meet my gaze with a polite smile.

It wasn't until I had sat down with tea and a book that Sandra reappeared, startling Saffy who was trying to get comfortable on my feet. She jumped up to her spot on the back of the couch but sat facing Sandra, very aware of our guest.

I looked down at my book to mark my page then back up at Sandra. "You disappeared. I'd hoped you'd be there while I talked to your old neighbor."

"Chelsea needed me more at the moment, but I did check in on you."

"And . . ."

"If you say he was my neighbor, then I guess he was my neighbor, but I don't remember him." She shrugged, then sat down on the couch beside my feet. "What was his name again?"

"Clayton Pierce."

As Saffy sniffed at her hair, Sandra paused a moment, her lips drawn to the side. "Nope, nothing. Doesn't even feel like I knew him. The woman with the baby I at least felt like I knew once upon a time." She sighed. "I'm really sorry I don't remember more. I'm not making this easy, am I?"

"No," I said truthfully, "but it's not your fault. I think it has to do with how you died."

"Likely for the best that I don't remember that, huh?"

I nodded. That was probably true from what I'd heard. "Don't worry about it. Memories or not, we'll help you and Chelsea." I closed my book and set it on the couch arm, then slid my feet down to the floor. When I looked back up at Sandra, she was gone, leaving Saffy to sniff the air. I had been about to ask her what Chelsea had needed, but as I took a sip of my tea, I figured I would find out soon enough.

CHAPTER 17

A week had passed since the swell of orders from Chelsea's future family. As much as I hoped for a nice, calm Wednesday like we were used to having at the bakery, the feeling that something else was on the horizon lingered all morning. It started a bit busier than usual, and I wasn't surprised when many of the customers to the bakery had Irish accents, some heavier than others.

"Here for the wedding?" I asked one strawberry-blond mother with her kids in tow.

"I love a good wedding," she replied in a thick brogue. "Came early to do a bit of vacationing first. It's the kids' first time in the States. I used to swim over every summer as a teen to hang out with my cousins here in town."

I'd never heard someone so open about their abilities, especially not to a stranger. Had Chelsea said something about me, or was where she came from more open than we were here? Thank goodness Sarah was out to lunch. For as much as she talked about my being a witch, Sarah didn't know about the supernatural status of the town. At least to my knowledge. Sometimes I wondered if she really believed I was a witch or if it gave her something to gossip about when strange stuff happened around here.

"Did you swim here for the wedding?

She laughed. "Oh goodness, no. We had all our things, and the kids' stamina isn't strong enough yet. Perhaps in another few years."

"I could do it, Ma," a young boy said, turning his head away from the cupcake case. That was at least one nose print to clean off this afternoon.

She gave me a wink then turned to her son. "You will soon enough."

Chelsea's family was huge. There were so many new faces along Main Street, and many came into the shop. Weddings were always big affairs in Heartwood Hollow, but this one might have taken the cake. I had a difficult time navigating around everyone as I made my afternoon deliveries, including a second stop to Donna who had not accounted for the extra foot traffic. She had a line out the door. Numerous restaurants along the street did as well. Over at the inn, Libby was loving the influx of visitors as she had a fully booked tea service and had even added a few extra seats to accommodate her guests. She also promised to serve during a special tea tomorrow in addition to her already full tea Friday.

When I got back to the bakery after grabbing a quick bite to eat at the coffee shop, having thought ahead to call in my order when I saw the line at Olde Templeton Diner, I hopped back into serving the curious customers who wanted a preview of the wedding cake—which we hadn't made yet—or to get a sample of the treats they'd have during the reception.

Although we were busy, the shop's atmosphere was a far cry from last Wednesday when the hustle and bustle was stressful. Today had been fun.

The door had been open all day. The early summer air was

warm and dry, and the wind was blowing just the right way to carry the smells of the bakery out of the shop and several feet down the street to lure in more customers. This was my favorite time of year, although I was sure I said that about other times too.

However, with the door open, I felt the shift in the mood well before Chelsea reached my shop.

Once I caught sight of her, I rushed out from behind the counter to wrap her in a hug.

"Oh, Joanie. I can't take it anymore," she cried into my shoulder.

"What's wrong?" Casting a glance to Sarah, I led Chelsea to the tables at the side of the shop, pulling out a chair for her so she'd sit.

"Do either of you want something to drink from Leafs and Grounds?" Sarah offered, knowing by my look that we needed a moment alone. "It's been a busy day, and I could use the pick-me-up if that's all right."

I nodded to Sarah as I sat next to Chelsea, and Chelsea asked for a salted caramel latte. Sarah ducked out of the shop, leaving the two of us alone.

"Is it the dress still?" I asked.

"Oh, the dress." she sniffed. "My grandma took it away and promised me that she'll come up with something great in time for the wedding. Something where I won't even recognize that anything bad has happened to it."

"Well, that's good, right?"

"That's only if there's going to be a wedding. They've all been so awful to me. From the dress to trashing the outdoor area where we were supposed to get wedding photos taken to what they did to you—"

"Don't worry about me. I can handle it."

"I think they're trying to make you tired of me. Tired

enough of all this that you don't want to make my cake anymore. And then the wedding won't happen because of that."

"I'd never do that to you. Plus, you've already paid me," I tried to joke, hoping to get her to crack a smile.

It didn't work. "I know you wouldn't, but I'm still afraid there's not going to be a wedding. David hates what his family is doing to me and is talking about skipping it altogether so that they aren't even involved."

"Like an elopement?" That wasn't such a bad idea.

"Yes, but that's never been what I wanted. And my whole family is coming. Most of them are already here. I'm sure you've seen all the redheads or heard the accents around town."

I told her about the many wonderful cousins of hers I had met today. *That* made her smile.

"You see? I can't elope. They all came here to see me get married. Now I worry about what will happen as more of David's family start to arrive. You saw what they did when just a few of them were here. Now imagine three times as many. His family isn't as big as mine, but almost, and when nearly all of them hate you?" She broke out into another round of sobbing. "It's all too much, and they are saying the nastiest things about me and my family. They've gone so far as to say my great-aunt deserved to be murdered, that the killer did them all a favor. How can anyone say that? It's terrible."

"It really is," I agreed.

She sniffed. "Do you see her often? Has she told you anything that would help her cross over?"

"I've seen her several times," I answered, then proceeded to tell her how Sandra didn't remember how she died, who killed her, or much of her life. I told her it was normal so she wouldn't worry and avoided saying anything about the rest of her memory. The truth was I didn't know if it was normal for ghosts to not remember their death. Over the years, I hadn't dealt with many who had been murder victims. A couple had known how they died, and with the others, it hadn't come up because that wasn't why they were still around. She didn't need to know that, though.

"Do you think she'll still be stuck in the tiara forever?"

"Goodness, no. I'm doing my best to free her, and I won't give up. It takes time. I bet she would be happy to witness your wedding from outside of the tiara, and I can make sure she's outside of it during your ceremony at the very least even if she is still tied to it."

I hadn't meant to, but that set Chelsea off into another round of tears.

"If there even is a wedding," she reminded me between shuddered breaths.

I gave her another hug. "Do me a favor, okay?"

She nodded into my shoulder. "Okay."

"Avoid David's family for the next few days. You have enough on your plate as it is preparing for the wedding. Hang out with the people who came here to support you. Your family is as excited to see you as they are to attend your wedding, and you never get enough time to see everyone on your wedding day as you'd like to. Go for a drive. Get good takeout. I highly recommend Mama à la Pizza. It's probably salty enough for all of you."

"Oh, I've been wanting to try that."

"Splurge. It's that good. Go crazy. Make it your bachelorette party with all your cousins. Then tell David you need a night just the two of you. No family talk allowed. After all, once the wedding is over, you two will be together. That's what matters. He's stressed too. It can't be easy to be in his position either."

She nodded again and wiped her eyes. "I'll try."

"Good. And don't worry about Sandra. I'll figure that out." At that moment, Sarah returned to the shop. She'd come in from the kitchen. Must have wanted to give us more time by going the long way. I turned toward her before she could come any closer. "Grab me a cookie, will you? One of the salted caramel ones."

I pulled away from Chelsea's embrace and walked over to the counter as Sarah reached in the case and pulled out a cookie.

She passed me the bag and the tray holding our drinks. "I threw in a brownie, too, because this also calls for chocolate."

"Good idea." I smiled at her, then walked back to Chelsea and handed her the pastry bag. "Here. On the house."

"Oh, I couldn't after all you've done for me."

"You've paid me plenty for the wedding cake, so think of it as a free bonus with purchase."

"Thanks." Chelsea reached into the bag and broke off a piece of the brownie and cookie, then popped both in her mouth at the same time. She chased the bite down with a sip of her latte. "Ah, true perfection. Thanks again, Joanie. I'm sure I'll talk to you soon."

"One way or the other. Now go get some pizza."

With that, she left the shop, leaving me with even more questions than I had previously. My window to figure it all out in was growing short. What would happen if I couldn't do it in time?

CHAPTER 18

With Chelsea's family already here en masse, and David's family starting to arrive, I increased our usual baking load to accommodate the boost in the town's population. It only made sense that we'd have to adjust our offerings along with the extra orders of muffins from both Double Aitch and Olde Templeton as well as the added tea service at the inn.

I had a firm belief that a cookie could make anyone feel better. Even if only for a moment. As I baked, I wondered how many cookies it would take to smooth the rift between David's and Chelsea's families. If it could work for tests and job interviews, it could work for decades-old grudges, right?

If only.

Business was steady throughout the morning, but the air was different. I'd felt it as soon as I propped open the door to the shop. On Wednesday, it had been cheery and full of excitement, at least until Chelsea arrived with her worries in the afternoon. People had been hugging on the sidewalk as family came together, seeing one another for the first time in however long. Today it was tense. People were all over Main

Street, that hadn't changed, but there was little if any hugging. As I made my lunchtime deliveries, it was easy to see the glares cast between family groups, some I recognized as Chelsea's family and others I didn't, who I assumed were David's. How had this grudge spread between states and even continents? This was feeling like the Montagues and the Capulets from *Romeo and Juliet*, only with added paranormal elements.

At this rate, the wedding needed to happen so everyone could go home and get on with their lives. I'd be able to help Sandra eventually, hopefully sooner rather than later, but right now, it seemed to be more than I was able to handle.

Chelsea texted me while I was in the driveway at the inn after making my delivery.

Chelsea: That pizza was amazing!

Me: I'm glad you liked it!

Chelsea: David came home and ate my leftovers. We might have to get more tonight.

Me: That sounds perfect.

She sent me a smiley face after that. At least she seemed to be doing well right now despite the shift in the air. I hoped she'd continue to take my advice and stay clear of David's family. If she avoided Main Street, she'd be fine.

The first argument started in front of the shop while Sarah was on her lunch break. Lauren and I were in the bakery and had just served a few of Chelsea's relatives who had heard nothing but good things about everything I made. As they left, they accidentally bumped into the husband of another family.

"Hey, watch it, merrow," the selkie father spat toward the family leaving my shop.

"Excuse me?" the merrow father said, incredulity in his voice. "You're the one who bumped into us. Don't you see this step? One of us could have fallen and gotten hurt."

"So?" the first man scoffed. "Would serve you right for what your family member did."

"I don't even know what you're talking about."

"*Sure* you don't."

The merrow wife gently placed her hand on her husband's back. "Dear, let's just get out of here, please."

"You're right. He's not worth it." The merrow husband put his arm around his wife, and they rushed up Main Street with their child in tow.

After witnessing the event, I would have refused to serve the family that had just harassed Chelsea's relatives if I didn't think it would have caused more trouble for her in some way. I didn't make small talk, though, and I was glad when they exited my shop.

The next argument was much worse. As Lauren, Sarah, and I cleaned the store in anticipation of closing, we heard shouts a little way up the street. Sarah popped her head out of the doorway to see what the fuss was about. As I watched for her reaction, her jaw dropped. She pulled the door closed and locked it, then flipped the sign from *open* to *closed*.

"We still have a few minutes," I told her, never wanting to close early in case someone was hurrying to make it in time when they needed a pick-me-up.

"Trust me, today you do. There's a fight happening in the middle of the street in front of Double Aitch!"

I hurried to the window, tossing my cleaning rag on the counter next to me. A crowd was gathering around what looked like two young men preparing for a fistfight.

Sh . . .ugar. The group of people around them was growing bigger by the second. It soon was larger than the turnout for when Lily chased John down the street with a knife, and that had probably been the most exciting thing to happen in town for some time. By the looks of it, this incident was going to top that one before long.

I rushed to the door, then flipped the lock and turned the knob.

"Joanie, what are you doing?" Lauren asked, worry in her voice.

"This is getting ridiculous. I need to do something."

"Let the police do something," Sarah urged, running around the counter toward the phone. I assumed she was calling the cops. I didn't stick around to find out.

As I ran across the street, I wondered how this decades-old, misplaced blame over someone's death had reached the point where people would fight in the streets. Did the people fighting even know why they didn't like one another?

I pushed through a group of onlookers, people I recognized from town, who stood gossiping behind their hands. A few words escaped the secrecy of their huddle.

Strangers.

Wedding.

Merrow.

The last sounded more like a question as if they'd never heard the term. I turned back a moment. None of the five gossipers had been to a paranormal support group meeting. For all I knew, they were completely human. So now this fight was jeopardizing the paranormal secrets of the town.

A proper circle had formed around the men who were still sizing each other up, their arms raised. All it would take is one push in the right—well, wrong—direction and the fight would start.

"Excuse me," I said, worming my way between two in the circle. They all might have lost their minds, but there was no reason for me to be rude and cause more problems for Chelsea or myself.

I strode up in between the two men. "What in the world is going on here? You are not in a boxing ring or on a wrestling mat. This is Main Street, Heartwood Hollow. Whatever problems you two have with one another, there must be a better way."

"Ha," the one scoffed. "I don't even know 'im. He's a merrow. That's good enough for me."

"And why is that a bad thing?" I asked the selkie. "Because they aren't the same as you?"

"Selkies are better. Always have been. We're smarter."

"Oh, yeah? We're faster," the merrow retorted, not helping the situation.

"Would you two listen to yourselves? You know what that sounds like, right? I don't care what you are." Lower in a warning voice, I added, "There are humans watching right now who don't know what any of this means. Do you want to jeopardize *all* the paranormals who call this town home, or do you not care because you don't live here? Because let me remind you, you have family here that does."

That seemed to sober them up some.

I sighed with hesitant relief. "Why don't we go talk about this over some cookies?"

"Hey, I thought I recognized you. You're the one who's bakin' this sham of a wedding's cake!" The selkie pointed at the merrow. "You're on their side!"

"I am on Chelsea and David's side! I am on the side of love. What's so wrong about that? Why can't you just let them love one another?"

"It's not natural!"

"It most certainly is." Taking a low tone again, I continued, "This town has trolls and selkies, and humans and witches, and dryads and lumberjacks. We all get along fine. You have to see that. And must I remind you humans are watching us? So please, stop!"

"Yes, *do* stop because if you all don't stop loitering in the street causing a disturbance, I'm going to have to write some citations," Seth, one of the town's police officers and my best friend's boyfriend, said over the crowd as he pushed his way toward us. "And possibly have to take the two of you in for disorderly conduct or worse. You aren't drunk, are you? Because that would be a public intoxication charge too."

The merrow shook his head. "Haven't touched a drop since we got here."

The selkie, too, shook his head. "Nothing here either. Savin' me limit for the wedding."

"Well, if you want to make it to the wedding, I insist that you all leave. Go about your business. Go eat at these fine establishments you've been preventing others from going to for fear of crossing the street."

Slowly, the crowd dispersed, mumbling things under their breaths.

Seth looked at me then. "Are you okay? These two didn't do anything to you, did they?"

"No, I'm fine. Thank you for coming."

"Glad you're okay. Courtney would kill me if I let something happen to you." He looked around at the several onlookers who remained standing around. "I'm serious. Get! I don't want to have to write citations for loitering this close to the end of my shift, but I will." He reached toward the pad in his breast pocket. That sent the rest of them away, including the two who had been in the middle of it all.

He let out a long sigh. "What it is about weddings that

brings out the worst in some people? I hope this is the end of it, but somehow I doubt it."

I did too. "You want a cookie? Might help." I knew I could use one.

"Nah, I'm good. But let's do dinner one night as a double date. Me and Courtney and you and your manfriend. What's his name, Ben?"

"Ken."

"Right. Ken. I'm better with faces, but I'll remember now."

"Dinner would be great. Sometime soon, but after this wedding, okay?"

He laughed. "Yeah. It's all hands on deck until it's over. A surge in visitors always puts us on edge." He cocked his head to the side. "You sure you're okay? You're looking a little pale."

I waved him off. "Yeah, I'll be fine. That was just a little tense, and I think I'm going to go have that cookie."

"Okay, well, you take care of yourself."

"You too." I turned and headed back toward the bakery, clasping my hands in front of me to prevent them from shaking.

One thing was certain. I needed more than a cookie to settle my nerves. This called for two.

CHAPTER 19

Sarah and Lauren were waiting for me at the door. Sarah pulled me in for a hug. "What are you, crazy?" My hearing seemed muffled.

"I might be," I admitted, still shaking.

"They could have hurt you. You can't go throwing yourself into every argument in town. First Lily and John with the knife, and now this? And you don't even know them."

"I didn't want anyone to get hurt and ruin Chelsea's wedding."

"I'm so glad you're okay." She squeezed me a bit tighter before letting me go. "*Are* you okay?"

"Yeah, I think I need to sit down is all."

"The adrenaline is leaving her system," Lauren said, placing a hand on my upper back. "Grab her a cookie. Come on, Joanie, let's go sit down." She led me to one of the chairs at the side of the room, and I slumped down into it before putting my head in my hands, my elbows propped up on the table I was leaning against.

The tears came unbidden. This us/them fight between Chelsea's merrow family and David's selkie family, the whole

Sandra issue aside, was my greatest fear about the paranormal secret of Heartwood Hollow. I'd seen how the rumors about me being a witch swirled when I moved here and continued to do so. I even encouraged them because they were harmless—even helpful to business. But since accepting who I was, I'd become protective of my being a witch. It was one thing to say I was a witch when gossiping but another thing entirely to believe it. What if the wrong person bought into the rumors as truth? What if they didn't like me because of what, no, *who* I was? What if that's why Sandra had died—because someone found out her secret?

A soft hand came to a rest at my shoulder, and a cookie appeared on the table below my face. "Here, chocolate always helps," Sarah whispered.

I lifted my head enough to eat a piece I broke off, and Sarah's hand slipped off my back. In the distance, I heard her voice, barely more than a mumble.

Sometime later, probably not more than a few minutes, a firmer hand pressed against my shoulder.

"Joanie?"

I perked up at the voice. "Ken?"

"Sarah said I needed to rescue you. From the tone in her voice, I thought you had been crushed by cookies for real. What's going on?" He pulled a chair up next to me.

"We're going to go," Sarah said. "Will you be okay?"

I looked over Ken's shoulder and nodded. All I had left to do was turn off the lights. "Yeah, it's all good. I'll see you tomorrow. And thanks." I cracked a small smile.

Sarah and Lauren ducked into the kitchen, and once I heard the back door shut, I told Ken everything that had happened. Unlike when he'd been upset about my rushing headlong to help Lily and John, he just listened this time.

It didn't keep me from apologizing, however. "I'm sorry. I

shouldn't have done it, but I couldn't stop myself. This whole thing isn't going to stop until I can figure out what's keeping Sandra here."

"What can I do to help?"

"Any chance you can get me some autopsy records?" Maybe they'd provide me with something that would help me solve this case.

He laughed but quickly sobered. "Wait, you're serious?"

"How else am I supposed to get them?"

"I dunno, ask her family?"

"But they already have so much going on."

He raised an eyebrow at me.

"Okay, okay. I'll ask someone."

"I wouldn't be able to give them to you even if I could access them. They aren't public record in Heartwood Hollow." He stood. "You ready to get out of here?"

"Yeah." I let him help me up, and after grabbing my purse behind the shop counter, I flipped off the lights and stepped out onto a much quieter Main Street with Ken, pulling the locked door closed behind me.

"Feeling better? Sarah had said you were pale."

"Yeah, just the adrenaline. The cookie helped."

"You want to grab dinner? Ivy is playing with a friend this evening."

"I think I want a nice cup of tea and to sit with my cat if that's okay." Part of me felt bad for passing on a child-free night with Ken, but the other part of me, the one that was speaking louder, wanted to be comfy and cozy under a blanket with my book.

Ken pulled me into a hug and kissed me gently on my forehead. "Of course it's okay. I am going to walk you home, though."

"I'd like that." Hand in hand, the two of us took the long

way back to my house. Being out in the early evening summer sunshine made me feel better, so much so that I almost changed my mind about doing dinner, but once my house came into view, I knew I'd made the right decision.

Saffy greeted me at the end of the couch he eyes wide and head darting between Ken and me.

As I ran my hand down Saffy's back, I assured her, "I'm fine. I promise. Ken made sure of that."

She turned to face him and partially squinted. After a moment, she finally allowed Ken to pet her for the first time since we got back together. She hadn't forgiven him, though. This seemed to be more of a thank you for his bringing me home. Then she hopped down to the floor and swishing her tail at him in a dismissive fashion before scampering off to the kitchen to wait for her dinner.

"Be there in a minute," I called after her.

"The way you talk to her, I'd think she was human some-times," Ken said, nothing but seriousness in his voice.

"Sometimes I'm surprised she's not."

"Well, it is Heartwood Hollow . . ."

I laughed. "She's not from here, though."

"And neither are you, yet here you are as if you've always belonged."

"I don't know about that."

He wrapped his arms around my back. "With everything you've been doing for this town and the people in it, I'd say you're right where you're supposed to be. I think she is too."

"Gram once said something about her being my familiar, but I don't know about that either."

"No, I can see it."

"You can? I thought you didn't know a whole lot about all of this paranormal stuff."

"I don't. Not the real-life stuff, anyway. But I am the dad to a seven-year-old, and I see a lot of this in her fairy tale books and movies. Nearly every witch has some sort of animal, even the good ones."

"Don't they all talk?"

"Some do, but not all of them. You should come by and have a movie marathon with Ivy. She'd love it, and you'd probably learn something."

"I'll have to do that. Mom and Gram didn't let me watch a whole lot of those movies as a kid . . . probably because of how they portrayed witches, now that I think about it."

Ken shook his head. "Some of them are pretty cute. Maybe if you had been able to watch them, you would have had an easier time accepting who you are."

"It's possible. At least I got here in my own way eventually. But, yes. When this wedding is over, I'll watch some movies with Ivy. But we might have to hold off on the ones with mermaids for now."

That made Ken laugh. "Yeah, I'm sure you'll be wanting some distance for a while." He took a deep breath and was serious again. "All right, I'm going to head back home. You sure you're okay?"

"I'll be fine. Thank you again for coming to my rescue."

He leaned down as he lifted my chin and kissed me softly on the lips. "Anytime." Then he trailed his hand down my arm and took my hand.

I gave it a reassuring squeeze. "Have a good night."

"You too." Ken pushed the door opened and stepped outside.

I waited until he'd reached the sidewalk and turned around to wave before heading into the kitchen after Saffy. We both needed dinner, and I wanted tea.

Saffy was sitting by her bowl, tapping it impatiently.

"You needn't be so rude to Ken. We resolved the issues we

had last month, and things are good now. He really helped me out today."

I filled her in as I prepared her dinner and started on mine, a Monte Cristo—turkey, ham, and Swiss cheese melted on top, then sandwiched between two slices of French toast—with a side of maple syrup to dip it in. Many people used Russian or Thousand Island dressing as a side, but I preferred mine to be sweeter. Sometimes I even sprinkled powdered sugar on top.

I'd just poured my tea, an herbal blend with orange and lemon peel, rosehips, and mango pieces, when Saffy darted toward the living room.

Curious, I followed her.

"He's right, you know," Sandra said. "About you talking to this cat like she's human. I easily could have thought you were talking to me or any of the other ghosts who hang about."

Did she mean there were other ghosts around me, or did she mean the others I occasionally talked to in town? I wasn't sure if I wanted to know the answer. All it meant was I needed Gram to visit sooner rather than later to reestablish the wards around my house and have her teach me to do it in case they broke again.

I changed the topic. "Did you see what happened today on Main Street?"

She nodded. "It really is awful. Tensions between our kind have never been higher. I had plenty of selkie friends growing up. It was never an issue. We just weren't allowed to date one another, not seriously anyway. It was no big deal the year I went with Norman to homecoming. He liked Rita back then, but she wouldn't give him the time of day. And that's how it had been with Brad, too, for much of our time together."

"Wait, you remember that?"

She thought a moment. "Huh, I guess I do. I remember a lot actually." She began talking about there being a general understanding between paranormals that they shouldn't be with one another romantically.

I waved her into the kitchen so I'd be able to eat and drink my tea while we chatted. She plopped down into one of the kitchen chairs. If anyone were able to see the two of us, they'd think me a terrible host not offering Sandra anything. That's how real she appeared.

"How did you all know about one another? Since learning about the paranormals here, it's seemed to me that the various groups only know about themselves except for the merrows and the selkies."

"The merrows and selkies have always been that way." She chuckled. "It certainly wasn't like I walked up to people when I got here asking, 'are you a merrow? I am.' But we all knew about one another and hung out together throughout school. My family was already aware of Heartwood Hollow and the underwater community when we came here. We all had lived together back in Ireland too."

Huh. Was that true for all paranormals in town? Greta had known about her friends even though she wasn't the same. But Vince hadn't known about all the dryads in the north woods several years later. Had events like Sandra's murder changed everyone's openness about who they were with those not like them?

While Sandra still remembered some things, I had to ask, "Do you remember who killed you?" I took a sip of tea while waiting for her answer.

Her eyes went up as if searching her brain for the answer. "Nope, it's not there."

I quickly changed to a related topic with the hope that

she'd remember what I needed her to if she talked long enough.

"So explain your friendship with Marvin Strong. Was he an underwater paranormal like you?" Marvin's family hadn't said anything that would lead me to believe he was, but that didn't mean he wasn't either.

"Marvin? Oh, he helped me find my lost cat when I was a little girl. He wasn't paranormal, I don't think—or remember —anyway, but he was very nice. I liked playing with him and his siblings and friends just as much as my other friends. Even better was when we could all hang out together. Everyone seemed to like him."

"So did you two ever date?"

She burst out laughing. The reaction almost made me choke on my bite of sandwich.

"Oh goodness, no. He was very sweet, and perhaps he liked me, but I liked Brad. He knew that. And even after the breakup, Marvin respected that we'd only ever be friends. I didn't see him that way. We still hung out, which was nice since few others seemed to understand why Brad and I broke up, but it was nothing romantic."

"Why did you and Brad break up?" Greta had said everyone was surprised when it happened, believing that they'd be the ones to defy the rules about paranormals being together.

"He was going to school." So that had been true. "Brad wanted to see what life was like outside Heartwood Hollow, and that meant all parts of it, including me. I was upset about it. I really liked him, but I guess I understood where he was coming from. If only everyone else had believed me when I told them. 'He'd never do something like that,' they said. Well, he did. His wanting to be apart from this town is why he stayed away so much. He should have at least told everyone that I didn't break up with him, but then he would have had to tell everyone the real reason he left. He wasn't ready. I was mad at him. That doesn't mean I wasn't sad when he died, though."

Sandra's revelation fit in with what Vince had said about him possibly having another girlfriend who wasn't from town, but would this be enough to shift people's opinions of Sandra? Could this help put a stop to their poor treatment of Chelsea?

No, they hadn't believed her the first time. They'd need proof, and only then would they *maybe* believe me.

"Marvin was the only one who believed me about Brad. Well, him and my new boyfriend, Greg. I hung around with them almost exclusively for the next year. We walked along the river a lot. Marvin loved to collect rocks. You should have seen his collection."

I didn't know if I should tell her if Marvin had been accused of murdering her. Would that force her into remembering or would it be too much to handle no matter the truth?

As I debated this, she told me about her boyfriend, how he was a merrow who had moved to the area the summer before she and Brad had broken up. That they weren't together until almost winter that same year, when she realized nothing she said or did could convince her friends that she hadn't broken Brad's heart. The more she said about him, the more his alibi grew stronger. Greg worked at the cider mill. Even now, they always set up a booth at the carnival in Knoll's Grove.

Finally, I figured out my wording. "Sandra, would either of them have been capable of hurting you? Of wanting to hurt you?" Maybe in coming to their defense, she'd remember who the real culprit was.

She squinted quickly and her head rocked to the side as if

I'd slapped her. "No. No way. That's not even possible. Greg was talking about wanting to marry me, and Marvin—"

Her face went blank.

"Marvin what?" I prompted.

"Marvin who?"

"You were just telling me about your friend Marvin."

"I was? Huh. I don't remember having a friend named Marvin. Can't say I even knew a Marvin." And just that fast, my hope of cracking this case crumbled like a cookie left in milk for too long. "I don't remember anything."

When my plastered-on smile felt like it was slipping, I looked down and shoved a bite of sandwich into my mouth. "That's okay. I'm sure it will all come back to you eventually."

I swallowed, then looked up from my plate.

Sandra was gone.

CHAPTER 20

I'd stayed up longer than planned combing through all the information I knew about Sandra's murder. I wrote it all down on recipe cards and shifted each fact around my table as I saw fit. For a while, Saffy joined me, standing on one of the kitchen chairs, her front paws on the table. It seemed like she was studying the cards with me.

"You see anything I don't?" I asked her.

She glanced up at me quizzically but soon focused back on the cards. If she was going to start talking, then would have been the time to do it. I could have bounced ideas off her.

"No, I didn't think so. Thanks anyway."

Eventually she went back to her food bowl. We'd been in here long enough that she figured it was time for her to have another snack.

The recipe cards were all blurring together. I needed to come back and look at them again after a moment away. No, what I really needed was to go to bed.

I gave Saffy a couple of her tuna catnip treats. She'd have the best of both worlds—food and catnip—and be fine for a few hours. Although I hoped to be fast asleep by the time she was ready for another round. She grabbed one of the treats with her mouth and carried it away. Maybe she was tired, too, and wanted one more snack before bed. Luckily she devoured these things, leaving no trace of their existence behind, so even if she did go upstairs to wait for me, there'd be no crumbs on my bed.

Sometime later, I gave up looking at the cards and left them on the table. Coming back in the morning to look at them again wouldn't change the facts, though.

On paper, Marvin still seemed the guiltiest. His collecting rocks gave him means, and their regular walks along the river gave him the opportunity and potentially put him at the crime scene. As for motive? Perhaps he liked Sandra more than she'd known, but that was only a guess. And I didn't like it. Despite what the cards told me, I didn't believe he'd done it.

I headed into the bakery tired and hungry. After sleeping later than planned, I didn't make myself breakfast. A Monday muffin from the refrigerator would have to do. I'd finally remembered to make extra so the bakery would have them on hand. Try as I might, the magic of replicating Monday muffins on any other day eluded me, no matter the flavor. I passed one of the muffins to Sam, who looked like he needed one too, then told the others to each grab whatever they wanted from the case. It was all destined for the day-old shelf, anyway.

After several moments, I started to feel better. Whether it was the muffin or the Irish breakfast black tea I'd let steep on my walk here, I wasn't sure. Perhaps it was the combination.

Sam, too, seemed to have perked up some by the time I got back from making my morning deliveries. Feeling like he needed to talk and would if given the opportunity, I asked him to help me stock the cases with what we already had done and to bag up the day-old goods as the others continued to bake. He followed me into the shop, each of us carrying a full tray.

I plopped my tray of scones on top of one of the empty cases then slid the door to it open. "I'd ask if you had a late night studying, but you've been out of school for a few weeks now. Everything okay?"

"Yeah. Just a lot on my mind about leaving." Sam handed me his tray of muffins so I could slide it into the case.

I wouldn't pry. It wasn't my place, but I'd listen and let him know I at least partially understood. "As someone who's done it, it's hard. I'm not going to lie."

"I'm excited, but I'm worried about leaving things behind." He passed me my tray of scones then headed back into the kitchen, returning a moment later with another tray of muffins. "Mostly I'm worried about Todd. The whole long-distance relationship thing. Have you seen it work?"

"Of course I have. But I've seen it not work too." My turn to grab a tray.

"Do you think it would be better if we broke up?" Sam asked when I came back. "He's still got another year here, and I'm going to meet so many new people."

I could have laughed at how close to home this line of conversation was going after talking with Sandra last night about Brad's reasons for breaking up with her, but that wasn't the reaction Sam needed.

"Do you love him?"

"Yeah," he answered without hesitation.

"Then let what's going to happen, happen. I'd hate to see you throw something good away for a what-if. If that time comes, then you'll know and can act on it then, but you don't need to do anything now. Enjoy your time together while you're still in the same place. Because it does get harder when the distance increases, but it could be worth it too. You don't find out until you try."

He grabbed a tray of day-old goods from the case next to this one, then set it on the counter. "Thanks. That makes a lot of sense."

"And no matter what you end up doing, be honest with him and anyone else who asks what's going on. You know how the rumors travel in this town."

I plopped the bags that we put day-old goods in onto the counter. As I priced everything, writing the amount on the bag itself, Sam put treats into the bags as I handed them to him. We fell into a rhythm, not talking again until the last bag was sealed.

Sam wiped his hands on his apron. "I feel like I should have called you at midnight when I was freaking out about all of this. Given how you were when you walked in, you were probably up then, huh?"

"I was. And you can call me anytime. Even when you're miles away."

He hugged me.

I sure was going to miss Sam when he left and gave him a final squeeze. "Okay, let's get back into the kitchen."

I wasn't sure what the day would bring for the shop, but Donna had already requested a second delivery because yesterday's increased order of muffins only got her halfway through the second wave of morning diners. There was always someone who wanted muffins at lunch, and even though it was her policy that when she ran out that was it, she hated to disappoint people. Libby had also asked for a few extra scones and cookies. In addition to running a tea service on a day when there usually wouldn't be one, she'd dug up all the chairs she could find and added another table in her tearoom to accommodate more people for her tea service than had ever been there before.

At least for them, the disputes between Chelsea's and David's families seemed to not be having an impact.

We wrapped up baking for the day shortly before I made my lunchtime deliveries. Main Street still felt tense, but there seemed to be an uneasy truce amongst members of the two families. If I had to guess, they were occupying opposite sides of the street, although they came together at Olde Templeton, keeping quiet and avoiding eye contact. Food brought people together.

Once again, I wondered if I could heal this divide with my treats. First with the cookies the other day. Now my thoughts turned to putting a spell on the wedding cake, but doing so wouldn't feel right. There was one other thing that could work. However, I didn't like that option either.

I took my lunch in Founder's Park, having called in a sandwich and marshmallow rice treat from Leafs and Grounds. I nodded to Arthur Miller and his dachshund, Bardi.

"Right fine mess this town is in right now. Sure hope you can fix it." It was the first time he'd talked to me since telling me he knew someone who could help me with the mystery up in the north woods.

"I hope I can too."

He stood and lightly tugged on his dog's leash. "Good luck to you." He turned away from me and his bench, Bardi trotting along beside him as they left the corner park.

"Sandra, are you here?"

She appeared next to me, her arms crossed over her red polka dot dress. Her hair was curled and her makeup done. She looked like a pinup model. "The answer is no, so don't ask."

"Hear me out."

"I know you're getting worried, but I refuse to leave. There's a reason I've been here all this time, and it isn't to witness the disaster that's going on right now."

"But what if your moving on and crossing over starts the process of everyone's healing? What if you're meant to find Brad and Marvin and Greg on the other side and fix it there so that it gets resolved here?"

"You know as well as I do that I would already be over there if that were true. So please don't send me away. I may not be much help, but I want to help you through this. This is my family. We have to finish this."

I set my lunch down and placed my other hand on top of hers. "I don't think I could send you away on my own. Not if you weren't willing. That would be cruel. And I'm sorry I suggested it. I won't make you go anywhere."

"Good. Because I believe in you. You can figure out whatever is going on."

I sure hoped so.

Then just like that, poof! She was gone.

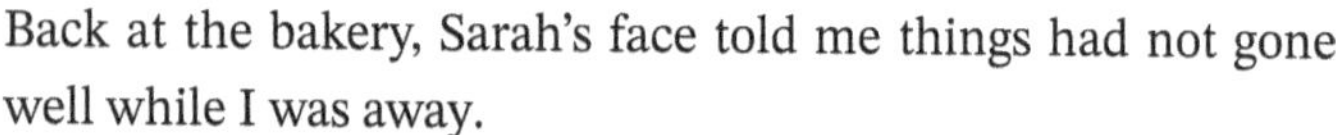

Back at the bakery, Sarah's face told me things had not gone well while I was away.

"What happened?"

"I don't know how to tell you this, but the wedding's been called off. David called to cancel the cake order. He said Chelsea was too upset to do it."

"Oh no, that's awful." It had been one of my biggest worries about this whole thing, that they'd bow to the pressures and the wedding wouldn't happen. But all hope wasn't lost. "Maybe they'll elope after all."

Sarah gave me a look that said she wasn't so sure. "You're such an optimist."

"It's my job to believe in love. I told Chelsea that at the end of all this, what mattered was the two of them. Eloping would still mean that they're together even if it's not the big wedding she'd been hoping for. Something smaller with fewer family members in attendance might be exactly what they need. Without a big wedding, their families will leave the town and things can go back to how they were."

"That's true. Plus, they have you and your witchy ways on their side." She wiggled her fingers at me. "I'm sure you have something up your sleeve."

Although I'd expressed hope about Chelsea and David eloping, I was at a loss on how to help them. I wasn't blind to the fact things looked bleak right now. Between the canceled wedding, the family tension, and the mystery surrounding Sandra's murder, a nagging feeling remained that things had to fall even further before they would rebound.

CHAPTER 21

Word must have spread that the wedding was off. Neither Donna at Olde Templeton nor Carter at Double Aitch ordered extra muffins for the morning. Without those and no longer needing to work on the wedding cake, it felt like a normal Saturday. We baked all our regular treats in their usual quantities, and when we were done, I sent everyone home, minus Sam, who was working in the shop with me today.

The immediate effect the wedding's cancelation had on the town made itself apparent as I made my deliveries. Fewer people walked along Main Street, and of those who were, they didn't seem as tense. I wondered if one family had left faster than the other or if simply knowing the wedding wasn't happening had appeased everyone.

Hopefully Chelsea and David would elope. That would show all of them that they couldn't mess with love.

I didn't have to wait long after returning to the bakery to realize something was going on, however. Saturday was our second busiest day of the week, and we'd only had a handful of customers. They'd all been Chelsea's relatives, stopping by for one last treat before heading home or venturing somewhere else since they now had more time to explore. One family was going to New York City. Another to Boston.

But beyond them, nothing. Not even our usual customers. Claire always came in for something after her morning run. Jenna would walk in with her sleeping child strapped to her chest, getting herself something to reward herself for getting him to sleep. To not see them was weird. Perhaps Claire had twisted her ankle and Quinton had finally started to take naps in his crib. What a relief that would be to his parents.

Maybe the humidity had kept people away. I'd been forced to have the doors closed all day, a change from the whole week when I'd let the scent of yummy treats waft out into the street. Nothing was luring in the passing potential customer. If I ever had to expand the bakery, perhaps I'd have to install a vent in the front of my store to blow the smells outside on days like this.

When I came back from a late lunch and Sam reported there'd been no new customers, I told him to head home. There was no need for him to stay when there was nothing for him to do. I could easily handle zero customers. After asking me five times if I was sure, he finally left, saying he was going to go surprise Todd, that he'd been taking my advice about making their time together count.

As I straightened things up, I contemplated closing early. But what kept me going was my unwillingness to disappoint someone if they wanted something right at the end of the day. So I held out.

One of my last tasks of the day was consolidating baked goods onto fewer trays within the cases. After a few minutes, I wondered why I was bothering since so few things had been bought today. I had one nearly full case left to go when the door to the bakery slid open. There was no need to look up to see who had come in. Chelsea's sniffle was enough to announce her arrival.

Knowing she needed a friendly encouraging face, I mustered up a smile as I walked around the counter, my arms spread wide. She came in for a hug, pulling me in close. We stood like that for a moment before she was able to gather her words.

"It's all over," she told me.

"I know." I patted her head, smoothing her hair. "David called yesterday to cancel the cake."

She shook her head, jostling my shoulder. "No, it's more than that." She sucked down a sob. "We're over. We split up."

"What? No . . ." Stopping the wedding was one thing, but ending their relationship?

"Everything got to be too much. His family, my family, the constant bickering between our relatives. I should have eloped like he wanted to. Then they wouldn't have been able to do anything about it." Another sob escaped. "But they've gotten their way now, though. Joanie, what am I going to do? He was perfect."

"He is perfect. I wouldn't tell you that if he wasn't. Let me see what I can do. I'm sure he's stressed over everything that's happened and just as upset as you are. He still loves you."

"I hope so. I don't want to lose him." She sniffled, then finally let go of me. "Since there's not going to be a wedding, I've come to ask if I can have my great-aunt's tiara back now. I thank you for all you did in trying to help unhaunt it, but I guess she can stay now that I won't be wearing it."

"Sure, let me grab it from my purse. I've been carrying it with me so I wouldn't lose an opportunity to talk to her." I walked back around the counter and pulled my purse off the shelf, then carefully removed the delicate tiara that I'd kept wrapped in tissue paper.

When I looked back up from the tiara, Sandra was standing behind Chelsea, her arms crossed, much like they had been when I talked to her yesterday in the park. "I don't want to go back to her."

Chelsea approached the counter, her hand outstretched, ready to take the family heirloom.

It slid away from her. Tissue paper and all.

"I'd rather be sent away at that rate," Sandra continued, "because going back with her means goodness knows how much longer I'd be stuck in a box somewhere, left to observe everyone living their lives only when I'm taken out for special occasions."

"What's going on?" Chelsea asked, her gaze darting from me to the tiara and back.

"Sandra doesn't want to go back with you."

"But the tiara belongs to my family."

"The tiara belongs to me," Sandra stated flatly. "Don't I get a say in these things? You're the only one who is going to be able to help me. Us. All of us." She disappeared, and the tiara skittered across the countertop, then in a deliberate zig-zag motion followed by a circle, began its return. It repeated the pattern two more times before settling in front of me.

"You can keep the tiara for now," Chelsea said shakily a moment later, visibly paler than she had been moments before. "I'll admit I had my doubts about it being haunted until seeing that. Sure, my mom and grandma would say it moved a little whenever it was out of storage, but I always thought it was coincidental, like through dusting or their not remembering they touched it. But having just seen that? She spelled out *no* right in front of us in capital letters. It doesn't get clearer than that."

So that's what it had been. It had been upside down for

me. "I promise you I'll continue working on this to free your great-aunt. She's been tied to that tiara long enough."

Sandra reappeared behind her great-niece.

"Thank you," they said in unison.

"And don't give up hope about David either." I bent back into the cookie case and pulled out a chocolate salted caramel cookie. "Here. On the house."

Chelsea shook her head. "But you can't. Before you gave me one because I was paying you for a wedding cake, and well, that's not happening anymore."

I held the cookie out and gave her a reassuring smile. "Not right now, it isn't, but it will. You'll see. It will all work out."

With a sigh, she walked over to me and tentatively took the cookie from my hand. "You're too good to your customers, Joanie."

"That's because you're more than a customer to me. You're also my friend. If a cookie is what you need to help cheer you up right now, I'm only too happy to be able to help. You take care of yourself, okay?" Tomorrow was going to be hard on her now that she wasn't going to be getting married in the afternoon.

"I will. My almost bridesmaids said they're going to take care of me. We're starting tonight with Greek pizzas from Mama's. Olives and feta. Gotta love the extra saltiness that combo brings."

"Sounds like a great girls' night. Enjoy."

Once she had left, Sandra stood in the shop for some time, staring at me while I finished consolidating the last case of baked goods.

I glanced up at her through the glass. "Is there something I can help you with?"

"No, just thinking, that's all. This feels familiar. Like a déjà vu moment."

I froze, the broom in my hand going still. "Did you remember something?"

She shook her head. "No. No, I don't think so." She sighed. "Anyway, thank you for not letting her take me."

"You did all of that yourself."

Her demeanor brightened, as did the lights overhead. "Yeah, I did, didn't I?"

"That was pretty clever moving the tiara like that."

"Thanks. I meant what I said, by the way. You're the only one who can help us." She disappeared then, leaving me alone in the shop.

As I locked up a few minutes later, I surveyed the still-full cases of baked goods, a pit in my stomach. Never before had I so poorly misjudged how much to bake. I'd barely sold anything.

What had happened today?

CHAPTER 22

In all my days as a baker, I had never cut the bakery's starting load. But after yesterday's lack of sales, I couldn't risk another day like that. If things went back to normal, I'd have to go into the kitchen and bake like crazy, but I didn't need an overflowing day-old shelf multiple days in a row.

After making my morning deliveries, I had the team help me box up the day-old goods. Some in single packs. Some doubles. Many more in half and full dozens. We decked them out in yellow ribbons and made pretty labels. If they didn't sell, then I'd be passing them out on the street and hoped the packaging would stick in people's minds the way it had after the cookie-decorating event.

Then I sent everyone home. I even debated calling Lauren and telling her not to bother coming in, but I knew she needed the money. She'd taken most of the last month of school off to prep for her college finals, and she was still trying to dig out of the hole that had created.

"Where is everyone?" Lauren asked as she walked into the kitchen to start her shift.

I placed my cleaning rag on the workstation I'd been

wiping. "Didn't make much sense to keep making baked goods when they aren't going to sell today."

She quirked her head to the side, and I filled her in on yesterday's lack of sales.

"Oh, wow. What do you think happened?"

"I'm not sure, but I intend to find out." The more I thought about it last night, the more I believed it was just as related to what was going on with the feuding families as the overwhelming number of orders from a week and a half ago. I'd talked it over with Saffy too, and she seemed to think the same. Well, she didn't say anything to disagree at least.

Between the two strange days at the shop, we'd broken even, but I didn't want to take another hit like this again. I couldn't.

A few people trickled in after church, and Claire's husband stopped by saying she wasn't feeling well so that's why she hadn't been in yesterday. Still, it wasn't nearly the foot traffic we got on a regular Sunday. As I made my way to the inn to make my delivery, taking the long way around to see if the lack of traffic was happening all along Main Street or only at the bakery, I spotted an unusual sight.

The Corner Bakery, the other bakery in town at the opposite end of Main Street, had a line out the door. Everyone was leaving with pastry bags and boxes. In my over four years here, I'd never seen people leave with more than a couple loaves of bread sticking out of plain brown paper bags or brown cardboard takeout containers with deli sandwiches in them.

I couldn't stop now and investigate, though. Libby was expecting me.

More than expecting me. She rushed toward me as I slowed to a stop near the inn's front stairs. Her tone was dead serious as she pulled one of the boxes from my bike trailer.

"We need to talk." As soon as I had the other boxes in my hands, she rushed me into the kitchen.

"What's going on?" I set my boxes down on the table next to the awaiting tea trays.

"I was hoping you could tell me. Is everything okay? Are you okay?" Her gaze darted all over my face as if searching for something.

"I'm fine. Why the concern?"

She reached for a flyer on the opposite side of the table. "I got this in the mail yesterday."

I glanced at the paper in her hand.

The phrase NOW BAKING UP YOUR FAVORITE SWEETS was printed in bold, bright-green lettering.

Below it was a picture of the Corner Bakery. The one I had to agree to not sell savory baked goods for if I wanted to open in Heartwood Hollow.

The Corner Bakery, your trusted corner bakery since 1986, is proud to now bring you cakes, cookies, pastries, and pies.

"I thought Zeke couldn't make sweets in the same way you can't make anything savory," Libby said, crumpling the flyer then throwing it into the trashcan.

"He's not supposed to, but it looks like he is."

She crossed her arms. "This isn't some retaliation for the pineapple bacon scones at the Love a Tree Day Festival, is it?"

I shook my head. "No, he had no problem with those and agreed I hadn't violated the arrangement because I wasn't selling them at the bakery. He even came back to the cart to say he liked the one he bought."

"Did he change his mind? I've known him for years. We sometimes get tea sandwiches from him when I'm too busy to do them, and this just doesn't seem like something he'd do for no reason."

"Oh, it's for a reason, all right, and I'm going to get down to the bottom of it."

"You're not in any trouble, are you? The bakery is okay?"

"The bakery is fine. It's not going anywhere. And no, I'm not in any trouble."

Libby placed a hand to her chest and let out a relieved sigh. "Oh, good. Goodness knows I can make cookies if I have to, but yours are so much better and free me up for other things I need to do around here."

"I appreciate your support." I really had to make a point of going to tea sometime soon.

She smiled at me. "All right. Let's get these onto their trays so you can go figure out what's happening with Zeke."

The line had died down at the Corner Bakery, and Zeke seemed to be managing a heavy but steady lunch crowd as opposed to the earlier pastry rush, but several people were ordering cookies with their sandwiches. How many people in Heartwood Hollow had gotten one of those flyers?

When Zeke looked up after ringing out a customer and saw me, his face went blank.

Part of me wanted to say something immature, like *busted*, but I had a sneaking suspicion he wasn't really behind this, so I said nothing. And if he wasn't the mastermind, then he likely was caught in the middle of all of this, too, for no other reason than he was the other baker in town.

I waited off to the side as he took care of the next three customers in his shop and admired his rack of bread loaves. He had the standard white, wheat, and rye but also things like cheddar scallion, spinach and feta, and garlic loaf. They were flavor profiles I hadn't worked with since culinary school with few exceptions of making bread and rolls at home for myself. Would his making sweet treats turn into my being able to make savory ones? Once again, thoughts of expansion entered my mind, but I pushed them aside for another time.

My gaze traveled down the case in front of me. Half the deli case had turned into a pies, pastries, and cookies case. Everything in it left much to be desired. Half of one pie was burnt. The pastries hadn't puffed enough, suggesting they'd been baked at the wrong temperature. The cookies had spread too thin, were too brown, and the chocolate chips were concentrated in the center. He hadn't used enough flour.

As I stood there studying the kitchen disasters before me, one customer came in holding a pastry box.

She placed the box on the counter. "Um . . . is there any way I could return the other ten of these? My daughter and I each had one and they just . . . weren't good."

As if he had said it many times before already today, Zeke replied, "I'm so sorry about that. You know how trying new things goes sometimes. Let me take care of that for you." He quickly processed the refund and took the box of baked goods back from the customer. I glanced behind him. There was a stack of used boxes piling up under the counter. No doubt the trashcan next to it held many returned treats.

"Thanks," the customer said, then quieter, added, "No offense, but this might not be your thing. My dad always told me to stick to what you're good at. Might be good advice for you too."

Zeke cracked a tight smile. "I appreciate it."

As the front door closed, Zeke sighed long and hard before taking the box and dumping its contents in the trash, never once looking my way.

"Why are you making all this, Zeke? You never made them before."

"Wasn't my idea," he said truthfully and without hesitation, defeat lacing the tone of his voice. "I know I stink at it. But I was pressured into it and promised I'd be paid for anything that comes back no matter what. Plus some extra for my trouble. Sure, I was skeptical, but the first check cleared. I couldn't pass up the money. You understand the penny pinching we have to do in this business. I didn't think anyone would come to me, not when your stuff is so popular, but I had a line out the door all morning, and yesterday's foot traffic wasn't too bad either."

"Did you know about the flyer?"

He tilted his head back to look at the ceiling in exasperation. "He made a flyer too?"

I nodded, wondering who this *he* was but having a sneaking suspicion. "I have no idea how many people got it, but some of my regular clients did."

"No wonder my phone has been ringing off the hook. It's too much."

"You could tell them no."

"I have!" Using his index finger, he made an *x* motion across his chest. "I'm no good at all those sweets. I stopped taking orders for anything but my regular stuff over an hour ago. Honest."

Right then, the phone rang.

"Hello . . ." He reached for his order pad but almost immediately set it back down. "No, I'm sorry. We're above capacity today on pie and pastry orders."

With that declaration, someone in line left, but two more people walked into the shop at the same time.

Zeke leaned to the side to look inside a case. "We have a few left, yes," he replied into the phone and then a moment later said, "Okay. Have a good day."

He turned back to me. "See? That was for a lemon

meringue pie. I'd probably be able to make the filling, but the crust and meringue part of it would not be good. You need to fix whatever you did to make Bruce Malloy your enemy so my bakery can go back to normal."

Just like Chelsea had suggested. "I didn't do anything to him."

"Yeah, well, then you should quit sticking your nose in other people's business."

I doubted that would happen but wasn't going to say that. "Thank you for confirming where this is all coming from. Good luck with the cookies. Helpful tip. Use a bit more flour. That will stop them from spreading out so much."

Zeke raised an eyebrow in confusion. "You're helping me? Aren't you mad?"

"At you? No. You're caught up in this the same as I am."

But I was going to put a stop to it.

I opened the bakery door and strode out, then called Lauren before hopping back on my bike to fill her in on what was going on. She agreed finding Bruce was imperative.

I had no idea where he lived, but I knew where to find someone who did.

CHAPTER 23

Greta's house was still packed with visitors who had been in for the wedding. Some sneered at me as I waited in the living room for Greta after I was let in by one of the younger family members. I remembered her from one of the orders I'd taken last week. She'd seemed pleasant. I wondered if she cared that Chelsea was a merrow. Did she even know of the history between their families?

Greta shuffled into the room. "Joanie? This is a surprise. What are you doing here?"

She appeared genuine, as if she didn't know why I'd be coming to see her. I'd figured Bruce was mostly a one-man show fueling the lingering tensions between the two families, but would he have hidden his misdeeds from one of his oldest friends?

My gaze darted around all the people still in the room before settling back on her. "I'm hoping you can help me track someone down."

"Come, come sit and tell me what's going on." She must have noticed then the looks some of the others were giving me as we passed. "Scram, all of you. Joanie's a friend, and as long as you're in my house, you'll show her some respect."

She ushered me to the couch, rolling her eyes. "This grudge is as strong as I've ever seen it. And I thought trolls were hardheaded."

"About that. I'm hoping to find Bruce."

"What did he do now? Oh, but first, can I offer you some tea?"

Usually, I would have agreed to some, but I had to get my information and leave. "No, but thank you. I assume you know about the cookie orders?"

She smiled. "Considering how many I have frozen right now as a result, yes. Once I found out, I wasn't going to let them throw away the non-salty ones."

They were going to throw out most of the cookies? What a waste that would have been. As annoyed as that made me, I wasn't about to take it out on Greta.

"Well, instead of the overwhelming number of orders coming in, I now have the opposite problem." I filled her in my lack of business these last two days and how Zeke was now trying to bake sweets.

"Oh, this is going too far now. Giving you a bunch of orders is one thing—it's at least more money in your pocket even if it leaves you exhausted. It's another thing entirely for him to be taking business away from you. He might not like whose side you're on, but you're good for the town. No one can argue against that."

"I'm not on anyone's side."

She sighed hard. "He doesn't see it that way, dear. He sees you as dredging up a past for someone he doesn't think deserves it."

"Well, then I'm just going to have to convince him that he's wrong."

Greta belted out a laugh. "Good luck with that." She got up and walked out of the room. Returning a few moments later, she held a slip of paper out to me. "Here's his address."

"Thanks for this."

"I doubt anything you can say will change his mind, but if anyone is going to do it, it will probably be you."

"What makes you say that?"

"You got me to tell you I was a troll," she began, her voice sincere. "It's not something I advertise. We're viewed as dull and curmudgeonly, and I don't like the stereotype." She shrugged, then waved her hand off to the side. "Many of my extended family members don't know what I am beyond the fact I'm not like them."

After what she'd told me last week, I found that interesting. "But I thought people didn't care that you were a troll who married a selkie."

"They don't, but that doesn't mean they don't still have a bias against trolls as trolls."

Was this why she was an early convert to liking Chelsea—because she understood what it was like to be different within this family? I asked her what I was thinking.

"That could be part of it, but I never disliked her before she got together with David. I remember her as a little girl in the town. Always so sweet to everyone. And the little ones love her. They're the best judges. They don't have any idea about the history between the families. Would be nice to keep it that way."

Knowing that gave me hope. "Thanks for helping me, Greta."

"It's the least I can do. All right. You better get. He'll be waking up from his midday nap soon, so it's the best time to catch him."

As I climbed off my bike, the beach-cobble path crossing the yard to the gray Cape Cod seemed to lengthen. My anxiety over direct confrontation was catching up to me. I'd been able to talk to Zeke because he wasn't behind all of this. I'd been able to rush after two strangers about to engage in a fistfight because I didn't want to see anyone hurt and the adrenaline had kicked in. This, however, felt like when I was younger and could tell a mean ghost wanted to talk to me.

That feeling had me wanting to turn back around, but I had to do this. I couldn't understand why my trying to help a friend made me and my business a target. Shaking my arms to loosen up, I took a deep breath and steeled myself for what I was about to do.

"Took you long enough," Bruce said when he opened the door. "Been watchin' you out the window for the last few minutes."

Drats. So much for the element of surprise.

"I've got nothing to say, so you might as well go on your way."

"Well, I have plenty to say to you, and I'd appreciate it if you would give me the courtesy of listening especially since I have some free time today thanks to you chasing away my customers."

He chuckled. "I thought that was pretty clever."

"You know you're hurting Zeke, too, right? He's not good at sweets. You're hurting his reputation. This could backfire for him."

"Eh, I'll give him another check. He'll survive."

"And if *I* don't?"

"Eh," he said again, shrugging. "I don't like sweets."

"Not even the salty ones? I can see the open pastry box on your kitchen counter from here." Surprisingly, he didn't close the door after I called him out. I'd been expecting him to shut it in my face since he first opened it. Still, it might happen at any time, and I had to say what I needed to before it did. "I've done nothing but contribute to Heartwood Hollow since I moved here. You don't want the bakery to become an empty storefront, do you?

Bruce scoffed. "You've done nothing but stick your nose in other people's business since you moved here, that's what you've done."

"David and Chelsea have been together for years. And yet you've had no problem with it until now."

"Oh, I've always had a problem with them together."

"Then why wait so long?"

"I always thought it would end. That David would come to his senses."

"So what are you more upset about? Her being a merrow and him a selkie or who her great-aunt is?"

"Bah! I couldn't care less about that whole merrow/selkie stuff." I somehow doubted that but said nothing. "But it did make it easier for me to turn everyone against Sandra once my brother left. A comment about merrows here, a statement about us selkies being better there. It fueled itself after a while. All I had to do was remind David's family about what Sandra did to stoke it back up against Chelsea and the wedding."

"And what *do* you think Sandra did to your brother?"

"She broke his heart when she dumped him before he went off to school. He never wanted to come home anymore because of her. It was like I'd lost my older brother a year before he even died because of how little I saw him."

"And you don't think he could have broken up with her so

that he wouldn't be tied down to anyone here in case he met someone else?"

He crossed his arms. "My brother was not like that."

I raised an eyebrow at him. "So there was no chance that he wanted to see what was beyond Heartwood Hollow? That he met someone else who he was afraid to bring home because of how different this place is or of what you all would think of her?"

"My brother wasn't ashamed of us."

Although I hadn't meant to imply that, he'd left me a good opening. "Would he be ashamed of how you're acting now?"

For the first time, he didn't have a comeback.

"From everything I've heard about your brother, he was an upstanding guy. Everyone liked him because he was so nice and charming. I don't think he would have done what you're doing."

He sighed and averted his stare slightly. Was I was getting through to him? "No, you're probably right. Doesn't mean I'm going to stop, though." His gaze hardened once more. So much for that.

"Why? You've got what you wanted. They aren't getting married anymore! What more do you want?"

"I want you to stay out of places where you don't belong."

"Why, are you hiding something you don't want me to find?"

His mouth dropped, but he quickly stifled the reaction into a scowl. "All right, I've humored you long enough. I'm done with this conversation." Without another word, he slammed the door in my face.

I spun on my heels and strode down the steps, my fists clenched to prevent them from shaking. My adrenaline level from our exchange was crashing. I hopped on my bike and didn't cry until I got home. That hadn't gone how I'd intended it to at all. Now he was even angrier with me, and my only concern was, what was he going to do to my bakery next?

CHAPTER 24

I'd barely started my morning, yet I was already looking forward to tomorrow being Tuesday. Tomorrow I would refuse to get out of bed except to get another cup of tea or a book to read. And feed Saffy. She wouldn't let me forget that.

Despite the lavender Earl Grey tea I'd had that was meant to calm my nerves and wake me up, I was still on edge. Jumpy. After my confrontation with Bruce Malloy, I'd been relieved to find my bakery in one piece when I arrived. Part of me had been afraid I'd find a window broken or the door busted in as retaliation. I doubted he would do it himself, but he easily could send someone else to do it for him. He seemed to prefer having a buffer between him and getting his hands dirty. But if that were true for all things, then he wasn't Sandra's killer. So who was?

"You okay?" Sam asked me from behind, placing his hand gently on my shoulder.

I jumped. "I'm good. What makes you ask?"

"You haven't rolled out the dough that's been sitting on your station for the last five minutes."

I looked down at the half-formed lump. "Oh, wow. Yeah,

yeah. Sorry. Just a lot on my mind, I guess. A little tired too. I should have a muffin."

"What's going on, Joanie?" Lily asked. "This isn't like you."

"Is the bakery in trouble?" Gina added.

"No. The bakery isn't in trouble." I sighed. It did no good to sugarcoat it. "But if we don't start selling, we eventually will be."

"Why aren't we selling?" Bryan asked, tossing me a muffin from the cooling rack. "This has never happened before." As one of my first employees, Bryan would know if it had.

I smiled sadly as I broke off a piece of the peanut butter and banana muffin. It was time to tell them what was going on. If I couldn't trust my team, who could I trust? I told them what I knew without going into any paranormal details. Lily knew of my abilities, and Sam had seemed open when I mentioned spelling the scones during the Love a Tree Day Festival. Gina and Bryan had been with me the longest back here. They joked about Monday muffins and good luck cookies as everyone did, but they weren't a part of this world. At least not that I was aware of. But either way, it wasn't right for me to divulge that Chelsea and David were anything other than human. So instead, I said there was a long-standing family feud, and my willingness to make the cake—as well as having gotten the two together—had made me an unknowing target. I told them about how Zeke was making sweets now and that he had a financial backer who would support him even if he was no good at it.

"So," I said, with a heavy exhale, "anybody got any ideas to drum up some more foot traffic?"

"Why don't you pass cookies out on Main Street," Sam suggested. "Kind of like a free sample sort of thing."

"Let's throw in a few cookies with your morning deliveries as a special promotion. You know Donna will talk you up," Gina said. I had no doubt Donna would pass out some of my cookies at her diner come lunchtime.

"Carter too," Lily added.

"What about flyers? If Zeke has them, you can too," Bryan said. "Ask Libby to put them out at the inn for her guests."

"Maybe it's time to add something new like him too," Sam commented.

I put a hand up to stop him from saying more. "I can't get the town council mad at me for violating my agreement with them."

"You wouldn't be. I wasn't thinking savory stuff." I quirked my head at him as he gave me a knowing smile. "What about fudge or other candies?"

"That would be great, but I don't have the recipes. Or the supplies."

"That's easy. My grama's still got all those. It's part of what she's been wanting to talk to you about."

It was yet another sign that pointed toward expansion. Maybe now *was* the time. That would certainly show Bruce I wasn't going anywhere. I added *Talk to Trudy* to my list of things to do tomorrow. Only she could get me to leave the house.

"These are all good ideas. And we can get started on some right away. Sam, at some point today, can you ask your grandmother if she's available tomorrow?" Sam nodded. "Thanks, and thanks, all of you."

"If you need anything, anything at all," Gina began, "don't hesitate to ask."

Carter called me into his office once I got to Double Aitch. He had also gotten a flyer and showed it to me. This one said Zeke was now offering muffins. Was this Bruce's retaliation?

"Whatever is going on, you have my business. One, after what you did for the town last month up in the north woods, I wouldn't leave you for the competition. Two, you've been my loyal supplier of muffins for years. And three, I had one of his cookies." Carter scrunched up his nose. "It wasn't good."

I raised my eyebrow at him in a teasing manner.

"Now, now, it wasn't my doing. Becca brought a few home. One of her coworkers had brought them into her office. I don't turn down free cookies, but I should have with these. Zeke may supply my bread for sandwiches and toast, but after that cookie? Guarantee you I won't be switching to him for other things anytime soon."

"Thanks, Carter. It means a lot. And speaking of free cookies . . ." I plopped the box I'd been holding when he asked to speak with me onto his desk. "I was hoping you'd consider handing these out to your customers or leaving them in a basket at your bar?" I opened the box, revealing four dozen individually wrapped cookies. Each in a clear cellophane bag and labeled with the cookie type and Suncraft Bakery scrawled on it. After this, I was absolutely ordering printed labels for my bags. This and the event at the senior center showed they were a necessity.

His eyes widened. "You're giving these away?"

"Trying to get some business. Even though his cookies aren't good, the publicity Zeke's been getting has left my bakery a ghost town." Ugh . . . had I really just used a ghost cliché? Oh well, it did fit the situation. Maybe a little too well.

"I'd be happy to. Let me try selling them for a buck. It's not what you charge for them, but my clientele isn't used to this sort of offering here. I'll get the money to you at the end of the day, and if you need to, you can bring more by on Wednesday."

I was touched by his offer. "That's more than I could ask you to do."

"That's the thing. You didn't." He gave me a warm smile. "If selling them doesn't work, I'll pass them out for free like you asked."

"Thanks. Okay, I must be off to Donna's." Walter and Paul would be waiting for their muffins.

"You have a good day. And Joanie? Try not to worry, eh? This will blow over eventually, I'm sure. Zeke will realize he's no good at this, or the town council will reprimand him for competing with you. I was at the meeting when you petitioned to open, remember?"

"I do. You stood up for me, saying how I would add something to this town with my bakery."

"And you have. More than I ever thought you would after last month. That was all you. No, you're not going anywhere."

I left Double Aitch feeling better about the whole situation. I'd needed to hear that someone else had my back. My team obviously did, but Carter's and my relationship had always been professional. Knowing he was on my side made me realize others would be too. Libby. Kim. Whitney at the portrait studio. Everyone at the real estate office. Those places where I'd made connections in the community on my own.

Donna had also gotten a flyer advertising Zeke's muffins. It had been waiting for her this morning. Paul and Walter were reading it as I walked in with their anticipated Monday muffins. Mine had already kicked in, and I was feeling much more awake now.

"What is all this nonsense about?" Paul asked, waving the flyer around as Donna wrote the muffin flavors on her whiteboard.

"Doesn't he know he'll never beat your Monday muffins?" Walter added. To Donna, he said, "I'd like mine grilled with butter today, please."

"Isn't he not supposed to sell the same stuff you do?" Donna asked, taking the box from me and pulling two out then handing them over to the kitchen to be grilled. Paul always had his grilled, but Walter sometimes took his straight from the box depending on how hungry he was.

"Not technically, but he is."

"That's going to come back to bite him. The town council won't take kindly to him going against his word, and doesn't he realize how this makes him look to those of us who use both of you? I can always go buy my bread somewhere else."

"That's very kind of you, but don't do anything hasty." I didn't want to go into why I wanted her to continue to use Zeke, it would only fuel the gossip and rumor mill in town if I did, but I had to say something.

She reached behind her to grab a pot of coffee to top off the men's cups. "It makes me mad that he thinks he can encroach upon your business like this. And the grocery store bakery will have everything I need."

"If you feel you must, but let me try talking to him again first, okay?"

"Fine. But if he doesn't stop this ridiculousness soon, I'm taking my business elsewhere."

She meant well. It wasn't her fault she didn't know the full story behind it, but I wasn't going to tell her. I'd seen Bruce eating in here before. Would he start to target her, too, for siding with me? I couldn't have that.

"Thanks, Donna. I do have a favor to ask you, though."

"You name it."

"Would you mind leaving some cookies on the counter for your customers? Free, of course. Trying to get back some of the foot traffic I've lost since this all started."

Paul's and Walter's eyes lit up as I opened the box of cookies.

"Go on, you two can take one too."

Paul stopped Walter's hand from approaching the box. Walter shot him a look, and after a silent exchange between the two of them, their hesitation was evident.

"What's wrong?"

Paul shook his head. "I can't take this from you after hearing what's going on. Dotty and I will be in later today to buy some from you like proper customers."

"Yeah, me and Martie too," Walter added.

Their proclamations touched me almost more than Carter's had. I was going to pull through this just fine.

Donna took the box from me. "I'll be happy to give them out today. Now you go on and give Zeke a run for his money."

CHAPTER 25

Feeling better about my situation, I pulled my bike around from the side of the diner, where I stowed it for safekeeping. The lights were on at the Corner Bakery across the street as they usually were at this hour. Inside, Zeke's nephew, Tyler, stood holding a large baking sheet at an awkward angle. Tyler wasn't a baker. He'd graduated from high school last year and was working at the gym to save up money for college. His mom, one of my regular customers until Zeke started selling sweets, had said he wanted to be a physical therapist.

The tray Tyler was carrying was full of cookies I could tell were burnt from here. Zeke was waving his arms wildly as Tyler walked over to where I'd seen the trashcan yesterday. Into the bin they all went. As I hopped onto my bike, I hoped for their sake that they were at least cooled down and that one of them had propped open the back door to the kitchen or turned on a vent to air it out. No one wanted to enter a bakery and be greeted by the smell of burnt cookies.

This was all getting out of hand.

No, this was *beyond* out of hand. At one end of Main Street, they were throwing away cookies because they didn't know how to make them, while at the other end, I couldn't get anyone to even come into the bakery for cookies I knew were delicious.

Although I had no plans of baking more once I got back to the kitchen, I did have ideas for the rest of my team to keep them occupied until their proper shifts ended. I couldn't send them home early a second day in a row.

After loading the cases with the half supply we'd finished baking, Bryan, Lily, and Gina wrapped up the day-old goods. I sent Sam off to visit Trudy to see about talking with her tomorrow.

Sarah walked in as the three were placing the individually bagged treats into baskets.

"You all look like you're on a mission," she said after putting her purse in the kitchen closet.

"We are. I'm going to need you in charge for a bit, although Lily will be around if things somehow pick up."

"I will?" Lily asked at the same time Sarah replied, "Sure thing."

"Uh-huh," I told Lily. "I want you to design me some sort of countertop stand for little fudge boxes. We'll start small at first, but Sam was right. It was time to add in a few new things to the mix. See how it goes."

"Sounds great."

Overhead, the lights brightened. It was nice to see after the last few days. It made me feel like we were going in the right direction by adding candy to the shop, as if the bakery approved of the decision.

"Get John involved if you want, but you can absolutely handle this."

She saluted me. "I won't let you down. I'll draw a few things up today and try putting something together for you by the weekend."

"Take your time. I need to be comfortable enough with the recipes before I sell anything."

"Wait, fudge? What's going on?" Sarah asked.

I quickly explained Sam and Trudy's offer, and with each word I spoke, Sarah grew more and more excited.

"That's a fabulous idea," Sarah said once I was done, "but what does that have to do with you leaving now if you haven't talked to Sam's grandma yet?"

"Gina, Bryan, and I are going to walk around the town and pass out free samples to whoever we see walking around."

Sarah gave me a look and tapped at her wrist as if she were wearing a watch.

"I'll stay close so I'm not late for Libby's delivery."

"Good. This all sounds fantastic." Sarah clapped her hands excitedly. Again, the shop lights momentarily grew brighter before fading back to their normal luster.

Bryan and Gina grabbed the baskets nearest them, and I took the one Lily had been filling. They led the way onto Main Street. As I followed them out the door, I flipped the sign to open. The humidity was lingering, so I didn't want to prop the door open just yet. I hoped some of the humidity would burn away as the day carried on.

"I'll try to catch some people in the park," Gina offered. "After that, I'll make my way up toward the hospital."

Bryan pointed a thumb over his shoulder. "I'll head out toward the golf course. There are going to be plenty of people there at this hour. It's a great day for it."

Through laughter, I said, "I'll take your word for it." The

only thing I knew about golf was to hope a ball didn't hit your windshield as you drove on the road running along the west side of the course. "I'm going to stick to Main Street. If I am out making my run to the inn when you get back, thank you so much for doing this."

"You got it," Bryan said. He began his trek up Main Street before turning down Pine. That would lead him to River Street at the end of Libby's property and the start of the golf course. He'd still have a bit of a walk before reaching the clubhouse.

"This is going to be fun! See you later!" Gina turned and jogged down the street.

Surveying Main Street, I planned my attack.

Donna's was at the top of the street and across from the Corner Bakery. I wasn't going to head up there. She had that area covered, and even though I had every right to pass my treats out, I didn't want to annoy Zeke by doing it right where he could see. He wasn't my enemy.

Double Aitch sat across the street from Donna's about halfway between there and here. If he was going to try selling my cookies at his bar, I wasn't going to undermine his efforts by handing them out to those people who may have just been in there or would be on their way to the restaurant. So I'd take my chances at the lower end of Main Street.

In the first half hour, I'd given out ten cookies, including an extra one to a dad and his son who had said his sister was at home and it wouldn't be fair if he had a cookie and she didn't. Although the dad told me the sister was too young to have cookies, who could argue with the kind logic from a five-year-old?

The atmosphere on Main Street felt lighter than it had over the last several days. The townspeople had taken it back over, giving me hope that everything would get back to normal once more after I'd finished helping Chelsea, David, and Sandra. As long as those issues lingered, I didn't think a true Heartwood Hollow normal would happen. At least for me.

I popped into the real estate office and gave them six cookies, one for everybody in the office. Then I crossed the street and headed toward the photo studio.

Whitney welcomed me in as the chimes above the door clinked together, signaling my entrance.

"What a pleasant surprise! I don't have anything on schedule with you today, do I?" She furrowed her brow in worry.

"Nope, just stopping in. It's a quiet day at the bakery, so I thought I'd hit the streets a bit." I reached into the basket and pulled out a cookie. "Here you go! On the house as a thank you for being a great neighbor to the shop."

She brought the wrapped cookie to her chest. "Thanks, Joanie."

"You have any sessions today?"

"A couple of senior photos later, why?"

I handed her several more cookies. "Give them my regards."

"I will, thanks."

"Have a great day!" I turned back around and headed out the door.

I caught Holly sweeping the ramp to Leafs and Grounds. "How's business?"

"It's a little quiet today." She held the broom steady. "I think all the hubbub over last week and into the weekend chased a few people away."

"You mean the whole wedding thing?" Not that I needed to ask.

"And the near fighting in the streets? Yeah, that. Did you

really charge into the middle of it again?" *Again* referring when I'd gotten involved with Lily and John's shouting match last month. Holly had seen the whole thing.

"Guilty." I gave her a sheepish smile.

Holly leaned the broom against the side of the building and crossed her arms as she turned back to me, putting her tattoos on full display. "You need to be careful. You could have gotten hurt."

"Lauren and Sarah said the same thing. Don't worry, I've learned my lesson." I held my hand up with a scouting gesture. "No more getting in the way of things."

She raised an eyebrow at me.

"Well, I'll try at least," I admitted with a shrug. "You know me."

"You still think Chelsea and David belong together?" Being Lily's cousin, Holly knew all about my matchmaking.

"I do." Although what I really needed was to get them together to see if I could still feel their match or if I felt a broken match. Then I'd know for sure. I'd never experienced the sensation of a match that had been broken, but Mom had described it as an achy hollowness where the tingling should be.

"They make a great couple," Holly agreed. "I'd hate to think that family drama split them apart. But not all hope is lost. If a lumberjack and a dryad can get together, anything is possible, right?"

I laughed. "That's about as odd a match as I can imagine. So anything is possible."

She finally seemed to notice the basket. "What are you doing with the cookies?"

"Free cookies to say thanks for being a great neighbor to the shop."

"Oh, may I?"

"Sure! Grab enough for whoever's inside too."

She took four cookies. "Thanks! I should get back inside. Are you coming in or . . ."

"Not right now. Gotta finish passing these out."

"All right, then I'll catch you around."

I made my way back to Main Street and popped into all the shops I passed. It was still early enough in the day that some of the restaurants weren't yet open for lunch. Some didn't open on Mondays at all. It was part of my decision to close on Tuesdays. That way there'd always be something open at this end of the street every day of the week.

By the time I was ready to head back to the bakery, With a Cherry on Top Ice Cream Shop had turned on its neon *open* sign with a large ice cream cone light next to it. Ken, Ivy, and I had already been here several times since it opened for the season at the end of last month.

I stepped inside. "Hi, Lucy, how are you today?"

"Oh, hey, Joanie. What brings you in? Aren't you usually in the bakery at this hour?"

"Yep, but Sarah's got it this morning. I'm making the rounds and passing out cookies to the local businesspeople to thank them for being great neighbors."

"That's so sweet! I keep meaning to get to your shop, but this place has been keeping me busy."

I handed her one of the few remaining cookies from the basket.

She looked at the label. "Salted caramel? Oh, my favorite!"

"I'm glad I had some in the basket then," I said, wondering if Lucy was an underwater paranormal. I pushed the thought away. There was no way everyone in Heartwood Hollow was paranormal, and it did me no good to assume based on Lucy's flavor preferences. I never would have batted an eye at her statement before learning of the existence of merrows and selkies.

Lucy unwrapped the cookie and took a bite. "Oh, so good. Thank you so much. Would you like some ice cream?"

"Before I answer that, what time is it?"

She pointed up and behind her toward a clock hanging on the wall. The numbers were painted on ceramic ice cream toppings, and the big and little hands were made to look like ice cream scoops. The whimsical clock made me laugh. It even had a cherry on top for twelve o'clock.

"I have to head back to the shop and go make a delivery, but I'll be back later. I can never have enough ice cream."

After making my delivery to Libby and grabbing lunch—an ice cream cone with a scoop of lemon and a scoop of black raspberry—I headed back to the bakery for the afternoon. Our efforts from the morning seemed to be paying off. Walter and Paul both came in with their wives and bought treats for themselves and their grandkids. Four golfers came in after they played their eighteen holes. And several diners from Donna's made the trek down the street to see what else we had today because the cookies they'd had made them crave more. Had I put a cravings spell in the cookies as an act of desperation? I didn't think I had, but it might have been unintentional. After all, I had been thinking about ways to drive more people into the shop.

Midway through a rush, well, a rush when compared to the previous few days, Sandra appeared in the middle of my shop. I glanced at her over one of my customer's shoulders. She waved animatedly. "I have to talk to you."

I nodded, hoping she'd realize I was telling her to continue. "Have a great day. Thanks for coming," I said to the woman in front of me.

"My killer," Sandra began. "He's not dead."

I froze. That meant it hadn't been Marvin, not that I'd ever truly thought it was him. "Sorry, can you repeat that?"

"He's not dead," Sandra repeated at the same time my next customer placed her order for six cupcakes.

I'd heard Sandra the first time and had actually needed my customer to repeat herself. "Who are you getting these for?" I asked as I boxed up the six cupcakes, addressing my customer but stressing the *who* while looking over at Sandra again. "Surprising anyone special?"

"I never would have expected him to do something like that, but they say that, don't they? It's the person you least expect?"

That, however, could have meant Bruce.

"Oh, that's wonderful," I told my customer, only having heard enough to know the cupcakes were for her grandkids. That's right, now I remembered. She had a grandson who was six. Her granddaughter was four. "They're going to be so excited. Have a great day."

"Do you know them?" I asked Sarah.

"Not well."

"Cute kids."

She nodded.

"They live up around the corner from the new pizza place. I bet it's popular in their"—I looked pointedly at Sandra—"neighborhood."

"Yes," Sandra confirmed. "Doesn't live there anymore, but I've seen him around." She gasped. "Oh, I remember it all. It was—"

She was gone.

If only had been able to ask her directly. I might have found out who her killer was or at least gotten more information. My only hope was that she'd return soon to tell me who had killed her.

CHAPTER 26

By Monday night, Sandra still hadn't appeared. Tuesday was no different. I tried calling out to her, but she never appeared. By Tuesday afternoon, I dug the tiara out of its tissue paper wrapping. I couldn't feel her in it at all, not the way I had before. It reminded me of the time Kate had retreated so far into the hairbrush she had been attached to that I thought she'd left for good.

But where had Sandra gone? She wouldn't have just left, not after her refusal to go.

I set the tiara by Saffy, who was soaking up the sunshine on my couch. She lifted her head and cracked open one eye. "Do you sense anything?"

Back when Kate had been in the brush, Saffy wouldn't leave it alone. She hadn't paid the tiara much attention before now, but then again, I'd been more careful about protecting this family heirloom. It would have done it no good for Saffy to knock the delicate tiara off my nightstand and break some of the shells that adorned it.

She craned her neck as she leaned toward the tiara and gave it a sniff. She cocked her head to the side, and her eyes slowly squinted. After a few moments, she lifted her upper body as if to shrug but settled back down.

"You neither, huh?"

Was that it? Was Sandra gone?

I picked the tiara up off the back of the couch and carefully wrapped it. If it still felt this way in a few days, I'd give it back to Chelsea. There was no point in me keeping it if Sandra wasn't in it any longer.

I sighed. I'd come so close to finding out who Sandra's killer was, and then *poof*. She was gone. This was worse than her constant remembering and forgetting of things. I couldn't blame her for something I thought was related to the blow that had killed her. But in all my years, I'd rarely seen a ghost still afflicted by what had killed them. Only the bad ones had still been scarred from their final moments or worse. But Sandra wasn't a bad ghost, so was something else going on? If only I could figure it out.

Saffy got up and stretched before heading into the kitchen, likely looking for a snack. I'd made her a new batch of cat treats this morning, and she'd been trying to convince me to let her eat them all. She'd already had three.

"One more, but then I need to head out," I told Saffy, following her to the cupboard. Spoiled cat.

She made a loud purting sound as I dropped a treat in her dish, her tail shaking in happiness.

"I'll see you later."

The drive to the nursing home only took about ten minutes. It was a little outside of town on a gently sloping hill with an expansive lawn set on an even bigger property. The nursing home was connected to the senior center. The assisted living facility was situated nearby. All the residents had access to hiking trails on the property, a pretty white gazebo where they sometimes had small outdoor concerts, and somewhere there was a lake with stocked fish. I didn't think they were allowed to go swimming in it, but given that some of the people who lived here had to be underwater paranormals, some probably did anyway.

Trudy and Sam were waiting for me in the nursing home's sunroom, although Trudy looked to be asleep. I'd been here once before to provide sweets for a resident's hundredth birthday a few years back. The sunroom itself was comfortably warm, and I could only imagine how popular this room must be in the cooler months. Trudy sat in a recliner, wearing a long-sleeve shirt, a knee-length dress, stockings, and penny loafers. It was the least dressed I'd seen her. She usually went everywhere with multiple layers on, making her look a little like a multi-colored marshmallow.

"Grama, Joanie's here," Sam said, patting her arm.

"I heard her Sammy, thank you." She cracked open her eyes. "Just soaking in the nice warmth of the room. These old bones are always so cold, but they aren't in here."

"It's so good to see you again," I said, taking the seat across a small tea tray from them. On that tray sat a thick leather-bound book. "How are you?"

"Oh, I'm good, dear. I'm so glad we're getting this chance to chat. I wanted to talk to you on the day of the cookie-decorating activity, but the excitement of all the children took a lot out of me. Looking at them was enough to make me tired."

Trudy giggled, and I imagined her laughing at the antics of the kids who came into her candy shop all those years ago. She looked at me, her eyes sparkling with a youth that made her seem younger than her wrinkled skin made her out to be.

"I'm really glad too." I shifted my gaze over to Sam. "Thank you for setting this up."

"No problem. I've been excited for this since Grama first mentioned it to me after she met you at the bakery a couple months back."

"Oh?" I looked back at Trudy. "Sam said you wanted to talk to me about your candy and fudge."

She slowly leaned forward and slid the thick book toward me. "This is my recipe book. Inside are all my time-honored, taste-tested recipes for every fudge and candy I ever had in my shop. I want you to have it."

"Me?" Sam had said as much yesterday, but hearing it straight from her had me in a state of disbelief. "Why me? Why not Sam?"

"Heartwood Hollow needs something more again. I have no doubt that someday you'll pass these on to Sam should he ever want or need them. But it's time this old grimoire found a new keeper."

I'd heard that word before, *grimoire*. It's what witches called their spell books. Was Trudy a witch, or had she known some growing up?

Before I could ask, Sam added, "Grama knows that candies aren't what I want to go into. I have always liked incorporating them into baked goods, though."

"Like the lavender in your cookies," I said.

Sam perked up, likely happy I had remembered the treats he'd made back in April. "Exactly. But overall? I want to bake. I love the bakery."

"Well, I'd be happy to share whatever you want to incorporate into your baked goods."

Trudy smiled at me. "And that's why you're perfect for this book."

Sam leaned in. "Joanie, after what's happened these last

few days in the shop, I think adding more to what you offer will be just the thing you need. And some candy keeps better than baked goods. You wouldn't have to make it every day, and not as much of it would end up on the day-old shelf."

"Are you really that worried for me?"

"You'll make it through this no matter what, but if Grama's recipes can help you in any way, I'm all for it."

I laughed, feeling a swell of emotion overtake me. If I didn't laugh, I feared I would cry. "I'm going to need a bigger shop at this rate. Or a second storefront. Thank you. Truly, thank you so much."

"I've been looking for the right someone ever since I retired. None of my children wanted to take over the business, and well, you heard Sammy. That baker down the street from you is fine with bread, but give him anything sweet and"—Trudy made a face—"no. And his heart isn't as in it as it once was, but you, you pour yourself into everything you do. I can feel it when I taste your treats. There's no one better for this, and once Sammy gave his blessing, well, that sealed it. He's told me what you mean to him and all the kindness you've shown him over the last two years he's been interning for you. It makes me wish I had met you sooner."

So much for not tearing up. I wiped my eye, then dried my fingers on my pant leg. Pulling the book toward me, I asked, "May I?"

"It's yours now. Go on ahead."

I spun the book around so that it faced me, then flipped it open and skimmed the first few pages, finding recipes for basic fudge, caramel, simple syrup, and more.

"Everything you'll need to form the base of more complicated recipes," Trudy pointed out.

I turned to a random page further on in the book. The handwriting had switched. I glanced at Trudy.

"I wasn't the first candy maker in town, you know. This was handed down to me the same way I'm giving it to you."

I flipped to another page. A recipe for candied bacon. "This would have come in handy last month."

Trudy laughed. "Probably, but you did fine with those scones. This recipe is great for bacon you dip in chocolate."

"This is going to keep me busy, that's for sure."

"I offer to be a taste tester," Sam said with the excitement of, well, a kid in a candy store.

"And I want to be there the day you start selling candy in your store," Trudy added. "Oh, to see some of these being made again."

"Well, what are your favorites?" I asked. "I'll start with learning those."

Trudy's eyes lit up.

We chatted for a good while longer, but eventually, Trudy grew tired. Sam offered to take her back to her room so she could take a late-afternoon nap. I hugged her and promised to come to her if I had trouble with anything, which she assured me I wouldn't.

I stopped at home to drop off the recipe book, and once there, I jotted down the ingredients I'd need to make Trudy's basic chocolate fudge.

Saffy looked up at me as I slid my shoes back on as I prepared to leave once more.

"I know I said I wasn't leaving the house today except to talk to Trudy, but I'm so excited to try this, I have to get to work." Plus, after the last few days of reduced baking, it would be a good time to take stock of my ingredients and make sure everything was still fresh so there would be no surprises tomorrow.

CHAPTER 27

Xavier and his cleaning crew were just locking the back door to the kitchen as I pulled into the parking lot.

"'Ello, Joanie," Xavier called as I stepped out of my station wagon. "Don't see you often when we're here."

"Hey, I wanted to experiment with a new recipe. Figured I'd come here to do it." I walked up to the steps as he and his crew came down them.

"Makes sense. Well, we're off to our next stop."

"Have a good day, and thanks for all you do. I love coming in and seeing how clean the bakery is."

"You make our job easy." He scrunched up his nose. "You should see some of the other places we do."

"Based on your reaction, I think I'd rather not."

I stepped into the kitchen to the sound of him laughing and then waved over my shoulder to him and his crew before the door swung closed.

As I searched for supplies in the basement, my thoughts drifted back to Chelsea and Sandra. I couldn't let my excitement for this added endeavor derail me of my promises made to them. Needing to check, I pulled the tiara from its tissue wrapping in my purse. Still nothing. Where had Sandra gone?

I returned to the kitchen, a few staples in one arm. For a small batch, what I had would do. The recipe called for milk, but I made sure to use up whatever I had on Mondays and bought fresh on Wednesdays. So instead, I had grabbed a can of evaporated milk that I'd water down to get the amount of milk I needed. The flavor profile would be slightly different than using regular milk, but for a trial run, this would be fine. I brought everything to the counter next to the stove and set up my *mise en place* so everything would be ready when I needed it in the proper amount.

An older recipe, there were no directions for how hot to get the fudge during the cooking process. Only a note that I wanted the consistency to be soft enough so I could flatten a small drop between my fingers after it had been in a cup of cold water. I mixed everything and brought it to a boil, stirring the entire time. As soon as the mix hit its boiling point, I cut the heat on the burner, setting it to low so everything would simmer. Immediately I took a spoon to collect enough to drop in the water. It wasn't ready. I repeated the process five more times. Finally I hit the consistency I believed I needed and turned off the burner. I carried the fudge mixture to my workstation, then added the remaining ingredients and kept stirring until it no longer looked shiny. As I did, an idea formed in my mind.

Once the fudge was in a baking dish to cool, I called Chelsea and then David, inviting them both to the bakery to be taste testers without telling them the other was going to be here. Chelsea agreed right away, but David needed a bit more convincing. It wasn't like I usually called him for things like this, and I hadn't spoken to him since the day in his tattoo parlor before the wedding got canceled. Eventually, though, the idea of a sweet pick-me-up won him over.

"What's going on? I thought this was a taste testing," he said as he saw Chelsea already in the shop a little while later. He gave her a sheepish smile. "Hey, Chels."

Her smile was small, but her eyes said so much more. She missed him and still loved him.

More importantly, my stomach was full of butterflies. Actually, my whole body tingled. It was almost overwhelming. There was no doubt—Chelsea and David were still meant for each other. Their match hadn't broken.

"It is a taste testing," I began, "but I also wanted to get you two together so you can talk. I hate what's happened to the two of you through no fault of your own. Your families may not like one another for something that happened long ago, but they shouldn't have taken it out on you and your relationship. Anyone can see that you two are meant to be together. Can't you feel it? It's almost palpable."

The room hung in a weighted silence a moment before David spoke. "I'm sorry, Chels. I shouldn't have let what was going on get to me like it did."

"And I'm sorry too," she replied. "I should have agreed to elope when I saw what the pressure was doing to you."

"But that's not what you wanted. I understand that. It was all so stressful."

She took a step toward him. "But I want you more than any wedding."

"I love you, Chels," he said, walking over to her.

"I love you too." Chelsea jumped into his arms, and he spun her around.

To give them a moment alone, I ducked back into the kitchen to check on the fudge. I stuck a toothpick in at one corner and pulled it out clean. Perfect. Using a knife I took from my block, I sliced into the fudge, cutting it into two-inch squares, then pried out the corner piece, which would be mine—the first piece out of a pan was never the best-looking one—and then used an offset spatula to lift out two more. Those two went into cupcake liners. I'd need to get something that fit better eventually, but these would do for now.

Before I walked back into the shop, I tried my square, needing to know if it was even worth letting Chelsea and David try theirs. If it was horrible, I'd have to grab out two Monday muffins for them. It wouldn't be much of a taste testing if I didn't have anything for them to try. I sunk my teeth into my piece of fudge, and the bite easily tore away from the whole. It was chocolaty, smooth, and perfect. I carried their squares back out into the shop, where the two were wrapped in a tender hug.

"Here you are," I said, cutting into their moment.

They pulled apart but remained side by side. Chelsea immediately held out her hand. I dropped a fudge square into her palm and then gave David his.

"Oh my goodness, it's fudge!" Chelsea took a small bite and gently closed her eyes.

David's bite was much larger, nearly half the square. His eyes rolled back as he chewed. "Mmm . . ."

"You like?"

"This is so good!" David put the rest of the fudge into his mouth. "Please tell me you're going to start selling this."

I nodded. "Soon. It's something I'm experimenting with for now. I took one candy unit in school years ago, so I'm still a beginner, but yes, I do plan on bringing this and more to the shop."

"We haven't had candy on Main Street in years." David

turned to Chelsea. "Do you remember that one store? We were still young when the lady retired."

"Oh, she was so nice! I wonder what happened to her. She was old."

I didn't know if Trudy wanted it known that I was using her recipes, so I said nothing about my fudge being what they remembered. I'd have to ask Sam to find out. But I did feel it was okay to tell them she was still alive. They could draw whatever conclusions they wanted to after that.

"She lives at the nursing home. You know Sam from here, right?" When Chelsea nodded, I added, "He's her grandson."

"Aww, good! I'm glad she's still with us. Maybe she can teach you a few things. Unless she's saving that for Sam, of course."

"That would be nice," I agreed, still not divulging the secret. "I don't feel comfortable selling what I made just yet. Need to be able to make it without looking at the recipe before I do, so can I get you two a few more pieces to bring home?"

Chelsea nodded enthusiastically. "Oh, yes please!"

I ducked back into the kitchen and returned moments later with two small boxes, each with another three pieces inside. "Here you go."

"Thank you," David said, wrapping his arm around Chelsea's back. "And I mean for more than the fudge." He kissed the side of Chelsea's head.

"You are so welcome. I'm happy to see you back where you belong. Together."

Chelsea leaned into David and wrapped an arm around his middle to give him a hug. "I can't imagine certain members of our families will be happy, but we'll get through it."

Now that they were together again, I had no doubt they would make it through anything.

If only I could say the same thing about figuring out the mystery surrounding Sandra's killer.

CHAPTER 28

The next morning, I rushed to the bakery. I was anxious to see Sam's reaction to the fudge I'd made using Trudy's recipe, minus the slight alteration with the milk. Although the weather was perfect, I ended up driving to work to get me there a few minutes faster.

Lily was first to the bakery, as usual, but Sam followed her in a minute or two later. I had to stop myself from grabbing him a fudge square, but it wouldn't have been right to do it before Gina and Bryan got in. Fortunately, they arrived a few minutes later.

"I have something special for you all, so gather in." I tapped one of the center workstations before rushing toward the baking dish I had covered on my table so no one could see and ruin the surprise. After I pulled out four pieces of fudge, I returned to the group and then set a square into each of their hands.

"Hey, you've already made some," Sam said excitedly.

The kitchen was momentarily quiet as my team tried the fudge. They said nothing as they chewed.

The silence was killing me. "Well?"

Gina, Bryan, and Lily all expressed how much they liked it and were eager to learn how to start making candies. Sam, however, was still quiet. He took another bite and worked it around in his mouth.

"What are you thinking, Sam?"

"It's good, but it's not quite the same. There's a hint of a toasty flavor."

"Can you figure it out, or do you want me to tell you?"

"Tell me. I'm not sure."

I filled him in on my ingredient swap. "Next time, I'll use whole milk."

"Mmm . . . huh, never thought it would change the profile like that. You know, with the right nut combination, it would be perfect the way you did it too." He took another bite. "I think Grama would be proud of this first attempt."

A swell of pride flowed through me at his approval. "Thanks, Sam. Okay, now let's get to work. Our usual amounts. I think our efforts Monday helped bring our customers back around."

The morning did indeed go smoothly. The air felt lighter both in and outside the bakery, and when we opened for the day, I propped the door open to let in the small breeze. Customers came and went in their usual numbers.

Everything seemed almost back to normal until I got a phone call while at the inn.

I dug into my pocket to see who was calling. "Sorry, Libby. No one ever calls my cell." It was so rare I regularly forgot I had one.

"Not a problem," she said, continuing to place scones on the lower tier of her tea tray.

I glanced at the screen. "It's the bakery. I need to take this." I slid my finger to the green answer circle and brought the phone to my ear. "Hello?"

"It's Sarah. I think you should get back here." Worry laced her voice.

"What's going on? Is everyone okay?"

"Everyone's fine, but there's a health and safety inspector here."

My stomach dropped. "Okay, I'll be there in a few minutes." I hung up the phone, then slid it back into my pocket.

"Is everything all right?" Libby asked, a look of concern on her face.

"Yeah, health inspection. I'm sure you can relate."

She rolled her eyes. "Always coming at the most inopportune times."

"Yeah." I sighed. Inopportune was right. It was part of the process for inspectors to show up unannounced to make sure we were always abiding by the rules, but everything else going on made me question if the timing was truly random.

"Okay. You should go. I can take care of the rest."

"Thanks, Libby. See you Friday."

I rushed to the bakery, parking my bike in the back, then running around to the shop to see if the inspector was there or in the kitchen.

Alone in the front, Sarah seemed to fill with relief as she saw me.

I stepped inside. "How long have they been here?"

"Thirty minutes? I called as soon as he walked into the kitchen. He's already come through the shop."

"Okay, well, let me go see him. Thanks for calling."

"Sure thing. But, Joanie, he made me nervous. He kept scribbling things down and taking photos. More than anyone else has ever done."

"I'm sure it will be fine," I lied. If Sarah was worried, then I had good reason to be too. But I was also confused. We'd just had our thorough weekly cleaning, so there couldn't have been any cleanliness violations, and I hadn't changed anything in the way I operated since the last inspection. What had caught the inspector's attention so much that he put Sarah on edge? There was only one way to find out.

I entered the kitchen, plastering a smile on my face, and guided the swinging door between the two rooms closed. The inspector's back was to me as he bent to look under one of the workstations. My team was standing back against the closet door and the door to the bathroom, clearly uneasy.

"Hello, there. I'm Joanie Sunevall, owner of the bakery."

The inspector straightened and turned around. I didn't recognize him, but that wasn't unusual. I stuck my hand out in greeting. He didn't take my hand, so I let mine fall back to my side.

"Allen Curd from the Health Inspection Program of the Center for Disease Control and Prevention. I'm here inspecting the premises for violations."

"I can assure you, Mr. Curd, my bakery is very clean. You won't find anything here." At least I hoped.

"Well, we received a call reporting a few issues that required us to come check."

"Oh, did you?" Only one person I knew would do such a thing. "He must have been mistaken."

The man's nose twitched. A coincidence or an indication he knew who had called?

I looked back at my baking team. They seemed so uncomfortable. "Why don't you three go on home? You were cleaning up anyhow. I can do the rest."

They gave me no argument, which was unusual for them. On a normal day, they'd at least attempt a token refusal to leave. But today, each of them told me what they'd already done and what they still had left to do in their cleanup routine. Gina, Lily, and Bryan pulled off their gloves and tossed them in the trash, and Sam ducked into the bathroom to wash his hands. Then they left with little more than a goodbye. I'd have to call each of them later to find out what I'd missed.

"The one wasn't wearing gloves," Mr. Curd said after the back door closed.

"Code doesn't require that gloves be worn during cleanup. When he handles ingredients or finished food, he either uses gloves or tissue paper as required for ready-to-eat food during production and after."

"None of them were wearing hairnets either."

Was he testing me? "Also not required. Three of them had their hair tied back, and the fourth was wearing a hat. I can show you where we keep hairnets in case that's ever different. Beard nets too." We'd gotten a small supply of the latter when Bryan participated in No-Shave November last year.

"Yes, please."

I crossed the kitchen to the closet, then showed him the shelf where we kept hairnets, extra boxes of gloves, our cleaning supplies, and spare components to our first aid kit.

"Mm-hmm . . ." was all he said, standing on his toes to see the shelf above that where I kept spare lightbulbs and a small toolbox in case I ever needed to make a quick repair. He stooped to look at the floor of the closet. "And these decorations?"

"Are decorations for the store. None of them ever come in contact with the food."

"It's being stored on the floor."

"As it can be because it has nothing to do with food." If he wasn't testing me, he was being wicked critical. Had he recently been reprimanded for being too lenient? Or was he being paid off? Given recent events, I leaned toward the latter.

Next, he thoroughly examined my dishwashing station, followed by my sinks, drying racks, ovens, and industrial mixers. "Your eye washing station?"

"In the bathroom."

"Right. Let me check there." After a few minutes, he exited the tiny space. "And now I need to check your food storage area."

"That's in the basement. Follow me." I flipped on the light by the basement door and then led him down the stairs. When I rented out the lower floor of this building to open the bakery, I'd had to pay to upgrade the wiring to run the extra refrigerators down here as well as seal the floor. It had been an added expense, but the location on Main Street was perfect. It had called to me my first trip to Heartwood Hollow.

Mr. Curd pulled open the large stainless-steel fridge. "Hmm . . ." He closed the door, took some notes, and opened the door back up.

I made a mental checklist of the fridge's organization. Everything should have been fine in there. We didn't use meat, so there were no contamination issues, and I kept the eggs in a separate section below everything else as was required. That way, if something ever caused a broken egg to go unnoticed, it wouldn't leak on other ingredients, thus keeping everything else safe to use.

He closed the fridge once more, hopefully for the last time. I hated the temperature fluctuations from repeated openings and closings, especially if the openings were for longer than it took to grab something out. It was a pet peeve of mine when people stood at the ice cream case in the grocery store with the door open for too long. All it did was start to thaw the front containers and cause the door to fog up. Then the next person had to stand there with the door open so they could see what was inside the case. If I ran a grocery store, I'd have a strict look, decide what you want, and then open the door policy.

The inspector walked the perimeter of the basement, jotting things down as he went. I'd never had such a long inspection before. Most commended me on how clean I kept things. Some made helpful suggestions like getting a rubber insert to span the small gap between the oven and the sink surround so that crumbs couldn't fall in between the two. I'd even decided to do that at home after learning such a thing existed.

But there were no friendly suggestions, comments, or conversation from this inspector. No wonder Sarah and the baking team had been so edgy.

Without a word, Mr. Curd headed back upstairs. I quickly followed him, tripping on the lower stair. I silently cursed myself, knowing I hadn't helped myself any. He glanced back over his shoulder, then continued up the rest of the staircase. Once back in the kitchen, he wrote a few more notes.

"All right, I'm all set here." He ripped off a sheet of paper and handed it to me. "You'll have the electronic report later today, but I'm sorry to say that until these issues are addressed, you'll have to close the bakery."

"What?" I fought to keep my jaw from dropping as the lead balloon that had settled in my stomach popped, spreading dread throughout my system.

"I'm sure this comes as unfortunate news to you—"

"You better believe it does. Improper storage of dry goods?"

"Yes, in the basement, you really should be keeping everything better contained. It's a basement. There might be pests, and the humidity is harder to control."

"In my four years here, I've never even seen a spider downstairs, let alone something that would get into a bag of sugar or flour and spoil it. I monitor the humidity levels with a datalogger. Everything is off the floor."

He didn't respond to anything regarding that and instead moved on to other violations.

"Your dumpster cover was open."

"I can go close it right now." Really? Why was I being flagged for something so minor? I made sure it was closed before I left every day.

"You'll need to replace the countertop in your commercial area."

"What's wrong with my counter?"

"You'll see in the photographs I provide in my report."

How ridiculous! I didn't say that, though.

"One of your refrigerator cases read at forty-one degrees."

Which was only a problem if my food was potentially hazardous, which baked goods weren't. And the remedy for it was to close the blinds so the summer sun wouldn't cause the temperature to rise or to have the thermostat on it adjusted. Not closing.

"Your cream of tartar is expired."

I'd have to check that, but again, that wasn't enough to close me down. I should only have had to throw it away.

"You have to do something about the decorations in the closet."

Fine, I'd get some shelving. Problem solved. Not that it was a real problem.

"Oh, and you need better tread on the basement stairs."

Point taken, although the tread had nothing to do with my tripping.

"There are more, but I should be going so I can get this report written. If you plan to reopen—"

"Of course I plan to reopen."

"Then I would suggest you get a move on fixing these issues. Someone will be back soon to check on your progress, and you won't be able to reopen until we see that these issues have been corrected. It looks like you need a moment to process all this. I'll see myself out." Mr. Curd exited the kitchen through the door to the shop. I rushed to follow. Then he crossed the bakery and left without so much as acknowledging Sarah.

I stood in the doorway between the kitchen and the shop, the door resting against my back, keeping it from closing.

"Well, what did he say?" Sarah finally asked after a few moments.

"We're being shut down."

She snorted a laugh. "You're joking, right?"

Holding up the list, I shook my head "Nope. It's all right here. We'll get the electronic report by the end of the day."

"Seriously? How is that even possible? You're always so careful about this stuff." She rushed over and took the list from me. "This is an outrage! It's been a few years since my food safety certification classes, but some of these shouldn't even be violations. Please tell me you're going to fight it."

"Doesn't matter if I am or not. We're still not able to be open until someone comes back out and agrees we're not in violation."

I dreaded making the phone calls to my baking team, but when they heard what happened, each one offered to help with whatever I needed, even saying they'd come in tomorrow to help do a deeper clean than we'd ever done before.

Instead, I invited them all to my house for breakfast. They needed to see the report for themselves, and we needed to come up with a plan.

CHAPTER 29

Saffy didn't know what to do with six extra people in the house when my baking team and shop staff arrived bright and early the next morning. She must have sensed our collective distress over Suncraft Bakery's closing because she rubbed up against each of our legs as we settled into the living room. Or she was hoping Lily or anyone else would turn their legs into wood for her to scratch. But after sniffing Bryan's legs, she skulked over to her cat tree in disappointment.

Ken arrived soon after with coffees for everyone but left after a quick hello and a kiss for me. He was meeting with a potential donor today but said he'd come over after work to hear what the plan was, promising to do whatever he could to help too.

As we let the caffeine kick in, I made scrambled eggs, pancakes, and bacon for everyone. It was easier to think with a full stomach, and the cooking was helping me get out all my nervous energy that had been building since being told I had to close the shop.

Once we'd all eaten, I dropped copies of the photographs

from the report onto the coffee table and passed around print-outs of the report to everyone so we could all be looking at it at the same time.

Sam closed his copy of the report. "I don't get it. We haven't been doing anything differently. Why is our basement shelving suddenly a problem?"

"Why is *any* of this suddenly a problem?" Gina echoed.

Beside her, Lily nodded in agreement.

"This isn't right," Bryan said, still flipping through his copy. "What was with that guy? It was like he was looking for things to fault us on."

"Well, that is their job," Gina said.

"Not to this extent," he replied. "I mean, docking us points for one degree off in a single case? I've worked in restaurants before, and usually they'd tell us to adjust the temperature and would recheck it at the end of the inspection. They don't make you shut down."

"So what are we doing about this? Please tell me you're going to file a complaint," Sarah said, reiterating her statement yesterday about fighting the closure.

"I'm going to call as soon as they open, although fighting may only delay our being able to reopen. Either way, we're shut down until someone else comes to inspect the bakery. Until then, we have to treat this as we would a legitimate report. There are things to fix and clean and take care of."

"What are you going to do about all of our orders?"

I sighed. "I made calls to everyone with orders into the weekend. Libby is going to make her own treats. Donna is going to the grocery store bakery. Carter, too, I think, or there's a baker in Knoll's Grove who is decent. No one said outright that they were going to the Corner Bakery, but some of them might be."

"Well, we know those people will be back. I haven't heard

one good thing about Zeke's baked sweets," Lily said. "That's the fortunate thing in all of this. Your customers will come back."

They would if I financially survived the closing of the bakery. A few days would hurt, but if this went on, if this attack on the bakery continued, I wasn't sure I'd be able to afford it. And that was what worried me the most. More loans weren't an option, and the Phoenix Foundation in town—who'd given me a grant to open—likely wouldn't help this time around because it wasn't a new business but a closed one.

There was a real possibility that I wouldn't be able to be a baker anymore. And if I couldn't do that, what could I do?

Matchmaking wasn't a job in the paying sense. Not for me. I wasn't one of those people who made connections for others and set them up on dates to see if they'd click. When I knew, I knew. And it felt weird to me to consider charging money to help someone find their true love. And without the bakery, how would I be able to see people regularly enough to feel their connection with someone nearby? For me, the two things went hand in hand. If I didn't have the bakery, I didn't think I could be a matchmaker either.

I'd find another job, sure. I had bills to pay and Saffy to feed, so I had to work, but it wouldn't be the same.

By noon, my team and I had devised a plan. We'd clean top to bottom, take things apart, and call Xavier and his team to go over it once more. I called a technician to look at the one case to be on the safe side. And then I put in another call to have someone take apart the exhaust system to give the fan blades a good cleaning and the rest of the accessible insides a vacuuming. Fortunately that tech lived in town and could fit me in tomorrow. Lily said she'd talk to John about a new counter and that he'd know people who would help install stair treads and a second—unnecessary —railing.

All steps in the right direction.

I needed to see my best friend, so I headed to Town Hall before lunch. Hopefully I could convince her to eat with me since I had the time as I waited for people to call me back. It didn't make much sense to clean the bakery before having a new counter installed and having service technicians come in and look at our equipment.

Courtney looked at the clock as I walked into her office. "It's a little late for your deliveries, isn't it?"

I couldn't even muster up a smile for my best friend. "Yeah, about that."

She stood and rushed over to me. "What's wrong?"

"Some bogus inspection resulting in my being shut down until I can make the required repairs."

She blinked a few times as if not believing me and waiting for the part where I'd say I was joking. Likely realizing there was no punchline, she said, "It looks like you could use a good lunch. Come on, you can tell me all about it as we eat. My treat."

We headed down to Leafs and Grounds, where Gary greeted us, relief on his face.

"Joanie, you're okay! When I heard the bakery was closed, I got worried. It's not Tuesday. I thought something had happened to you."

"I'm fine. Physically, anyway." I grabbed a rice treat from the counter. This would, at least, start to make me feel better.

"What's going on?"

"Health inspector shut down the shop."

"That's not possible. You've always had glowing reports." Drats. I forgot that the violations were made public. Now everyone would know. No doubt some wouldn't realize they were bogus, though, especially if Bruce found a way to exploit the information. One more thing to worry about.

"Well, not this time, not that these were warranted. I had one ingredient from last month's special that was expired still in the storage fridge that I got marked on—"

"He didn't just let you throw it away?"

"Nope," I answered, shaking my head slowly. "Didn't let me adjust the thermostat on the one case that was a single degree off either."

"That's ludicrous."

The more my fellow food-service entrepreneurs agreed with me, the angrier I was getting over the whole incident. Bruce Malloy had gone too far by getting Mr. Curd involved. This was the difference of me being able to be a baker, something I'd paid good money to go to school for. This was the difference between six other people being able to have a job that they'd come to depend on. I knew why Bruce wanted me gone, but what had my team done to get caught up in this? Nothing.

"You don't even know the half of it," I said, widening my eyes in the hopes of cluing him into that other half being paranormal since I couldn't come out and say that in front of Courtney. I still hadn't told her anything about me or my abilities.

"So you're drowning your sorrows in a panini and soup?"

"You got it. Plus one of these." I held up the marshmallow rice treat, then glanced at the daily soup menu. "I'll take the chilled cucumber melon soup. A chai tea too, please."

"Can do." Gary looked at Courtney.

"The same, please, but make mine iced."

"Coming right up."

We took our usual seats to wait for our food and drinks.

Before I'd even had time to set my bag on the empty chair next to me, Courtney said, "Tell me everything."

As I munched on my rice treat, I told her all about what I thought was retaliation for being involved in Chelsea and David's love life, starting with the swell of orders until now, obviously avoiding anything paranormal.

"Ugh . . . he's been a miserable man since I was a kid. What are you going to do about him?"

"I'm not sure. Confronting him certainly didn't work. That only resulted in him reporting the shop for violations."

"Hmm . . . yeah, any escalation from there could only get worse."

"Do I try to ignore it?" I popped another piece of the crispy, marshmallowy goodness into my mouth. Half the treat was already gone.

"I bet nothing would annoy him more than to see you open back up with an even nicer storefront than you already had. Plus, with Chelsea and David being back on the track to the altar? Might be the perfect revenge."

It was more my style, too, succeeding in the face of adversity.

We chatted all through lunch and our walk back to Town Hall, promising one another to do this again soon. "Oh, we need to do a dinner together too, Seth's request," I said as we walked up the tall marble steps to the building's main entrance.

"Oh, that's right. He told me he saw you. Were you really trying to bust up a fight?"

"Pretty much."

"But you hate confrontation."

"I know, but it seems I've been dealing with a lot of them lately. I couldn't let the now non-wedding get off to such a poor start by having their guests fighting in the streets."

She sighed, a small smile on her face. "Can't say there's anything you wouldn't do for the couples you've gotten together, huh?"

"You have no idea. All right, I'll let you get back to work."

She held out her arms, and I stepped into her hug. "You take care of yourself. And if you need any help, call. Seth is great at moving stuff."

With a laugh, I said, "I may just need to take you up on that offer."

From Town Hall, I continued up Main Street. As I came upon the Corner Bakery, motion in the shop caught my eye. Zeke was in the window, waving frantically at me. I nodded in greeting, but he banged on the window and pointed to the door.

Fine. I detoured into the shop, wondering what he could possibly need me for.

CHAPTER 30

Zeke's shoulders sagged. "Joanie, I need your help."

"I'm not sure I'm in the helping mood right now."

"I heard about your bakery."

Everyone in town surely had by now.

He stared at me, eyes full of worry. "Please help me. The orders are pouring in, and I can't handle all these sweets on my own."

Zeke's plea tugged at me. He hadn't created this mess. "You should take it up with Bruce Malloy for reporting bogus allegations. This wouldn't be happening to you if it weren't for him."

"Oh, believe me. I'll be saying something the next time I see him. This is too much." He sighed. "I don't know how you do it."

"I have a great team behind me, that's how. A team that's hurting and out of work."

"The shop isn't big enough for all of them, but I could fit you and one more in back with me as we got control over these orders."

Pick only one of my bakers? How would that be fair? "Can I rotate between them?"

"I don't care as long as you're here."

I mulled it over. The others could work on getting the shop ready when it wasn't their turn here. "I'll do it on one other condition."

"Name it."

"I get to fulfill the orders of my regular customers."

"Done. Can you start now?"

Still waiting to hear back on the couple of phone calls I'd made, I didn't have anything else to do today. "Do you have an apron? I'm not really dress—"

"There's one in the back." He placed his palms together in front of him. "Thank you, thank you."

He led the way into his kitchen. If I had been shut down for such minor violations, he definitely should have been forced to close too. It wasn't dirty, per se, but it looked like the stress of trying to fill so many orders for things he wasn't used to making was taking its toll.

"All right, let me make a few phone calls, and I'll get started."

"Phone calls?"

"I'm going to need a little help getting all of this"—I waved my hand around—"under control."

He held his hands up in front of his chest. "I'll let you do your thing." He retreated into the shop.

I called every member of my team to let them know what was going on. Both Lily and Sam offered to come in and help right away. Zeke had said one, but if he wasn't going to be back here, we'd fit. Gina offered to come in tomorrow, and Bryan took the day after that. As I waited for the two to get here, I called everyone who usually placed Friday orders with me and let them know of my arrangement with Zeke. Carter had already ordered from the bakery in Knoll's Grove but said he'd see me Saturday. Donna and Libby would be back on my schedule tomorrow.

When Sam and Lily arrived, we set to work cleaning the work surfaces and took stock of what ingredients Zeke had on hand for today and tomorrow. I'd have to go put in an order to get supplies for my customers' orders, but that was fine by me. As soon as we had a list of what we needed, I called my supplier, filling him in on the temporary location.

Feeling good about tomorrow, we rushed through the orders for the rest of the day. There weren't that many, making me wonder how much word had spread about Zeke's bad cookies. Then again, he wasn't used to making them, and without that familiarity with what he was making, he was likely finding everything harder to juggle. I understood how Zeke and his nephew were getting overwhelmed. They should have stuck to the basics and not tried to offer everything I did at my shop.

Once Lily, Sam, and I were done with the orders, we made a couple dozen more cookies to sell through the afternoon. If we were truly going to help Zeke while we were here, then the burnt offerings he had currently in his case needed to go.

I headed out with a tray of cooled cookies—chocolate chip and sugar for now. His shop was busy, as it was toward late afternoon as people arrived to pick up bread and rolls for dinner. They oohed and aahed over the fresh batch of baked goods. Six were purchased before I even had time to put the tray on the counter and open the bakery case. Zeke came over and boxed up the half dozen, a genuine smile on his face for the first time in I don't know how long since this whole charade began.

As I swapped out my supply for Zeke's cookies, the bells above the door chimed.

"What is she doing here?" Bruce Malloy's voice, although it sounded surprised, was unmistakable.

I felt everyone's gazes dart to me then away and back before I stood and faced him. He wasn't alone. Greta stood there with one of her nieces, or at least I thought she was a niece. She was from out of town. Greta looked uncomfortable, probably just as surprised as Bruce was but not upset like him. She gave me a strained smile.

"Zeke, I asked, what is she doing here?" Bruce demanded again.

Zeke stood there, his mouth partially agape. I wondered if he saw his money disappearing before his eyes.

Well, if he wasn't going to say anything, then I was. "Hi, Bruce. Just helping out Zeke while my shop is being updated. I help him with some of his orders, and he lets me fulfill the orders of my regular clients. It's a win-win."

"Zeke, I want her out of the bakery this instant."

That seemed to snap him out of it. "And who are you, exactly, to be issuing me demands? I'm the owner here. You don't get to tell me who I do and do not allow in here."

All eyes turned toward Zeke, then to Bruce, who crossed his arms and said, "It didn't seem like that was your rule when I was in here last."

"And I was wrong about that. You played up the insecurities I had about the popularity of Joanie's bakery, telling me I'd be better off if her business went away. Well, guess what, you got Joanie's business shut down"—with this revelation, customers began whispering amongst one another—"and I've been swamped with orders for things I'm no good at." He lifted his arm and pointed at me using his open hand. "She's been nothing but kind to me, and now she's helping me stay on top of these orders and possibly saving my reputation. Do you know how fast word travels about bad cookies?"

Greta placed her hand on Bruce's arm. "Is this true?"

He glanced down at the short woman beside him. "Of course it's not." He shot me a look before setting his sights back on Zeke. "Well, I never—"

"No, *I* never. Never should have listened to you. You can take your last check back. I didn't deposit it." Zeke pressed a button on the cash register and the drawer popped open. He reached in and pulled out a check, then stuck it out toward Bruce. "And when you take this, you can leave my bakery."

Rooted in place with my tray of cookies, I realized I had none of the anxious side effects I had before. It was much easier for me to watch someone stand up to Bruce than for me to do it myself. And although he kept looking my way, there was nothing that Bruce could do to me. My bakery was already closed.

Bruce stepped toward Zeke and ripped the check away from him. "See if I ever help you again."

"Help me? You practically ruined me with your stunt. I don't need that sort of help. You can show yourself out." Zeke turned his attention to Greta and her niece. "Ladies, I'm sorry. You are welcome back anytime as long as Bruce isn't with you."

Greta nodded at him before turning to me and mouthing "Sorry."

I gave her a small smile. I genuinely didn't think she'd known what had happened to me and my shop.

Once the door had closed on Bruce, someone started a slow clap in the shop. Soon, the other customers joined in. Zeke flushed a brilliant shade of red. This would likely earn back some of the reputation he had lost with bad cookies. I doubted many would remember that he had originally been complicit in Bruce's scheme after that showing.

"Is it true, Joanie?" Lichelle, one of the college-aged residents of Heartwood Hollow and also Ivy's babysitter, asked.

"Sadly, yes. Bruce filed a false complaint about the shop and got it shut down. Don't worry, though, it will be open again soon."

"And until then," Zeke began, "you can find her operating her shop out of mine. This way you can still get the breads and cookies that you know and love from your two favorite bakers."

I looked across the small shop at Zeke and, with a nod, whispered, "Thank you."

Somehow, we'd make it work.

CHAPTER 31

Despite the cramped quarters, Zeke and I were making the two businesses, one bakery arrangement work. That was if you ignored the fact Gina and I had waited outside for twenty minutes for him to show up and open the kitchen for the day. Then there was the constant having to wait for something to come out of the single oven so we could get something else into it.

But once we got going for the day, all of that was forgotten as we worked on our muffins for Old Templeton Diner. We doubled the recipe to have what I hoped would be enough for the bakery today too. Never once had I run out of things in my shop, but it was a different story here. I couldn't monopolize the kitchen, so once we ran out, we ran out. While I was here, I had no other choice than to keep a light menu, but something was better than nothing.

"Zeke, do you have any boxes larger than this?" I asked, searching through one of his cabinets. "These aren't tall enough for my muffins."

"Well, they were tall enough for mine."

I'd seen his muffins. They were half the size of mine. I wasn't going to point that out, though. "Do you?"

"No."

Great. How was I going to get these muffins over to Donna's?

"I have bags for my rolls that you are welcome to use."

It was either that or carrying the muffins over in their tins. I glanced out the window. My occasional klutziness and the threat of rain made the bags a better option. "Fabulous, thanks."

The bags weren't huge, only five muffins fit into each one, but they'd work. I took six bags full of muffins across the street to Olde Templeton Diner. Thank goodness I didn't have to transport my baked goods like this regularly, but I sighed when I realized I didn't know how long I was going to have to keep doing this. At least the diner wasn't too far away. The rest I could ride my bike for.

"Well, aren't you a sight for sore eyes!" Donna rushed out from behind the corner, throwing her rag to the nearest table as she did. She enveloped me in a side hug, my hands full of muffin bags braced against my chest preventing her from doing anything more. "It is so good to see you."

I returned her smile. "It's really good to see you too."

"I'm so glad Zeke came to his senses and is letting you do some stuff in his bakery. Really, that's how we should all be in a town this small. None of this family feuding or trying to get people cast out nonsense."

Had something else happened while I'd been dealing with my bakery and working with Zeke? "Cast out? What have you heard?"

Donna walked with me up to the counter, scooping her rag back off the table as we went by. "Oh, Bruce Malloy is up to his old tricks again, but that's nothing new to you. Why didn't you tell me he was hasslin' you?"

I shrugged. "Thought I had it all under control until he set the health inspector on me. And you know that I don't like to start anything." The truth was I wasn't going to give her gossip material, but she didn't need to know that.

"Honey, he started this a long time ago. You just got caught up in it, that's all. He's been after everyone in Chelsea's family for years. Seems he can't let a grudge go. I get he lost a brother and all that, but really, he can't be taking it out on his brother's ex-girlfriend's family. One, they had nothing to do with it, and two, it's a mouthful for the gossip. Though, him getting you and Zeke involved is somethin' else."

I sighed. "Hopefully he'll put it past him now that we're on to him."

She barked out a laugh. "Doubt it. He might leave you alone now, but he's on a crusade to make living here unbearable for them. Called the cops on them over that near street brawl the other day."

"But he wasn't even there, and nothing happened. Everyone walked away in one piece."

"Something about intimidating his family or some such. It was in the police blotter." She rolled her eyes. "He's also filed a petition to make the beach over by Point Judith a private beach. His family's owned it for forever, and he technically has the right to revoke the public trust it's been held in if he chooses to do so."

"I always thought it was private. Everyone always calls it a private beach."

Donna shook her head as if I didn't understand. "*Private* as in secluded."

I bet the picture of the human pyramid Greta had shown

me was taken at that beach. I'd never been, thinking it to be closed to the public, but if it was as secluded as Donna suggested, then it was probably a safe place for all the underwater folk to change into their other forms to swim. If Bruce removed access, he'd be denying the merrows something they'd had for years. They'd either have to break the law to continue to use the beach, go to public places on off-hours when it was safe, or leave to secluded beaches elsewhere. At the same time, Bruce could continue to allow the selkies the use of the beach, so they'd continue to exist how they had for decades. Wow, he really was doing everything in his power to make the merrows unwelcome in their own home.

If only Sandra could tell me who had killed her so I could wrap up this case. If she was still around, that is. It had been days since I'd seen her.

"Well, thanks for the update. I should head back to Zeke's. Don't want him meddling in my sweets."

"I am glad he's letting you have a bit of space. But you'll see, everyone will have your shop up and running again in no time."

I didn't know what she meant by everyone but doubted it would be "in no time." I hadn't put any work into it yet myself beyond phone calls. Some I was still waiting for replies on. It was going to take a while at this rate. There was no reason to worry her with that, though. We waved goodbye once I reached the door, and I headed back across the street.

CHAPTER 32

Zeke was fuming by the time I reentered the kitchen. "How much longer are you going to need? I have to get these in the oven for eight thirty when Ed Peters comes to pick them up. He pointed to a full tray of rolls. I can't be a moment late because he has to be at work for nine and they're doing some sort of lunch."

I glanced at the clock. Not even seven a.m. Then I looked over at my cooling trays to assess where we were.

"This looks to be the next to last batch of scones. Why don't you hop in with your rolls when these come out. It's what, ten more minutes?"

Gina nodded at my estimation, a look of relief on her face. He had to have been going on about these rolls since I left.

Zeke groaned. "This was more trouble than it's worth." So much for what he had told Bruce yesterday.

"You have over two hours to cook these twenty-four rolls." He only needed twenty minutes to cook the tray he had.

"And I have to bake everything else I need for the day, but these have to be done first."

I wasn't going to point out that he had several loaves of bread already cooling.

"Do you bake during the day at all?" He hadn't yesterday, but I wasn't sure if he'd been trying to give me space.

"With what help? I do everything. I come in, bake, run the shop, clean, go home."

"Wasn't your nephew here a few days ago?"

"Only to help with all the cookies." He shrugged. "I was desperate."

Gina stopped cleaning the mixing bowl in her hand and stared at Zeke, one eyebrow raised. "It's really just you? All day? Why don't you hire someone?"

"Bah!" He waved his hand dismissively.

I believed Zeke had a micromanaging problem, but I wasn't going to tell him that. "She's right, you know. If you hired someone, you'd be able to come in later and bake longer into the day so people could come in and practically have their rolls still hot when they picked them up for dinner. Or if not that, then maybe someone to help clean in the evenings." Xavier would probably love to have another client in town.

"Hmm . . . It's no secret that I don't like mornings. I'll think about it." He was quiet a moment before grabbing the tray of rolls. "So am I going to be able to get these in or not?

Had he not heard a thing we'd said?

"Five more minutes, then you can pop in your rolls or whatever else you need to until . . . let's say nine thirty. We'll prep everything else we need to bake, but then we'll have to get in Libby's order for her tea service."

That seemed to appease him. His shoulders relaxed, and his face softened. "Well, all right. Can't have your customers getting upset after I agreed you can fulfill their orders."

For the next hour and a half, Gina and I prepped the rest of the day's baking, including some of Zeke's, and covered everything with a layer of plastic wrap so the doughs and batters wouldn't dry out.

Zeke had to be the most disorganized baker I'd ever seen. He ran here and there for ingredients as he baked, rather than gathering everything all at once. He set three timers in addition to the one on his stove, all as warnings so he could be prepared to pull things out of the oven on time. In the down moments, he didn't clean up. He just stood there. Waiting. How had he survived all these years without help?

Fortunately, Ed Peters walked in right on time. Zeke stood ready and waiting, prompted by two more timers in his shop as a reminder to bag up the rolls once they'd cooled and another to unlock the front door. In the few minutes Zeke was taking care of Ed, Gina and I loaded up his dishwasher for him and set it to run. It took him a moment once he'd returned to realize what we'd done. He grumbled his thanks and continued to bake until it was our turn again.

We fell into a steady rotation of sliding trays into the oven, cleaning, then pulling trays out of the oven and immediately putting more in. With only one oven, getting everything done was slow going, but we got Libby's order and some scones for the shop done before Zeke took over again.

When I got back from Libby's, Gina was helping Zeke organize his workspace, putting all of his most-used ingredients in the same area. Okay, *helping* wasn't the right word. A takeover was more like it. I entered the shop to him yelling, "What are you doing?" from the doorway to the kitchen.

"It will be so much easier for you if you keep it all together," Gina shouted back.

I listened a moment before coming in any farther. The scene was almost comical, and I had to press my lips together to stop a chuckle from interrupting the moment.

"But I knew where everything was before," Zeke complained.

"And you wasted so much energy going back and forth to get it. You'll be able to do everything so much faster now, and you won't be scrambling for time at the end."

"Bah!"

"You can always move it back later, but try it, will you?"

"Humph!"

Unable to contain it any longer, I giggled to myself as I crossed the shop then scooted past Zeke to get into the kitchen. It seemed he was coming around to the idea.

One of Zeke's timers went off, and Gina grabbed the baguettes from the oven before he even had time to turn around. She placed them in the cooling rack and added in the next trays for him.

As he passed by me on his way back to the front with a tray of rolls to bag, he mumbled, "You may be onto some-thing with this whole help thing."

"I think he likes you," I told Gina as I loaded up a dish-washer rack, hoping she knew to not take it in a love match sort of way.

She laughed. "I thought he was going to have a fit at first, but I couldn't take it anymore. I was hoping to get it done without him seeing me, but then another timer buzzed, and he came running back here, catching me in the act. He'll thank me later."

CHAPTER 33

Running the two shops out of one storefront wasn't easy. It was at times crazy as customers came in for the both of us, and chaotic with our varying work habits, but somehow we survived the first full day. I sent Gina home after we finished the rest of our baking and had cleaned up the area we'd been working in.

With my baking done, I stayed in the shop while Zeke continued his baking. Whereas Suncraft Bakery was busier in the morning, especially in the summer, Zeke was busier from lunch to dinner.

About a half hour before I would usually close, though Zeke would still be open for a while longer, Ken came in, looking visibly shaken.

"Ken, what's wrong?" I asked.

Likely hearing the door chime, Zeke came out to investigate.

"It's Clayton."

Thinking something tragic had happened to the old man, I said, "Oh, I'm so sorry."

He shook his head, realizing where my thoughts had

jumped. "No, he's still alive, but after he volunteered with me, I sent him down to his new therapist. While there, he attacked her. She's in the hospital."

"That's awful. Is she going to be okay?"

"Yeah, thankfully. I'm on my way to make a statement at the police station now." He cast his gaze to the floor before directing a worried glance my way. "Could you come with me?"

I looked at Zeke, who made a shooing motion. "Go on, get. I can handle things in here. You allowing me to bake all afternoon got me ahead for the evening. I'm all done and have even started to clean back there already. I might make it home at a reasonable hour."

"Thanks." After telling Ken I'd be right back, I pulled off my apron, then put it where I'd been working and grabbed my purse from the kitchen closet. I met Ken back out front, and we left for the station.

We hurried down Main Street, Ken gently pulling me along. Anytime we'd been out together, we'd always walked side by side, but this time he was a full step ahead. Still, he didn't let go of my hand.

"Has he ever done anything like this before?" I asked.

"No. Clayton never would have been able to be a volunteer if he had. He was fully screened when he signed up. He didn't get special treatment because of his family connection. This came out of nowhere and surprised everyone."

"That's terrible. I wonder what happened."

"I don't know, but I obviously can't have him back after this." He scrubbed at his face. "He's been around Ivy. What if it had been her instead? What if Kelly uses this against me in the custody case?"

Giving his hand a slight squeeze, I said, "I'm glad it wasn't Ivy, but don't let yourself get caught in the what-ifs. It didn't happen, and you'll make sure it won't happen. You're a great father."

He took a deep breath, and his pace slowed. "You're right. Thanks. I thought I knew him, that's all."

We passed by my shop, and the lights were on. It wasn't surprising to see the closed store with its lights on. The team had shifted their hours during the remodel since we weren't doing baking in the early morning. I felt bad for not having gone in at all today to see how things were going. Lily stood over by the new tables, looking toward the counter. She saw me and waved. I waved back. At that moment, John came through the kitchen door. He pulled out what looked to me to be a measuring tape then bent down near the counter. I was glad he'd agreed to help. With him and Lily taking care of the issue, I'd never have to worry about replacing my counter again.

We turned up the street a block over from the library and headed toward the police station. Ken grabbed the door and held it open for me. I stepped through, giving his hand one more squeeze before letting it go so he could walk over to the officer at the desk. If it weren't for the uniformed officers staffing the desks that I could see, this could have been a scene in any office building. I hadn't been inside the station in two years, not since the retirement party for the former police captain.

I glanced at the waiting area, the one where those who weren't in trouble waited to talk to someone. On one side of the room sat several members of Chelsea's family. Marina stood and rushed over to me as Ken continued talking with the desk clerk. "Please tell me you're here to file a complaint about Bruce Malloy too."

"I heard he was causing trouble, but what's going on?"

"He's trying to out us. Hanging red caps from our

mailboxes."

That was one of the strangest things I'd ever heard. "I'm sorry, I don't understand."

"It's not true, but lore states that merrows needed red caps to take on our aquatic form and swim in the deep sea. Bruce had some of his boys go around with red caps, effectively outing us to anyone who knows what to look for. And while it may be okay with some of us that a bunch of others know what we are, it can't be said for all of us. Most of us love what you're doing with the support group and all, but this sort of thing is too out in the open. What if there are people who aren't okay with what we are? It might not be safe for so many people to know, you know?"

I nodded. This had gone too far. "Is that what all of you are here about?"

"Uh-huh. All of our houses have been marked this way."

"So what about Dylan?"

She glanced at the other side of the room where one of David's cousins sat. She shrugged. "Don't know. Can't say I care given everything that's been going on, but he's been here since before we were."

"All right, let me find out what's going on, then." There was no way he was here for something unrelated.

Marina returned to her seat next to Chelsea's grand-mother, who smiled softly at me. She didn't need to be going through this. None of them did.

I approached Dylan and took a seat next to him. He sat on his hands, his arms stiff, back straight, and head down. "Heard this was the place to be tonight," I joked, trying to lighten his tense mood.

"He snorted. Sometimes it's rather entertaining."

"Sounds like you've been here a time or two."

He cracked a smile. "Yeah. When I was younger and more

irresponsible."

"So why are you here now?"

"I'm done with this whole thing that's going on with Bruce Malloy," he mumbled. "I used to help the old man out, doing favors for him and whatnot. Mow his lawn, shovel his sidewalk and driveway. When he called asking for a favor, I never expected it to be what he asked. It's not right. I got a wife and kids to think about. I don't want to get in the middle of whatever he has against Chelsea's family. David's not only my cousin but one of my closest friends. I was supposed to be in the wedding. So I came down here to give the cops a heads up."

One of the doors in the hallway opened, and I heard Clayton shouting, "But I don't know why I'm here. What did I do?" The door closed again, and an officer turned away from us and walked down the hall.

"When the old man got brought in, they asked me to wait out here. Then they came, so I can only guess Bruce found someone else to do his dirty work."

I tipped my head toward the hallway. "About the old man . . . Did he say anything about what happened?"

Dylan shook his head. "Only what you heard."

I glanced up at the front desk. Ken was gone. "Excuse me for a moment." Dylan nodded, and I stood, then walked to the desk. The officer sitting behind it said, "Your boyfriend is currently giving his statement. He got to skip the line because the incident it's related to is more urgent."

"I heard what happened. I feel so bad. The old man, Clayton, he has memory problems from an old injury."

"Guess that explains why he keeps saying he doesn't remember." His face went slack. "I shouldn't have said that."

"It's all right. I won't tell anyone. Besides, we all heard him yelling just now." Could Clayton have forgotten or blocked out what he'd done to his therapist? Could their session have triggered some sort of erratic behavior that stemmed from his injury? No matter the answers, I hoped they'd be able to help him despite likely having to punish him for this incident.

The officer sighed in relief.

"Thank you for your help."

Rather than return to David's cousin, I walked back toward Marina. "You know, you should talk to Dylan about why he's here. Seems like you may have more allies than you think."

"Really?" Her tone sounded half skeptical, half hopeful.

"I wouldn't lie, but you should go find out for yourself. You can't expect things to get better if you aren't willing to put in some work to help get it there."

Resolve settled over her, and she nodded. "Okay."

Marina stood, and I smiled as she approached Dylan. He looked panicked but calmed as I gave him a thumbs-up. She sat down next to him, and the two began talking.

I took the seat Marina had just vacated so I could chat with Nancy. I'd been hoping to chat with her about Sandra before now, but things kept getting in the way. At least we were finally getting the chance.

"Those two were in the same grade all through school," Nancy started, "but I doubt they said more than a few words to one another. There was a lot of distrust between us all after what happened, and now look. Both of them are smiling."

With Chelsea and David back together, perhaps this here was the first step in turning things around for the rest of the merrows and the selkies.

If only Bruce could see what was possible when people made the first step toward being friendly and moving past their differences.

CHAPTER 34

Zeke surprised me by being on time the next morning.

"Amazing what happens when you get enough sleep," he said, a genuine smile on his face.

"I'm glad. Sleep always makes me happy." I, however, was running on a slight lack of it. Ivy was spending the night at a friend's, and there had been no stomach issues before leaving this time. So we took advantage of it. After Ken made his statement at the police station, we went to dinner, then walked along the path in Riverview Park until late. He was still trying to wrap his head around what had happened at the hospital with Clayton, and I filled him in on Bruce's efforts to chase the merrows out of town.

We'd talked about so many things that my brain continued to think about them long after we said goodnight. When I woke up, I left my tea in longer than recommended, hoping to cut through the fog in my head with every bit of extra caffeine I could get. Fortunately, the tea I used didn't turn bitter with added steeping time. By the time I made it to Zeke's, it had mostly done the trick.

Bryan and I immediately got started on our muffin orders.

Carter at Double Aitch was back with his, and we still had Donna's. Because it was busier on Main Street on weekends, both were larger than their usual weekday ones. I hoped we wouldn't set Zeke off with our monopolizing the oven until these got done. But he surprised us, pulling a couple batches of bread dough from the refrigerator that he had let rise in there overnight and then revealing another one that he'd let rise at room temperature. Like Gina and I had done yesterday when we were waiting on him, Zeke waited for us to be done by prepping multiple trays of rolls and baguettes. Thank goodness we hadn't needed the sheet trays yet or else I don't know what he'd have done.

As the muffins came out of the oven, we set them to cool, and as soon as they were, I quickly boxed them up—I'd asked Bryan to bring some boxes from the shop since he was there yesterday—and delivered them to Double Aitch and Olde Templeton Diner.

When I got back, part of me was expecting the first part of the morning to have been an illusion or that I was still asleep in my bed, dreaming about an uncomplicated day at Zeke's after the chaos of yesterday. But everything was still going well when I walked inside. Zeke had already stocked some of his baguettes, and two trays sat on the counters with rolls waiting to be bagged. Inside the kitchen, he was pulling another tray of baguettes out of the oven, whole wheat from the looks of it.

As Zeke moved out of the way, Bryan slid two cupcake trays into the oven. Had this been our bakery, we'd have made two more, but forty-eight cupcakes would have to do today. We still had cookies to make.

Right before the shop opened, I headed to the front. Bryan had a handle on the cookies, and Zeke was working on his bread. I figured my being out here to help customers would allow Zeke to get ahead and possibly get another decent night's sleep. He was like a completely different person today, and if all it took to have the pleasant version of him was more time for him to sleep, then I'd do all I could while I was here to keep him well rested. Hopefully, he'd see the use in having a second person in the bakery if for nothing else than to run the front end while he baked.

The bakery seemed busier than what I could remember seeing on previous Saturdays when I'd made deliveries nearby. I had a steady stream of my own customers, but just as many came in for a loaf of bread or two. As it drew closer to lunchtime, Zeke came out from the kitchen, a glorious rosemary smell wafting out from behind him.

"I have to be out here to make sandwiches. You can go do whatever you have to. I won't need to be back there again until the lunch rush dies down."

Having no experience on a deli slicer, I gladly stepped into the kitchen to let Zeke take over the shop once more.

"It smells amazing back here," I said, then took a deep breath in.

Bryan was cutting out another batch of cookies, likely the last of what we'd need to get us through the day.

"Focaccia rolls. With feta. Zeke said he hadn't made them in a few years. Guess they had been his wife's favorite."

Zeke had been married? That was news to me. He'd been running the shop by himself for as long as I'd been in Heartwood Hollow.

"I might have to get some to have with dinner tonight," I said.

Bryan laughed as he placed the last cookie on the tray in front of him. "They'd end up being my entire dinner based on the smell alone."

I pointed to the tray. "Is that the last of the dough?"

He nodded.

"Fabulous. Thanks again for taking care of things back here."

"It's no problem. We get that this is an unusual circumstance. Things will be back to normal soon enough."

"I hope so."

"Have you gotten a chance to head to the bakery since we closed?"

I sighed. "No, and I'm feeling wicked guilty over it. I saw Lily and John there yesterday afternoon on my way to the police station."

"Police station? Did you file a complaint about the false report?"

I quickly filled him in as best as I could without giving details. "I should have stayed and told an officer about the false claims made against my bakery." Maybe I could still tell Seth.

"You should, and once you get out of here for the day, you also should stop by the shop and check things out."

"I was thinking of heading over while I got lunch."

Bryan's eyes grew wide. "No. Later. At the end of the day."

"Why not lunch?" I'd just told him how I'd been feeling about not being there. Why was he trying to stop me?

"Trust me on this one. Come at the end of the day."

"Does this have something to do with John and Lily and the counter? Or at least I assume it's the counter."

"Sure, let's go with that." He glanced at the clock. "Please don't go now, okay?"

Like that wasn't the least bit suspicious . . . but if he was telling me not to do something, he had a reason. Bryan didn't do things just because.

I held up my hands. "Okay. I'll go later. But speaking of lunch,

I'm going to go grab mine, and when I'm done, you can head on out. I know you don't have a lot to do left, but I don't want to leave Zeke alone. He's been doing so well with someone else here."

"Yeah, I wouldn't have believed this was him given what the others had told me."

I raised an eyebrow at him.

"We're in a group chat with one another. We tried adding you once, but—"

"I never check my phone. Besides, it's good you have that. You don't need your boss knowing everything you all talk about. I think it's sweet." I walked over to the closet and then grabbed my purse. "All right, well, I'm off to lunch." As I left the kitchen, Bryan was sliding the last cookie tray into the oven.

I headed down Main Street, stopping at Double Aitch. As much as I could have gone for a marshmallow rice treat and my usual panini sandwich, passing by the shop on my way to get there would have been too much temptation for me. I'd have ended up checking out what was happening inside the bakery.

"Hi, Joanie," Lichelle greeted me once I stepped inside the restaurant. She wore a gray Double Aitch shirt and had a black apron tied around her waist.

"Hey, Lichelle. I didn't realize you worked here."

"Uh-huh. Started a couple weeks ago for the summer. Picking up the odd shift here and there. No need to worry your boyfriend, though. I'm still able to babysit at night."

"I'm sure he'll be glad to know that. Ivy adores you."

"She's a fun kid. We've been doing a lot of baking recently." She gave me a pointed look, then smiled. "I wonder where she gets that from."

I laughed. Since getting Ivy to help me make cookies, one

of her favorite activities had become experimenting in the kitchen.

"So just one for lunch?"

"Yes, please."

"Follow me." Lichelle turned and led me through the restaurant.

As we wove around tables, I said, "Since I don't have long, I'd like to order now. I'll have a Brown Cow and a Greek Burger, extra dressing on the side."

"You got it." She sat me at a two-seater, then headed into the back before coming out with my root beer float using chocolate ice cream. I rarely drank more than tea, water, or the occasional cup of milk, but Double Aitch's Brown Cow floats was a special treat. I stirred the blob of ice cream around a minute before devouring it with a long spoon, but the root beer I'd have with my burger.

Seven minutes later, Lichelle placed my lunch in front of me. I usually went to Olde Templeton if I wanted a burger, but Donna didn't have this amazing combination of feta, banana peppers, and Greek dressing topping a burger patty. The extra dressing was for my fries. Steph and Alex had turned me onto this meal during my first few weeks in Heartwood Hollow. This was their regular hangout.

Usually, this was a meal to be at least semi-savored, but with needing to get back to Zeke's, I didn't spend as much time enjoying the meal as I would have liked to. Still, I was grateful for Lichelle rushing the order so I'd have as much time as I did. After I paid the bill, I headed back onto Main Street, nearly bumping into Chelsea's grandmother.

"Oh my goodness, Nancy, I'm so sorry. I didn't even see you there."

"It's all right. These things happen, and I'm glad it did. I was hoping to talk to you again."

"Oh?" Had Bruce done something else after our chat last night, or was this about Chelsea and David? Maybe the wedding was back on.

"I know you were concerned about the old man who was brought to the police station yesterday while we were there."

"He's one of my boyfriend's volunteers at the hospital, but they've known each other since Ken was a kid."

"Well, I wanted to tell you to be wary of him. He was one of our neighbors and was always telling me how pretty I was. As a teen, I was flattered. He was handsome and a few years older, but I wasn't interested. Then one time he cornered me behind his toolshed. You know, as if he wanted a moment of private time with me. He didn't do anything, but I avoided him after that. His charm had turned creepy. It's been years since I thought about it, but after hearing about his outburst with his therapist, it came back to me. I wonder now if nothing happened only because Sandra had come looking for me and interrupted whatever was going on."

"Oh, I'm so sorry you had to go through that," I said, placing my hand on her upper arm.

"I'm fine. No harm done. But I thought you should know since you remind me of how I looked when I was younger. My hair was on the redder side of brown, but yours is like how Pam's was when she was younger. Brown, but with red highlights when the sun catches it just right."

I pictured the woman in front of me as a younger version of herself, with reddish-brown hair and no wrinkles. Our eyes were the same color, and it wasn't difficult to see the slight resemblance with the years stripped away. "Thank you for telling me."

"You're welcome. Now go on and get. You have places to be. You take care of yourself now. I hear there may be a cake order coming your way once your shop opens back up." She winked.

Upon hearing that last sentence, I brightened. "Oh, that's wonderful news. You take care of yourself too. It was nice talking with you."

Nancy stepped up onto the front steps of Double Aitch and headed inside. As I glanced up the street toward the Corner Bakery, all thoughts about my conversation with her vanished. I hadn't seen a line this long before, not even on the day when Bruce first sent the flyers to everyone about Zeke's sweets.

I took off running.

CHAPTER 35

The smell hit me before I reached the shop, and I understood then why the line existed. Zeke had employed the same method I'd been using the week prior with my cookies. Leave the door open and lure customers in with the scent. Only in this case, it wasn't cookies and sweets permeating the air, it was the warm oil and rosemary from his focaccia bread. Hopefully there would be some left at the end of the day. I absolutely had to get myself some. Even though I'd just eaten, I was already salivating.

"Excuse me, excuse me," I said trying to get through the front door. When people realized who I was and that I wasn't trying to cut the line, they parted, allowing me access into the store.

"Great! You're back," Bryan said with an exasperated sigh as he looked up from the cash register and saw me. It was something I'd never trained him on, and I didn't know if he had any experience with them.

I rushed behind the counter and around to where he stood.

"Help!" He stood there with a ten-dollar bill in his hand,

the drawer closed, and a customer in front of him who was trying to be understanding but likely only wanted her change.

"What were you trying to do?"

He explained, and I quickly remedied the situation.

"What are you doing out here?"

"You see this line, right?" When I nodded, he replied, "Zeke got worried he wouldn't have enough focaccia for everyone, so he asked me to come out front and ring people out while he baked more. Said it was dummy-proof, but I have no idea what I'm doing."

"I can take over." He scooted out of the way but stood to the side of me, still looking frazzled. "If you're all done cleaning, head on home."

He ducked into the kitchen and returned a moment later with a bag of rolls. "These are mine." With that, he rushed from the shop and headed down Main Street, the opposite direction from his house. I had a sneaking suspicion he was heading to the bakery, but the line in front of me prevented me from thinking about it beyond that.

We saw a steady stream of customers for the rest of the day. Every single one of them wanted focaccia rolls.

"They smell delicious," I agreed with one customer in the late afternoon, "but what's making them so popular?"

"Have you ever had one?" the woman asked.

I thought back to all the times I'd come to the Corner Bakery. After moving here, I'd avoided it for the first year, feeling awkward and a little bitter that the town council had made me agree to not bake anything that Zeke made. Then one afternoon, I wanted bread with caramelized onion in it and Zeke's was my only hope if I didn't want to make it at home, which I'd had no time for that night. He didn't have it, but I loved what he did have and ended up taking home a garlic loaf that went as well with dinner as the onion would have. After that, I regularly stopped in his shop, especially when I had a feeling my neighbor Matt would be coming around for dinner. In the now over three years I'd been a customer, not once had he ever had focaccia on the shelves. I would have remembered this smell.

"I can't say that I have," I said, turning back my customer, two bags of rolls in one hand and a baguette in the other.

She scrunched her face in thought. "He probably hasn't made them in about five years. You haven't been here that long, have you?"

I shook my head. "Not quite."

"After his wife died, I don't think he could bring himself to make them. They were by far the best bread he made, so as soon as the smell hit me, I rushed over. Called a few of my friends to let them know too." She turned and waved to two of the other women in the shop.

"How nice of you to spread the word like that. I'm sure Zeke really appreciates it." He'd spent most of the afternoon in the back continuing to bake, coming out only to resupply the focaccia rolls and round loaves. Every time he saw how busy it was without it being overwhelming chaos, his eyes lit up.

The woman dug through her purse. "It's good to see him returning to what he's best at. For a time, we all thought he'd close the bakery. This had been her dream. But instead, he stopped selling sweets—those were her forte—not his, and he tightened up the bread menu. At the same time, he started with the sandwiches. Half the time, I wonder if he remained open because you, in a way, were competition. He didn't want to see you come in here and take over. Would have been one more thing he'd lost, you know?"

Grief forced change on people. If the focaccia had been his wife's favorite, I understood him not being able to bring himself to make it anymore. A lot of what I'd seen over the last few days began to make sense. But what had caused the change?

"I know you have your own bakery"—the woman pulled out a twenty from her wallet and then handed it to me—"and that you'll go back to it soon enough, but I think your being here has been good for him."

In some weird way, I guess we had Bruce Malloy to thank for that. My team and I never would have been here had we not been shut down and had he not gotten Zeke involved in the first place. It didn't excuse what Bruce had done, and I couldn't overlook the possibility that he was a murderer, but for a moment, knowing we'd helped Zeke lessened the sting of everything that had been going on with the shop.

I rang the woman out, then handed back her change. "Well, I'm glad I've been able to do my part in helping him. He's seemed happier today. I hope it keeps up."

The woman smiled. "Me too. I've missed this bread. She took her food, then headed out of the bakery, pausing to say a few words to her friends."

A half hour before closing, Zeke came out of the kitchen, one last load of rolls on a tray ready for bagging. When that was done, he handed me a bag of six. "All right, I can handle the rest. Go on home and enjoy these."

"Are you sure? You've been in the kitchen all afternoon."

He nodded. "I'm all set in the back already. Now go on."

"All right." I grabbed my bag from the back counter. With Bryan's call for help and the constant flow of customers from that point on, I'd never gotten a chance to put it away. "I'll see you tomorrow," I said, walking out from behind the register.

Instead of saying goodbye, Zeke took care of the next person waiting to buy rolls. Had I not known better, I would have said he put some magic into his rolls to make them fly off the shelves. But the real magic was the shift in his attitude over the last few days that called to people. As I headed out the door, holding it open for another person to scoot inside behind me, Zeke laughed. Actually laughed. If this continued, and he got the help he needed so he could get enough sleep at night, Zeke and the Corner Bakery would be fine.

The pink door of my bakery was open, able to be seen even from a distance. No surprise there as people were still likely working inside to fix it up, but when I saw Ken come around the corner and head into the shop, my curiosity grew. Adding that to Bryan's insistence that I not come until the end of the day . . . Just what was going on?

Then the door closed, and the lights went off with Ken still inside.

CHAPTER 36

I picked up my pace, hoping there was a simple explanation, but part of me worried if Bruce had gotten wind about the work we were doing and had done something else.

Ken came back out of the bakery and turned toward me, a smile on his face, instantly flooding me with relief. He was okay.

"What's going on? Why were you in the bakery?"

His smile widened and turned into one of an excited child as he approached. I'd seen the same expression on Ivy's face many times. "You'll see." He extended his hand out, and I took it.

Ken led me the next twenty feet toward the bakery. The blinds were down, and I couldn't see a thing inside. He stepped in front of me, blocking my view of the interior through the six panes of glass that made up the top portion of the door. With his back still to it, he grabbed the knob, twisted it, and cracked the door open.

"Close your eyes," he ordered, a light chuckle to his words.

"What?"

"Close your eyes."

I did as told, and the soft gliding noise told me Ken had pushed the door the rest of the way open.

Ken tugged lightly on my hand and then guided me inside the bakery.

The shop smelled different. The fresh baked good smell had dulled and been replaced by the stronger combination of paint, lacquer, and cleaning products. When I concentrated on the smells hard enough, I could smell the focaccia rolls inside the bag I was still holding too. No wonder there'd been such a line at Zeke's.

"Ready?" Ken's voice held an edge of anxious delight. He gave my hand a slight squeeze.

"Yes."

"Open your eyes."

The lights above me brightened as I took in the space, reacting to the cheery emotions in the room. My bakery had been transformed. I had a new front counter and back shelves, the bases of my bakery cases had been given a fresh coat of white paint, and the tables and chairs that were only a few weeks old had been joined by a new matching corner shelving unit where I put my day-old baked goods. The walls remained a happy shade of yellow, but a new coat of paint had been applied to them.

Standing in the middle of the room was my entire bakery team. Sarah, Lauren, Sam, Gina, Lily, and Bryan. Lily's boyfriend, John, was there too. So were Holly and Gary from Leafs and Grounds, Rachael's husband Mark, Chelsea and David, Rich and Ashley, Courtney and Jill, Billy from the inn, Ivy, and a handful of other Heartwood Hollow residents who regularly frequented the bakery.

"Surprise!" they shouted in unison. Even the lights above us momentarily brightened as if shouting along with them.

"You all did this for me?"

Ivy came running forward and stopped before me, bouncing on her toes. "Yup! Come see!" She took my hand out of her father's hold and led me around the shop, pointing out little details she thought were neat. The highlight by far was the front counter. A wide slab of a tree trunk with one cut-smooth end facing the back counter and the tree bark facing the rest of the shop. But in the cracks and splits of the trunk was this gorgeous shade of pink that matched the other pink pops of color I'd put in the shop over the years.

"It's a pink resin that we poured in," John explained, "and it's just as thick as the wood portions. The whole counter is coated, even the trunk, so it's all food safe and hygienic. No violations there."

"It's from the north woods," Lily continued. "One of the fallen trees that John and his team cleared during the tree planting. She didn't need to tell me it wasn't sacred wood, wood that had once been a dryad. Although they typically left sacred wood to return to the earth, the north woods had become a nature preserve. In a few short weeks, it had become a popular destination for outdoor enthusiasts. The remaining dryads had decided to burn all the sacred wood in small funeral pyres along the river's edge near Dunmore Falls to prevent the possibility of pieces being taken as souvenirs.

I looked at Lily, tears welling in my eyes then turned to face John. "Thank you so much. Truly. This is beautiful."

Lily clasped her hands over her heart, and John gave me a small smile before continuing to tell me about the custom shelving in the back that I could use to hold candy jars once I got to that point or faux cakes to showcase what I could do. Then Lily pointed out the day-old goods shelf, which she had designed and made herself then painted pink to match the counter. I was thrilled to see her beaming with pride over the beautiful work she'd done. As much as I wanted to keep her here, I knew she would eventually leave the bakery to do woodworking full time. She hadn't said anything yet, but it was coming. Selfishly, I appreciated that I'd have these reminders of her in the shop once that happened.

"We also refreshed a few of my gram's old candy stands for you," Sam added, pointing to three small tiered shelves on top of my pastry case. "My parents still had them, probably in case I ever took up the business, but they're yours now."

"And all the cases have been given a clean bill of health by the tech who came out to service them," Bryan said.

"But that's not all," Gina jumped in. "Wait until you see the kitchen."

My team filed into the next room, but I hung back a moment to hug everyone else who was there. I didn't know what they had contributed, not that the specifics mattered, but they had all done something to get the bakery back up and running. That meant more to me than words could say.

"I called a friend of mine who knows a different health inspector," Billy said as I gave him a squeeze. "And while I can't *guarantee* she'll be your inspector because of how they do things . . . let's just say, she'll be here Monday morning to get you up and running again."

Two more days and I had no doubts I'd get my bakery back. "Thank you." I stepped back from the group. "All of you. Thank you so much for getting this all done so quickly."

"Well, when we heard what that Bruce did to you the other day at the Corner Bakery, we couldn't sit by and do nothing," Mark said.

"It was around-the-clock work to get it done," John added.

"And more of us helped out than are here," Gary finished.

Wiping a fresh round of happy tears from my eyes, I said, "I don't know how I will ever be able to repay you all."

"No repayment needed," Rich said. He took Ashley's hand and held it up. "You got me and Ashley together. I owed you this and more."

"Same with Chelsea and me." David pulled Chelsea into his side.

"And you sure help keep Libby sane by doing the baking for her," Billy chimed in.

Holly gave me a small shove. "Now go see your kitchen."

I pushed open the familiar swinging door separating the bakeshop from the kitchen. It had been painted a brighter shade of pink but was otherwise unchanged.

I couldn't say the same for the kitchen. It was gleaming. Nearly all the stainless steel in there looked new. That's how good they'd cleaned. The walls had been painted a light mint-green, the floor resealed, and the shelving system in the back corner reconfigured. I crossed the kitchen toward the closet and then opened the door. The cardboard box of decorations was gone. In its place now stood a clear plastic container system, lifted off the floor. The decorations had all been sorted into bins for their respective holidays along with a general decoration box. The best part was there was room for more in each tote. And the closet still had plenty of space for our coats and bags as needed.

Next, I moved into the bathroom. It had new tile flooring, a new toilet, and a brand-new vanity instead of the old pedestal sink, giving us more storage room in here for anything we might need.

I stepped back out into the kitchen.

"That's a new exhaust fan," Sam told me. "The rest of it was cleaned extensively by the tech."

"I can't believe you all did this in a matter of days. I never even heard back from everyone, and here you are, the work done. It's all wonderful."

"I *may* have called everyone after you did to have them call me instead of you," Sarah admitted.

"And if you think this is great, wait until you see downstairs," Lauren said.

My team led the way to the steps leading into the basement. Many of the boards had been replaced, and a new tread system had been installed as well as a minimal hand railing on the wall opposite the one we already had. I ran my hand along it to see how it felt. Smooth. Comfortable.

"It's small," John said from behind me, "but it's sturdy and meets code. It'll pass any inspection you're given."

I had intended to reply, but the words died on my lips when I saw the basement.

"This is beautiful!"

"Never thought you'd say that about a basement, huh?" Lily said with a chuckle.

"I can honestly agree with that. What did you use on the floor? It's gorgeous and sparkly."

"It's an epoxy paint that has a bit of a crystalized look," John answered. "Lily said you'd like the purple."

"I *love* the purple." Thanks to the sparkle, it reminded me of one of Gram's crystal rings. I couldn't wait to tell her about this when I talked to her later.

Sam continued across the floor. "You haven't seen everything yet."

When I realized where he was heading, I gasped. "I have a washing machine?"

"Yep! No more having to take our aprons and rags back to your house or the laundromat."

Lily pointed across the basement. "And don't forget the dryer!"

John pointed overhead. "One of my buddies came and installed them. Due to where your piping was, we had to place them at opposite sides—"

"I have no problem with that. I'm thrilled to have them in the first place."

"And we upgraded your shelving down here too," Lily said.

"Not that they needed it," Bryan added.

"No," Lily agreed, "but now there will be no question as to them passing."

I wandered to the shelves. "This is all wonderful. I'm so touched that you would all do this for me."

"Why?" Gina asked. "You've been there for all of us time and time again."

"And took chances on us when it was a risk," Sam stated. "Do you know how few people would have said yes when I said I wanted an internship at their bakery? Never mind someone willing to work around my school schedule like you have."

"Or let us take time off for finals," Lauren added.

"You're all going to make me cry," I said, fully aware that the tears had been building since I first stepped foot into the shop and saw everyone standing there.

"It's okay to cry," Ivy chirped. "It means you're letting it out. Daddy says it's not good to keep things in."

I smiled at Ken and Ivy, who were standing by the stairs. "Your dad is a smart man."

"And one last thing," Sam said as he crossed the basement again toward a refrigerator that hadn't been there previously. "We have a secondary storage area for any of the candy stuff you end up needing, so you can keep everything separate since sometimes they have different requirements than baked goods. My grama gave me some specifications, and we made it happen."

I slowly walked around the basement, taking everything in another time. Then we all headed back upstairs, where most of the others were still waiting in the shop.

"So what do you think?" Ken finally asked once we were all together.

"This might be the only time I'll ever say this, but is it Monday yet?"

CHAPTER 37

Sunday crawled by despite the busy nature at the Corner Bakery. I was so excited for Monday to arrive. Things had been going smoothly between Zeke and me since our initial hiccups, but now that he was starting to bring back some of his old recipes, I bet he was looking forward to having all the space on the shelves and in the cases again.

At the end of the day, Zeke handed me another bag of rolls, this time a spinach and feta bread. "We're closed Mondays," he reminded me.

I'd already told him the inspector was coming to check out my bakery in the morning. "Any plans for your day off?"

He smiled. "You know? I'm going to experiment a bit. I haven't tried out new recipes in a long time."

"That sounds fabulous."

"I'm looking forward to it. I can't believe I'm going to say this, but I think I'm going to miss having you around when you don't show up Tuesday morning."

"Well, there's always a chance—"

He held up his hand to stop me. "You know as well as I do that you never should have been closed down. You'll be fine."

"And you will be too."

Zeke nodded. "Although I do think I'm going to need to hire someone to run the shop. You've reminded me how much I can get done when I'm not trying to be everywhere. I don't know if you know, but my wife used to run the front end of things and bake all the sweets, leaving me to do what I was good at."

"One of your customers mentioned it to me. I'm sorry for your loss."

"Thank you," he said with a small smile. "I'll be with her again someday, but in the meantime, it's time to start living again."

"You've got the right idea on things."

"I do now. It was good working with you." He stuck out his hand.

I took it and we shook. "You too." Releasing his hand, I then turned and headed for the door.

Zeke stopped me before I could open it. "Oh, and feel free to make those pineapple bacon scones in your shop."

I glanced back at him. "You sure?"

"I won't be candying bacon anytime soon, so I declare that to be squarely in the sweets category. Besides, they were really good. I can't imagine having to wait for another big event so I can have another one."

Although everyone had said I had no reason to be worried about the inspection, I was. I couldn't help it. Part of me wondered if Bruce had something else up his sleeve so he could mess this up. But the inspection came and went without a problem and plenty of compliments on how nice everything was. Sam and I spent much of Tuesday restocking the kitchen and storage area with everything we'd need to move forward.

On Wednesday morning, we had a small ribbon-cutting ceremony when the shop opened. Several people from town attended. Steph even covered it in the paper. She'd already run a small piece to announce the reopening. I'd been hesitant to allow her to publish the first article, but she told me to not let Bruce make me afraid. She said that he'd been put on notice after the confrontation at Zeke's and that if anything more happened to me or the shop, he would be an immediate suspect. That made me feel better about that whole situation.

The whole day was busy. Everyone who came in had missed my baked goods. Several were excited to see the pineapple bacon scones on my shelves. They all loved the updates, even those who weren't in love with the color pink in general. They said the brighter colors suited me.

It seemed that those who couldn't come into the shop called to get something for later. Aside from the day when Bruce had purposefully swamped us with orders, there hadn't been a time we'd been this busy. Fortunately, not all the orders were for today. We'd be busy through the weekend.

The yoga girls all cheered when I arrived at the studio for cheat day. It was crazy to think of all that had happened in the week since I'd last dropped off cookies.

I headed to Libby's next, where she was waiting for me with one of her big hugs.

"So glad to see you back at your own store. I missed you on Monday," she said as she led me into the kitchen, carrying one of the boxes for me.

"It felt weird to not see you," I replied, putting my two boxes next to hers on the table by the tiered tea trays. "How did you make out?"

"Well, I survived, *we* survived, but you're back in business now, so that's all that matters." She laughed. "May have driven Billy crazy, though. I made him be my gopher to help get everything set up since I was stuck here in the kitchen."

"Please thank him again for me. I don't know how long I would have had to wait if he didn't have a connection to someone else who could inspect the shop."

"I'll tell him, but he'll just say he was happy he could help."

"And please give him these from me." I passed her the smaller box that I'd carried in.

She peeked inside. "Oh, are those?"

With an exaggerated smile, I nodded. "They sure are. Zeke gave me his blessing to let me sell them in the bakery."

"That's wonderful! We'll have to put these into the tea rotation."

After we'd finished setting up her trays, I left with one more stop to go before I could grab a quick lunch.

I pulled my bike up to the side of the Corner Bakery, then pulled out the last small box from my trailer.

"Back so soon?" Zeke joked when I stepped inside the shop.

"I wanted to come say hello and see how you were doing." I placed the box on the table. "And give you these."

He opened it and smiled. "Well, it's just gotten better, that's for sure."

My smile fell. "Things not going well today?"

"Bah," he began with a dismissive flap of his hand, "it's nothing I can't handle, but I do need to hire someone. If you know of anyone . . ."

"I'll be sure to send them your way."

A customer walked in at that moment, and I used the

opportunity to duck back out of the shop, giving Zeke a wave. I looked forward to having a stronger and friendlier business relationship with him from here on out.

CHAPTER 38

As soon as I flipped the bakery sign from *open* to *closed*, I headed home to feed Saffy and get ready for my date. It had been a while since Ken and I had gone out for a nice dinner, and celebrating the bakery's renovations and reopening were as good of an excuse as any. I'd been looking forward to it all day.

"Okay, Saf, which one?" I laid out two potential outfits on my bed. She'd just finished eating, and I was keeping her from her nap, so hopefully she'd decide quickly and with minimal fur on my clothes.

She squinted at me.

Once again, I hadn't given her the option of choosing my black dress, her favorite. "I know it's been a while, but it has long sleeves. No can do this close to summer. I don't know how you lay in the window all day like you do. Your fur gets so warm."

Eventually, Saffy lay down facing my green dress with yellow and pink flowers. I wasn't going to burst her bubble by saying I'd been leaning toward that one on my own. She always seemed so satisfied with her choices.

As I looked at myself in the mirror, I thought of Sandra. The first dress I'd seen her in had been this color. It had been a week since she'd last made an appearance, and short of a séance—and having one was becoming an increasing possibility—I was at a loss of what I could do. A séance, however, wasn't guaranteed to work. When we'd done one for Kate, she'd been anchored to her brush. I felt nothing within the tiara. But if Sandra didn't come back soon, I'd have to try it. Maybe we'd have a strong-enough energy field to draw Sandra back from wherever she was with more people. She certainly had enough family still around who I hoped would be willing to help.

I headed back downstairs, Saffy hot on my heels. So much for that nap. She was likely hoping to get treats before I left, and she got exactly that. Who was I to disappoint my cat?

Ken knocked on the door as she munched away. She didn't even bother to greet him when I let him inside for a few minutes.

"I'll see you later, Saffy," I called, slipping my shoes on by the front door.

"Is she ever going to forgive me?" Ken asked as we reached the sidewalk. He opened the passenger side car door for me.

"Eventually." I hoped that, in time, she would, but I'd never known her to keep a grudge this long. He closed my door and walked around the car. When he was in his seat, I added, "You should try getting her a gift. Girls love presents."

He chuckled. "What do you suggest?"

"Some catnip toys might do the trick. Or those little foam golf balls. She carries those around in her mouth."

"All right"—he started the car—"I'll bring them over next time."

We drove out to a brewery south of town. They'd recently

opened a little restaurant, and we'd been meaning to check it out. The route took us over the river, past Dunmore Falls, and then followed the river until pulling away as it veered into the hills, where the rolling landscape had once been wooded but was now all farmland and cow pastures. Silos and barns dotted the view until we turned down a short driveway where a barn had been converted into a store, tasting room, and now a restaurant, too, for the larger brewery building out back.

Ken and I walked arm in arm into the rustic space. Once we were seated, I immediately recognized the handicraft in the dining area.

"John made this," I said, trailing my fingers along the golden-colored resin that filled in the gaps of the wood-slab table. "This is similar to my counter at the bakery."

"He does great work. Did you know some of the waiting rooms in the hospital have furniture that he made and donated?"

"Seems he donated furniture to a lot of places over the years. Probably trying to make amends for everything he felt his family did to the community." I opened my menu. "I'm glad that's likely past him now that the north woods is thriving. Now he can donate things because he wants to, not because he feels he has to."

"You were right about him and Lily," Ken admitted. "It was nice getting to know them better over the few days of renovations."

After his initial worry about the two of them, which resulted in our short breakup, his agreement made me happy. I couldn't blame him after the way they'd met, but I'd known it was meant to be all along.

We sat in companionable silence for a few minutes as we looked at the menus, then placed our order with the waiter. He returned with our drinks moments later.

"I can't believe I wasn't there to help with any of the renovations," I said, swirling my straw around my glass.

"Don't worry about it." He placed his hand over mine. "Besides, had you been there, there wouldn't have been anything to surprise you with. Seeing you and your shop light up like that when you first laid eyes on the updated space was awesome. You're always beautiful, even covered with flour, but seeing you at that moment? Stunning."

Heat rose into my cheeks. As much as I appreciated his compliment, it didn't make me feel better about not lifting a hammer or a brush. "But I didn't do any of the work. And no one is letting me pay them for the time they put in or what they did beyond parts, not even the HVAC guy, and I had called him before you all took my being gone as an opportunity to transform the bakery."

"You were busy trying to run your business out of someone else's to keep your customers happy. That was plenty of work."

I squeezed his hand before releasing it as the waiter came back with our appetizer, Belgian pretzels with three different dipping sauces. "You all did a wonderful job with it. I love the colors," I replied once the waiter left.

He chuckled. "Just so you know, Ivy picked out the pink."

"I'll be sure to mention her fabulous color choice the next time I see her."

Dinner was amazing, and it made the date night on a night before work worth it. The brewery served typical pub food with a bit of a twist. I had the Barbequed Cuban Sandwich with maple pulled pork in it, while Ken had the Morning Burger with his egg sunny side up. And our fries came with one of five types of ketchup, none of which were the traditional plain tomato.

Despite the hour, I had to try the dessert. As we waited, Ken and I held hands, not really talking but not really not talking either. We were enjoying each other's company, something we hadn't been able to do in a while. Then dessert came. Fried banana cream pie with a caramel drizzle. It was so good, it made me want to become friends with the chef so I could get the recipe.

As we waited for the check, however, Sandra appeared right in the middle of the table. And she looked scared. There'd have been no other reason for her to appear between us with the table interrupting her physical form, something I'd seen few ghosts ever do as most avoided going through physical objects.

"Are you seeing what I'm seeing?" Ken asked, his eyes wide.

"You mean—"

"Yeah. There's a woman standing *in* our table."

I scanned the rest of the restaurant. It was full, but no one else seemed to be witnessing the ghost at our table. I'd never been so relieved that only I could see ghosts.

Well, except for Ken this time.

"I think it's because we're holding hands. I can let go."

He gripped my hand tighter. "Is this—"

"Sandra," I said, both answering his question and trying to get her attention. "Are you okay? Where have you been?"

She didn't look at me. She didn't even seem aware of my presence. What was going on?

She took a step back toward the wall.

"What are you doing?" Her voice wavered.

"Sandra," I replied gently. "It's Joanie, and this is my boyfriend, Ken. You just appeared inside a restaurant."

"Get away from me," she said a bit louder, taking another step back.

She was mostly out of the table now, and I was able to see that the tight green top she had on wasn't a top at all but a bathing suit from her era.

I realized then what was happening. "Sandra," I said now at a normal volume, a bit of assertion in my voice. "Sandra, it's Joanie. Look at me. This isn't happening right now. You've already lived through it."

"What's going on, Joanie?"

"You don't need to see this." I tried to pull my hand away, but Ken grabbed my hand tighter. I tore my gaze away from Sandra to look Ken in the eye. "She's reliving how she died. She hasn't remembered her death until now, and I only know she was either struck in the head or hit something with it as she fell. *You* don't need to see this."

"I might see something you don't. Let me do this with you."

I nodded and looked at Sandra once more.

She'd backed up another step or two. Her legs had scales on them, although they were separated from one another. So had someone caught her as a merrow or mid-transformation from one? I could have kicked myself for not asking her family about autopsy records. Surely, those would have revealed an unfinished shift.

"But you've known me for years," Sandra said calmly as if she was trying to talk whomever down, her statement eliminating the idea that her killer had been a random stranger.

Another step back. Why didn't she run? She'd been found at the private beach where there was plenty of open water to dash into. Was she somehow unable to get to it? I felt like kicking myself for never going to see how it was situated, but

Bruce immediately would have pulled public access to it if he found out I'd been poking around there.

"Why now? I've never done anything to you. I've always been friendly."

This didn't sound like someone she was friends with but had at least been on good terms with until that point.

Sandra stopped short in her attempt to take another step back, and she placed her hands behind her flat as if they were against a wall. She lifted a foot behind her, then the next, but slid back down.

Then she barked out a laugh. "That? You're blaming me for that?" Her voice had grown stronger as if this show of bravado was her last attempt to get free. She kept trying to find purchase against whatever she was backed up against but failed.

The answer she received seemed to anger her. "I'd do it again too."

Then her image disappeared. I pulled my hands away from Ken and covered my mouth to stifle a gasp. I knew what had happened then and was grateful we hadn't been able to see more.

We drove home in silence, the scene replaying itself in my mind and no doubt in Ken's too.

"Are you going to be okay? I asked him as he dropped me off at my house and walked me up to my front door. Saffy knew something was wrong with me. Instead of staying in her spot or running to the end of the couch to say hello before dashing off into the kitchen, she stood on her hind legs at the window, her front paws on the glass.

"I still don't understand what I saw. It's all so new that it almost feels like it was a clip from a movie where they haven't put the CGI-animated killer into it yet." He rubbed my arms, which were covered in goosebumps despite the heat. "Are you going to be okay?"

I nodded. I'd be okay, but I wasn't right now. Maybe I needed to tell myself that Ken was right. Convincing myself that it had been an unfinished scene from a movie and a cup of calming tea might help me sleep tonight.

Ken kissed me goodnight and held the door open for me as I stepped inside. Saffy rushed to the edge of the couch, and she looked at Ken as if to ask, *what happened?*

"I hate to have to leave you," he said.

I gave Saffy's head a quick scratch. "I'll be fine. Saffy's here with me."

Ken looked at my cat. "You take care of her."

Her head dropped momentarily in what seemed like a single exaggerated nod.

Once Ken left, I kicked off my shoes, put on my slippers, and shuffled into the kitchen. Saffy stayed right by my feet, something she rarely did given the destination. I heated the kettle for tea and scooped some loose leaf into a strainer, all the while Saffy sat in front of the oven watching me.

"How about a treat?" I grabbed one out from the container in the cupboard, then dropped it in her dish.

Although she followed me to her bowl, she didn't dive in for the treat like she usually did and instead stayed watching me.

"I'll be fine," I assured her. And I would be fine, just as soon as I figured out who had killed Sandra.

CHAPTER 39

Two things were certain. Based on what Sandra had said, her killer hadn't been a stranger but hadn't been a friend either. That ruled out Marvin. So who killed her? Who blamed her for something so much that it made them turn to murder?

"Morning, Joanie," Lucy said as she walked into the bakeshop close to lunchtime, snapping me from my thoughts.

"Almost good afternoon. What's up? Shouldn't you be at work?" Lunchtime was a busy time for the ice cream parlor that Lucy ran diagonally across the street from the bakery. I'd seen the line out the door some afternoons.

"I finally feel comfortable enough to let my summer-help staff the counter by himself." She turned to Sam who was working with me in the shop today. "Todd says hello, by the way."

"Is that why you've been getting ice cream for lunch every time you have a shift in here?" I teased. Todd and Sam had been together for some time now, and their relationship was fully out in the open as of a few weeks ago. It was good to see Sam comfortable in his own skin and no longer needing to hide who he loved, and I was happy Sam wasn't letting his going off to school come between them.

Sam's ears turned a slight shade of pink. "Well, that and the ice cream is spectacular."

"I'm glad you like that too," Lucy said with a laugh.

"Speaking of ice cream," I began, "why don't you go grab some. Get me a cone of Buzzin' Bee's Knees before you head back."

I didn't need to tell him twice. He took off his green apron, stashing it on a shelf under the cash register, and then sped out of the shop.

Lucy clapped once. "Okay. I'm here to run a bit of a business proposal by you."

That piqued my curiosity. "Oh?"

"What are your thoughts on making cookie dough?"

I raised an eyebrow at her. "Well, I do it regularly."

She laughed again. "I don't mean in general. I'm talking about the raw kind that you can eat without worrying about getting sick."

My mind filled in the blanks. "Thinking about a new ice cream flavor?"

"A few of them, all depending on whatever cookie dough you felt like making. I'm thinking limited batches, when they're gone, they're gone until the next time you make that one again sort of thing. The standard chocolate chip for a sweet-cream ice cream and how about some peanut butter that I could put into a chocolate-based ice cream."

I liked where she was going with this and smiled. "I can make brownie batter too."

"Oh, that would be amazing. I'm so excited. I've been thinking about this since the day you walked in with your free cookies, but you know how crazy things can get, and then you were closed, and now here I am. So, when do you think we could get this up and running?"

"I'll have to try out a few things regarding taste and texture, but I'm sure we can roll it out soon."

"We can work on all the specifics later regarding amounts, payments, and whatnot, but any chance we could announce this tonight at the stroll?"

The Stroll Along the Street was a monthly event where the businesses stayed open later on Main Street and had taste testings and specials set up on tables in front of their stores. It was a fun way to spend an evening, and a good way to see people who usually couldn't make it into the shop during regular hours.

"I don't see why not," I told her.

"Awesome! Okay, I'm going to run and make up some sort of flyer for our tables to help spread the word tonight." She stuck out her hand, and I took it. "To the start of a great partnership."

We shook, and then she headed out of the store and back across the street.

In the time between Lucy leaving and Sam returning, I had a quiet moment to think. First candy and now ice cream. Seemed I was doing fine with expanding on my own after the misunderstanding between me and the investor from Astoria.

Sam rushed in with an already dripping ice cream cone. Today was the warmest day of the year so far. "Better eat this fast!"

I scooted around the counter and took the cone from his hand, then licked the drips. "Mmm . . ." As I ate my ice cream, I filled him in on my new deal with Lucy.

"I'd love to help you with that," Sam said. "Anything I can learn before I go is only going to benefit me at school."

"Hey, whatever happened to that person you said you knew who might want to work for me?"

"I haven't forgotten, but she only just finished school for the year. I got out a few weeks early because I was a graduating senior."

"So I'm going to have another budding culinarian from the high school?"

"Quite possibly. I still need to bring it up with her, though. Didn't want to add to finals stress."

"Sounds good. I look forward to meeting her."

Once I finished my ice cream cone, Sam and I continued working in the store, gathered supplies for the bakery's stroll table, and prepped a sample tray. Shortly before our usual closing time, Lauren arrived to relieve Sam. She and I would work the table together for part of the evening's event, then we'd swap solo shifts so each of us could enjoy the rest of Main Street's offerings for a while.

The first portion of the stroll was busy. The town had arrived en masse to Main Street. Regular customers, sporadic customers, kids, families. Everyone was happy and smiling. But by far, the happiest portion of the evening was seeing Chelsea and David walking arm in arm. Before I even spotted them, the matchmaking tingle rushed up from my feet to my stomach. I waved as they approached, a smile on my face.

Chelsea stopped at the table with a small bounce.

I folded my arms onto the table. "It's so good to see you two. How are you?"

"We have a new date." She beamed.

"You do? Wonderful!"

"And we're hoping that, despite everything that you've been put through, you'd still be willing to make our wedding cake." She pressed her palms together in front of her.

"I would be delighted."

"And some of those cookies we'd talked about," David added.

"Of course." I pushed the basket toward him. "We have them as samples tonight. Dig in."

Each of them grabbed a cookie before saying goodbye and continuing on their way.

Seeing them provided me with another theory about Sandra's murderer. Could it have been someone who was angry over her new boyfriend, obviously not Brad, but perhaps an ex of his blaming her for their breakup? Love or the rejection of love could make people do extreme things.

I shook my head. That didn't seem right.

But speaking of boyfriends . . .

A large bouquet covered Ken's face as he walked toward the table.

"Oh wow, those are beautiful." My gaze followed the flowers as he placed them on my table. "What did I do to deserve those?"

"Well, I wanted to apologize for how I behaved last week." I looked up at the man speaking. Not Ken. Instead, it was Nelson James. "I shouldn't have called you crazy. It was out of line. This whole town seems to be a bit . . . different, but that's part of its charm. So what do you say we try again?"

"Hey, Joanie. Um . . . What's going on here?" the voice I had been expecting to accompany the flowers asked.

I jumped from my seat. "Ken, this is Nelson James, that investor from Astoria who I met with about possible expansion opportunities for the bakery." I was suddenly glad I hadn't told Ken what had happened the last time Mr. James was in town.

Mr. James stuck out his hand. "Nice to meet you."

Ken took it, sizing him up, and they shook.

"Nelson, here, was asking if we could have another

meeting about expanding, but you know? I'm good right now. I just had the bakery redone"—I wasn't about to admit why— "and now isn't a good time to expand the business physically." Plus, I was doing a fine enough job on my own with my two new endeavors. If I ever needed more space, or another space, I'm sure I could do that on my own too. I grabbed the basket of samples. "Thank you for stopping by. Please, have a cookie."

"Oh, uh, okay." Mr. James picked one out and then took a quick bite. "Mmm . . . These are good. Well, if you ever change your mind, you know how to reach me."

I nodded. "Have a good night."

Mr. James turned and walked away, leaving the flowers at the table.

"I don't have to worry about him, do I? Those are some expensive flowers."

I looked at the beautiful arrangement. "Him? No."

At that moment, Lauren returned from her break. "Those are so pretty. You did a great job picking them out," she said to Ken about the flowers.

Before Ken could correct her, I replied, "Didn't he? Feel free to bring them home. Saffy is going to eat them if I take them. If you don't want them, we can split the bouquet among the tables in the shop in the morning."

"Really?" Her face lit up.

"Absolutely. You going to be good here?"

"Sure will!" She shooed me away. "Go have fun."

I walked out from behind the table and took Ken's hand. "Ready?"

"Lead the way."

Ken and I spent the next forty-five minutes strolling along Main Street. We tried cheese samples from Cheese Louise, sliders from Double Aitch, garlic knots from Nick and Etta's, bread samples that we dipped in oil from the Corner Bakery—I was doubly glad to see Zeke as he hadn't partaken in one of these events since I'd been here—drinks from the brewery collective's satellite location, ice cream from Lucy's, and shots of coffee and tea from Leafs and Grounds. By the time I arrived back at Suncraft's table, I was stuffed.

"Your daughter came by looking for you. She headed that way," Lauren told Ken. She pointed up Main Street.

Ivy had been walking around with her group of friends and two of their moms. We hadn't run into them, but she was easy to spot in her gold glitter pants and bright-pink shirt in front of Nick and Etta's table.

Ken laughed. "I should head over there. She loves their garlic knots. She'll eat them all if they let her." He gave me a quick kiss, said goodbye to Lauren, and then jogged away to catch up with his daughter.

"Thanks for the flowers!" Lauren shouted after him before flopping back in her seat. "You are so lucky."

"Yeah," I said on a happy sigh. "I am, aren't I?"

As the stroll wore on and the crowd began to dwindle, my thoughts returned to Sandra. As I thought more about the potential whodunnit, I kept coming back to something Vince had said when I talked to him about the murder. And the more I thought about it, the more I kept returning to one question, was Bruce Sandra's killer?

Bruce blamed Sandra for his brother's death. As I contemplated the case during the quiet moments between customers the next morning, I couldn't think of a motive stronger than revenge for taking the life of a loved one.

Then there was his spearheading the effort to cast Sandra from their friend group when she and his brother broke up.

And the timing between Brad's death and Sandra's.

The graveside confrontation between Sandra and Bruce that everyone attending saw.

His knowledge of the private beach where she was killed was as well as his owning the land.

His continued dislike of anyone from Sandra's family and all merrows in the ensuing years.

His behavior surrounding Chelsea and David's wedding. All that he did to prevent me from operating the bakery normally and looking into Sandra's murder.

What did he have to have to hide?

He'd also been avoiding Main Street from what I'd heard in bits and pieces in hushed conversations of customers and from Donna the gossip queen. He'd been a regular at her diner for years, but he hadn't been all week. She hadn't barred him from it, but she had told him he needed to wisen up. She and several other business owners were fed up with his behavior between stoking the near fights in front of where they worked, trying to sabotage me, and making a public spectacle of himself at the Corner Bakery. He didn't show his face last night at the stroll from what I could tell, not that he would have come to see me, anyway.

By the end of the evening, I'd come to one conclusion. As much as I didn't like confrontations, it was time to face Bruce again and get the truth once and for all.

CHAPTER 40

"Are you sure you want to do this here?" Ken asked as we neared David's parents' house. They were hosting a dinner party for their family, Chelsea's local relatives, and their friends. With the engagement back on, the two families had to learn to get along, and since David's parents supported the relationship, they were going to try to mend fences.

Outing a killer seemed to be a good way to get rid of one obstacle in the happy couple's path to marriage.

"I'm sure. There are other people here who need to hear this. They should know why he's been causing so much suffering. Not just now but for years. They need to be able to move on. If I confront him alone, all he'll do is deny it, and then it won't go anywhere." Been there. Done that. Almost lost my business.

"Can't you go to the police? You have a friend there, don't you?"

I nodded. "Seth. Courtney's boyfriend. Oh, that reminds me. They want to do dinner some night soon."

"Okay, we'll plan something, but don't change the subject. What about going to Seth with your theory?"

"And what evidence? The statement that I saw a ghost relive her last moments? Ha! I haven't even told Courtney that I can see ghosts. Even if Seth and the entire police force did believe me, it's not like that sort of thing is admissible in court. I need him to confess in front of witnesses. Besides, he won't want to cause a big scene in front of others. We can do this quietly and calmly." I hoped.

Turning into Celia and Steve's driveway, Ken sighed. "I don't see this ending well, that's all."

Truthfully, I saw this ending with me in tears or passing out from the fear of confrontation. I was always a little on edge at large gatherings because of the potential for multiple matches to be present, sending my system into overdrive since I never stopped feeling them, but this conversation with Bruce had to happen.

I said as much to Ken before he turned the car off. He got out, then came around and opened up the passenger side door for me. Together we headed up the driveway to the side gate. The backyard barbecue had been fully decked out with long tables, chairs, and sunshades. Unsurprisingly, the merrows and the selkies were at opposite ends of the yard, with friends mixing in the middle as a buffer between the two families.

"Joanie! I'm so glad you made it," Celia called from inside the house as I stepped onto the deck to find the drink cooler. My mouth was dry from nervousness.

Celia stepped out of the house holding a tray of watermelon cubes and feta chunks on toothpicks. She held the tray out to me.

I grabbed a toothpick and then popped the fruit and cheese end into my mouth. "This is delicious!"

"Thank you. And with this, the added salt on top isn't just because we like extra on everything."

"It helps enhance the flavor."

"Exactly. Thanks for coming. You've been so good to David and Chelsea through all of this." She walked away to offer the appetizer to others before I could respond.

I gulped. The momentary refreshment from the watermelon had already dried up. Was I really doing the right thing by confronting Bruce here? Or was it only going to hurt Chelsea and David more?

Ken tapped my shoulder, and when I turned toward him, he handed me a water bottle.

"Thanks." We headed down from the deck to the mingling crowd. Many greeted us with smiles, but over on the selkie side, Bruce scowled at me from under a sunshade. Greta next to him gave me a small wave. I took a small step toward them, but Ken grabbed my arm.

"I'm going to ask you one more time. Are you sure?"

I took a breath to steel myself. "Yes."

Ken let go and held his hands up in surrender.

Thinking it best to get this over with right away, I walked over toward Bruce, saying my hellos to all who stopped me along the way. Meanwhile, my heartbeat struggled to keep calm.

"Oh, what do you want?" Bruce groaned once I was a couple feet away from him.

"I'd like to talk with you if you don't mind."

He rolled his eyes. "I have nothing to say to you, witch."

"Witch, huh?" Sounded like someone was grasping at the town rumors to throw me off guard. Too bad for him I had embraced those rumors as the truth they were. Still, my anxiety rose a notch from his unpleasant manner.

Next to him, Greta gently smacked his arm. "Be nice. Haven't you done enough?"

Seemed even Greta was tired of his behavior now.

"Fine," he grumbled to her before turning back to me, his arms crossed. "I still have nothing to say to you, so make it quick."

Maybe Ken was right. Maybe this would be better if it were just Bruce and me. I gave him a final out. "A moment alone please?"

"Oh, come on. What do you have to say to me that you can't say to the few of us around here?"

Time to come out with it, then. "Did you kill Sandra O'Grady?"

His mouth dropped open. "What?"

I swallowed hard. "You heard me."

A slow murmur started at the table closest to us and it spread from one end to the other before hopping to the other scattered groups sitting and standing around. Soon, all eyes were on us.

"Why would you think I killed her?" He sounded taken aback.

"I think the better question is why wouldn't I think that?" I started laying out my evidence. How he blamed Sandra for his brother's death. How his hatred for Sandra morphed into hating all members of Chelsea's family. "You all got along just fine as friends for your whole childhood until Sandra and your brother broke up."

He rolled his eyes. "They didn't belong together, and I think you know why." A few nodded in agreement.

"There was no problem with their relationship before then. So why the anger regarding their breakup?"

"As I told you before," Bruce said with a huff, "he loved her. She hurt him and chased him away."

"You hated her so much that you took it out on Sandra's whole family and beyond." I brought up the red hats as best as I could without mentioning merrows directly to keep their secret safe from the humans in attendance.

Someone on the other side of the yard gasped. "That was you?" I hadn't realized how quiet everyone had become.

"Still doesn't prove I killed her," he said louder.

"You were last seen together having a massive argument. Were you mad enough to kill her soon after?"

"Yes. But it doesn't mean I did."

"You also own the land where she was killed and had direct knowledge of where she'd go swimming."

"As did many of her friends. Could have been anyone."

At this, Greta shifted slightly away from Bruce but remained in her chair.

"And you're trying to prevent us from using it now," someone else said from the merrow side of the yard.

"Still doesn't mean I killed her. I'm shocked you'd think that."

"I'm not," another voice said. Many others nodded as well, more than who had agreed with Bruce's implying that merrows and selkies didn't belong together.

Someone else shouted, "Here, here!" over the murmurs that were building in volume once more.

Then the first person who had spoken stood in the central area of the yard. I recognized him from the event at the senior center. He looked to be around the same age as Bruce and Greta. They might have been friends once. It didn't seem they were now.

"And then you go and get Joanie's store closed down because she's baking their cake."

"That wasn't the only reason." Dylan, who I'd talked to at the police station, stood from his seat at a picnic table on the selkie side. "He didn't want her poking around in the past and was sending her a message."

"Why? Do you have something to hide?" a female who didn't stand asked from the merrow side of the yard. I wondered that myself.

Bruce looked around at the party-goers. "You all think I killed Sandra?" With few exceptions, David and Chelsea's family members nodded.

Was this it? Was he going to confess?

"Well, sorry to disappoint." Arms still crossed, he stuck his nose in the air. "I didn't do it. Besides, I have an alibi."

"Which is?" Drats. A sinking feeling settled in my gut. I'd forgotten Vince had mentioned something about an alibi when I had talked to him. I never should have confronted Bruce.

Bruce clamped his lips shut. If he had an alibi, why wouldn't he have said that to start with? Why wasn't he saying anything?

Slowly, one of Chelsea's older relatives stood up. "He was with me."

Several merrows gasped.

"Sally, what do you mean he was with you?" Nancy asked.

Sally's eyes widened as she lowered her head, her face flushing.

Nancy's face also took on a red hue, and heat rushed into my face as well.

"Dagnabbit! We agreed we'd never talk about it," Bruce yelled.

"You'd rather have everyone think you're a murderer than that your deep-seated hatred of merrows doesn't stem from my cousin and your brother's breakup? I knew you wanted to keep us quiet, but I thought it meant more to you than that."

So Bruce had been hiding a former relationship with Sandra's cousin all these years? Wow, I hadn't seen that one coming, but as I shifted my gaze back and forth between the two, I felt it. The hollowness my mom had once described. It was faint, but there. A broken match. It had been drowned out by the tingling sensation I got from the matched couples at the party. And it was coming from one source. Well, two. Bruce and Sally.

"Don't you get it?" Sally continued. "The only reason anyone cares about this feud between mer—*our families*—is because you kept it up. Anyone you were worried about finding out the truth about us is long gone." She turned to face Nancy, then to her other family members, then finally to me. "Bruce couldn't have killed Sandra because we were together that day. I'd found him at the bar the night before and said his brother wouldn't want him to drown his sorrows. We took a drive then ended up at the winter carnival in Knoll's Grove. Not the most conventional place to go after the death of a loved one, but we were doing anything to get his mind off his brother."

Bruce looked at me, anger and a hint of sadness mixed in his gaze. "Can't you see what you've done? I don't need my mistakes coming back at me." At that moment, all I felt toward Bruce was pity.

Sally snorted. "Mistakes? Ha! We were together for a long time. That's a lot of mistakes, then. But if you ask me, your only mistake was thinking we couldn't be together. And now look at you. An angry old man who's not even mad at the right person."

"Oh, I'm mad at the right person, all right." Bruce's gaze hardened as he continued to stare at me. "Why couldn't you let this go?"

This wasn't how I saw this going at all. "I'm, I'm sorry. I never meant—"

"You *certainly* meant for something to happen," Bruce

spat. "Accusing an old man of murder when you had no proof."

"But—"

Ken gently tugged on my arm. "Come on, Joanie, let's leave Mr. Malloy alone. I think he's had enough of you for now."

I turned to leave, Ken's hand gently pressing the middle of my back as he guided me from the hurting selkie.

Chelsea and David approached us as we crossed the yard.

"I am so sorry," I told them.

"Joanie, what were you thinking?" Chelsea asked, tears welling at the corners of her eyes. "This was supposed to be a happy event."

"I just thought that if everyone heard him confess that he killed your great-aunt then—"

"But he didn't kill her, did he?"

I looked at the ground, unable to meet her gaze. "No, but we did find out that all of this hate he's been stirring up is because of him trying to hide the truth that he'd once cared for one of your relatives. And maybe he still does. Now, hopefully people will realize how silly they've been all these years and drop this nonsense."

"That may be, but it's taken on a life of its own. You know that. Joanie, you embarrassed me. You were here as a friend, someone who supported us."

"And I still do. You two are perfect for one another." I let out a defeated sigh. "I'm really sorry."

"Me too." She sniffled. "I'm going to have to ask you to leave."

"Understood."

"And I need to think long and hard about having you make our wedding cake."

"If it weren't for the deposit, we'd be going elsewhere," David said.

"If that's what you decide, I'll refund your deposit. I'll go now. Please apologize to your parents for me. And to anyone else, *everyone* else."

Chelsea gave me a small nod and a halfhearted smile before she and David walked away.

As Ken and I drove home in silence, I hoped the party could recover from this, but that was only second to the question, if Bruce didn't kill Sandra, then who did?

CHAPTER 41

Ken walked me up to the house. "I'm sorry things turned out like this."

"You tried to warn me. I should have listened. I'm sorry for ruining our afternoon."

"It doesn't have to be over. Lichelle is still with Ivy for another few hours. I don't have to go home."

"I don't know that I'm going to be much fun to be around."

"You don't have to be fun. I'm not looking to be entertained. I'm happy to just be with you. And if I can cheer you up a bit, all the better."

"Okay," I said on a sigh, unlocking the door and letting it swing open.

We stepped through and were greeted by Saffy standing at the end of the couch. She plopped down onto her behind and stared at Ken.

He held out his fingers for her to sniff. After a moment, she leaned forward and smelled them before hopping down and trotting off to the kitchen.

"Am I forgiven?" he asked, turning back to me. "I wasn't expecting to see her today, so I didn't bring her anything."

"She's probably not totally over her grudge, but it's a start. How about you give her the treats I keep in the cupboard? I'll make tea."

Several minutes later, all three of us returned to the living room, Ken and I sitting next to one another and Saffy behind me in her spot. I was sipping a fruity tea blend, trying to lift my spirits as Ken read on his phone.

"Boy, you sure are fun at parties," Sandra said, making me jump and slosh tea over the rim of my mug. She sat on the armchair to the side of the couch.

"What's wrong?" Ken asked, once more unable to see or hear her.

"Sandra stopped by for a visit." I pointed at the chair. To her, I admitted, "It wasn't my finest hour."

She crossed one leg over the other. "I could have told you it wasn't Bruce who killed me. I had no idea about him and my cousin, though. That explains a lot."

"What do you mean?"

"Bruce and I always got along. I think I was the first girlfriend of Brad's who didn't mind that Bruce regularly hung out with us. I had Nancy. They were the same age. I got it. Bruce couldn't drive when Brad and I first started dating. He needed rides. That sort of thing. He never seemed to have a problem with what I was back then. But a year or so before Brad and I broke up, he started going off on his own a lot. I didn't think much of it. He could drive then. And Brad and I had been together for long enough that people in town started thinking we'd be married right after school. We were always just keeping each other company, though. I knew that, but I guess that's when all the talk got to his parents because they started talking about how it wasn't right for us merrows and selkies to be together. I bet Bruce heard it way more than Brad ever did. Things like that aren't said unless it's behind someone's back. I bet it ate at him. I bet he'd already been seeing my cousin and didn't know what to do."

It certainly seemed possible. Sally had said they were together for a long time. She didn't say whether it was before or after Brad and Sandra had died. Maybe it was both.

"When Brad moved away," Sandra continued, "it wasn't as easy to get away to be with her. And to cope, instead of resenting the rules his parents made, he started to dislike us merrows. He was never going to disappoint his parents. Not when he lived in Brad's shadow. I almost feel bad for him."

"Almost?"

"Joanie, what's she saying?" Ken asked.

I patted his leg. "In a minute."

"Well, from the way Sally acted today, she's still hurt over this. I knew she had liked someone then, but she wouldn't tell me who. Guess I know now. Can't fully feel bad for a guy who hurt my cousin like that and continued to make life difficult for her family."

"So why didn't you tell me it wasn't Bruce?"

She shrugged. "You never said you were looking into him as a possibility."

"Well, it wasn't Marvin either."

"No, it would never have been him."

"Sandra, who killed you?" I asked pointedly, hoping she would tell me while she still remembered.

"It was . . ." She scrunched her face. "Well, huh, I don't remember now. It had been on the tip of my tongue."

Had I asked when she first appeared, would she have remembered? As I thought about cursing my bad timing and deciding that probably wouldn't be a good idea given my abilities, Ken said, "Joanie, I need to go. I just got a message from a friend of mine at the hospital. They admitted Clayton after he had another outburst."

"Oh no. Did he hurt anyone this time?"

He shook his head. "Only himself. He punched a window at the assisted living facility. He's asking for me again."

"All right. Call me, okay?"

He leaned over and kissed me before standing. "I will." Then he rushed out the door. The noise of it falling shut startled Saffy awake, and she made a squeaky half-meow. I turned toward her, cracking a smile for the first time since getting home because of her funny noise. She stared past me at the chair Sandra was sitting in.

I looked back at the forgetful ghost.

She was gone.

Again.

CHAPTER 42

At lunchtime on Saturday, Ken and Ivy came to the shop, a takeout bag from Dawg Pound in hand.

"Hi, Joanie!" Ivy chirped. "We brought you lunch."

"Why, thank you. That is so nice of you." I stepped out from behind the counter.

"Daddy told me you were sad, and hot dogs and fries always make me feel better."

I peeked back at Sarah. She seemed more interested in their being here than she had been a moment before. I hadn't told her what had happened at the barbecue. Since she hadn't said anything about it, she either didn't know—which I doubted—or hadn't wanted to bring it up. Either reason was fine by me, though. As I'd told Sandra, it wasn't my finest moment, and I didn't want to talk about it.

"Seeing your faces makes me feel better, hot dog or no, but I appreciate the lunch. I forgot mine today." And I hadn't wanted to go out and risk running into anyone from the party. It had been hard enough making my deliveries this morning with all the people walking their dogs, the early morning running club, and one of the biggest gossips of all—

Donna. But she must have sensed something or taken a good look at my face because she hadn't said anything about the barbecue either, and she always came to me to find out the real story of something that had happened. Not that I always knew, but lately I had. I looked forward to being out of the gossip game.

"Sarah, why don't you take lunch now since I'll be eating mine in here? I can help anyone who comes in."

"Sure. You want tea when I come back?"

"That would be fabulous, thank you."

She pushed through the kitchen door and returned a moment later with her purse, then headed out the door.

Popping a fry into my mouth, I asked, "How's Clayton?"

"His hand's cut up pretty bad, but he's going to be okay."

"Daddy thinks he might be getting his memory back. Isn't that neat? It's like in a story!"

"Really?" Hopefully he'd remember something that would help point to who killed Sandra. As her neighbor, he was my last shot at getting answers. "Do you think I could talk to him again?"

Ken pursed his lips and drew them to the side. "Hey, kiddo, how about you go choose something from one of the cases?"

"Okay, Daddy." Ivy popped out of her seat and scurried across the room.

The shop wasn't big, she'd still be able to hear what Ken wanted to say, but she'd probably be too distracted to pay much attention as she looked at the treats.

"I don't think that's such a good idea," Ken said. "These outbursts that he's been having, they're violent. Not like him at all from what I remember as a kid."

"Well, you only knew him post-accident. What if he was like this before?"

"My dad and grandpa never would have been friends with him if he was." He sounded a little defensive.

"Is it possible that he hid that side of him from your family?"

"I guess he could have. But either way, I'd rather you not go see him on your own. I don't want him to hurt you or . . ."

As he hesitated to find his next words, something occurred to me. "You don't think—"

"Think what?"

"You don't think he"—I lowered my voice—"killed Sandra, do you?"

He stared at me, blinking. "Wait, you're serious?"

"They were neighbors. He would have been aware of her comings and goings and could have easily followed her if he saw her leaving."

"But why would he have done something like that?"

I shrugged. "I don't . . . Wait. Her sister said something to me the day after he was taken to the police station. She called him creepy and said Sandra had saved her from him one time."

He raised an eyebrow. "What does *that* mean?"

I quickly recounted the story Nancy had told me. "Was that what Sandra meant by being blamed? Could he have blamed her for Nancy getting away from whatever he was going to do?"

"I don't know." Ken opened his mouth to say more, but Ivy hopped back over.

"I've made up my mind." Then she looked down at the table. "You haven't eaten your hot dog. Did I not pick good toppings?"

While the chili, cheese, caramelized onions, and banana peppers weren't a conventional choice for someone who would have to interact with customers for the rest of the day, it was a tasty combination. "Oh, that's not it at all. I got so wrapped up in talking to your dad that I forgot to eat." I grabbed the hot dog and took as big a bite as I could manage. Once I finally swallowed it—an act that seemed to take forever to get to—I asked, "So what would you like?"

She hurried back toward the cases and pointed to a key lime whoopie pie.

I walked behind the case and pulled out the tray so I could get to the one with the most frosting in the middle. I glanced at Ken. "Are you going to have this here, or should I box it up?"

"Box it."

"Aww, but Daddy . . ." Ivy leaned forward, her arms hanging down limply, then turned around to face him.

"I know, kiddo, but we need to let Joanie get back to work. Maybe she can call me or come over later?"

Grabbing one of the smaller boxes, I nodded. "Sure. I'll see what time it is after I talk to Gram for our weekly call."

Ivy straightened as she looked back at me. "Don't forget about your hot dog!"

"I won't," I promised, taping the box closed with her whoopie pie inside. I held it out to her. "Here you go."

She took the box from me. "What do I owe you?"

I bit back a laugh at her question considering her dad always paid. When he made me let him. "You brought me lunch. Let's call it even."

I called Gram shortly after getting home, earlier than our usual time. The whole possibility that Clayton had killed Sandra wouldn't leave my mind, and I wanted to head to Ken's so we could talk more about it as soon as possible.

"Hello, Joanie. How are you? Still got that sassy cat?" Gram asked like she always did.

"Hi, Gram. Of course I do. She wants to know when you're going to come visit."

"Still having ghost troubles?"

"I don't mind the ones I've had recently, but I don't want the house to be a waypoint either. They can knock on the door like everyone else if they want to talk to me."

"Hang on. Let me get out my calendar."

"Are you so busy that you need an appointment book?" I hadn't lived at home in years, but I still knew my grandmother's schedule by heart.

"Well, I do have that commendation soon." She chuckled. "Have to schedule around that. Are you coming?"

"Of course I am. It's not every day that my grandmother helps solve a murder." Gram had recently helped uncover who killed her best friend. Seemed we had solving murders in common right now. If I could figure out if Clayton had killed Sandra, of course. "So why do you need a calendar? The real reason."

"A lunar calendar. To tell me when the full moon is."

"Okay . . ." Lunar cycles were important to witches like Gram, but I didn't know why.

"I'll come then. That's when any of the wards we'll reestablish will be at their strongest. We can recharge your crystals too."

"You can charge crystals?" Then it dawned on me. "Wait, I have crystals?"

Gram sighed. "You really should spend some time researching all of this." She wasn't wrong. I'd been so busy lately. I promised myself I would do some research when things settled down. "And yes, you do. They're above your doors and windows. Go check."

I walked to the back door and then reached above it. On top of the door jamb was a textured lump. I pulled it down, revealing a stumpy black rock with ridges. "Huh. Why, so I do."

"They're meant as protection for your home and hearth. We should put some in your bakery, too, with all the ghosts you've been getting in there."

I contemplated that a moment before dismissing it. "No, the bakery can stay as is. I don't want to harm anyone that happens to be tagging along with a customer. And without the bakery, I wouldn't have been able to help two of my cases." Had the bakery been warded, the hairbrush may never have moved because I hadn't invited Kate in. And Dale may never have gotten my attention by pacing the shop. Only Sandra had come to me outside of the bakery first, and even then, she'd been in the shop several times since. With her memory problems, if she remembered something, I wanted her to be able to access me there.

"All right, then. It's going to be a few weeks away. We had one the other day, but I had to make sure of the date for the next one. Shall I make sure your mom is free too?"

"If she is, great"—it had been a while since I'd seen her too—"but if not, I still want you to come."

"I will. Now, how are you and your man doing?"

We chatted a few minutes about Ken before I admitted that I was going to talk to him after this.

"Well, what are we doing still on the phone?"

"Gram, we always talk on Saturdays."

"And we have. Now go out and have some fun." I imagined her pushing me out the door.

"You sure?"

"You're only young once."

"Well, all right. I hadn't meant to end the call so quickly."

"It's all right. You tell your sassy cat that I'll see her soon."

"I will." I looked down to find Saffy waiting by her dish. She must have come looking for me after hearing me get up to grab the crystal.

"I'll talk to you later. Love you." She hung up before I could say goodbye.

I switched the phone off, then back on to call Ken.

"You still up for my coming over?" I asked when Ken picked up.

Without hesitation, he answered, "Absolutely."

"Great. I'll see you in a few."

CHAPTER 43

Saffy had migrated to her food bowls by the time I hung up with Ken. She likely knew what was coming next.

"Heading out for the evening, Saf." She squinted. "Now, now, I know you're not happy with him still, but he's a good guy, I promise." First outfit advice from a cat now I was seeking her approval with Ken? I really was a cat lady.

She glanced at her bowl.

"Yes, dinner's coming, you silly thing." That seemed to perk her up. Maybe her look hadn't been about Ken at all. Reaching into the cupboard for her food, I continued, "You know I've had a lot going on lately with the shop and trying to catch a murderer, but did you really think I'd forget to feed you?" Like she'd ever have let me.

Saffy didn't answer, too busy staring at the bag of her crunchies as I approached her bowl.

"Here you go." I poured her food, and she dove in. "See you later."

The door flung open as I arrived at Ken's. Ivy bounded down the steps and across the yard. "Hi, Joanie! Bye, Joanie!" She righted her scooter lying in the driveway, then hopped on. She gave me a quick wave as she kicked off and coasted toward the sidewalk.

When I turned back to the house, Ken was waiting for me. "Tea? I bought a kettle."

"Finally," I teased, unable to hide my grin. Neither he nor Ivy drank tea—yet—so this was a purchase all for me, and the knowledge warmed my heart. I lifted onto my toes as I reached his doorstep and kissed him. "Yes, please."

He led me into the kitchen where he filled the purple teapot with water, then set it on the stovetop. "You'll have to forgive the fact I only have stuff in bags, but I got a variety." He opened the cupboard where he kept cups and glasses, revealing four different types of tea. I took a closer look. A plain black tea, a green chai, and two herbals. I grabbed the fruitier of the two herbals as well as a mug and then dropped a tea bag into it.

As the water heated in the kettle, Ken and I sat at the kitchen table. I'd been thinking about what I'd say and the implications of my words my entire walk here. Given what had happened at the barbecue with Bruce, I had to be absolutely certain before I cast any more accusations. When the whistle boiled, I hopped up to pour the water, then brought the mug to the table. I wrapped my hands around it. It may have been summer now, but I found it comforting to have a warm cup in my hands.

"Let's say what we're both thinking," Ken suggested when neither of us had spoken after several moments.

I sighed hard, using the air to blow on my tea. "Okay."

Ken leaned forward as if to tell me a secret. "Do you really think Clayton killed Sandra?"

"I haven't seen her since yesterday, so she hasn't confirmed it. But he had the means and opportunity. Possibly a motive. When did Clayton have his accident?"

"My dad was fifteen or so. So the early seventies?"

I did a quick estimate. "Sandra died a few years before that. If these violent outbursts are indicative of how he acted before the accident changed him, then maybe he did kill her. I don't know."

"Let's say he did. Why did no one look at him?"

I shrugged. "They thought Marvin did it. And Nancy said she never thought about the incident with Clayton again until seeing him at the police station, so she never said anything to shed light in his direction. What other reason would they have had to look at him?"

"It's all so strange. I mean to kill Sandra and then have these outbursts years later?"

"Like you said a while back, some people never go on to kill again, thinking they got away with it." I grew quiet. There was something I was missing. As I sipped my tea, a thought came to me. "But what if he didn't stop? What if the next time wasn't viewed as related?"

"What do you mean?"

"Marvin's family told me that other girls disappeared in the few years following Sandra's death. One was found murdered."

Ken straightened in his chair, doubt crossing his face. "So now you think Clayton is, what, a serial killer?"

"I don't want to but . . . hang on." I rushed over to my bag by the door, then dug my phone out. "Hey Steph, you busy?" I asked when my newspaper reporter friend answered.

"What's up?"

"I'm going to owe you another girls' night, but can you do your research magic and locate some info for me about three girls who disappeared or were killed from town several decades ago?"

"I don't need to. We've been working on a special tribute article because the fiftieth anniversary of the last girl going missing is coming up. It's still an open case, but it's been cold for decades. We run something every few years on it but are doing a big push this year, hoping someone will come forward."

"Is there any way you can send me what you have? Photos or anything like that?"

"Yeah, I'll send you the last article. It has photos in it. Give me a few to pull it up."

"Thanks, I'll talk to you later. Hey, they weren't paranormals, by chance, were they?"

"One was a dryad, but that's all I know. No one was talking about it openly. No support groups back then."

"Okay, thanks again." I pressed the button on my screen to hang up. I joined Ken back at the table. "Steph is sending me an article." As we waited, I sipped on my now lukewarm tea. Perfect.

A moment later, my phone buzzed with a text. I clicked on the link Steph sent. The article quickly loaded on the newspaper's website, and I scanned it looking for any information that could tell us one way or another if Clayton was involved.

"Says here the three girls started to disappear a year and a half after Sandra's murder. The first disappearance resulted in a body being found just outside of town in the woods." Was this the dryad? "They never found the second, who disappeared a year later, or third, who disappeared the year after that. They probably weren't in the woods if the first girl had been found there."

I handed Ken the phone for him to read it himself. "So

these three were all the same age when they disappeared or were killed. How old was Sandra?"

"Twenty."

"That doesn't fit this. These girls were younger. Right out of high school." He scrolled some more. "And didn't you say she died in the winter? They were taken or killed in the summer. If we're trying to find patterns, I guess they all look similar to one another, but they don't look like Sandra either."

I raised an eyebrow at him, momentarily forgetting he had seen her during our date. He turned the phone back to me so I could see.

A weight settled into my stomach. "No, but they look like her sister, and she was their age when Sandra stopped him from doing whatever he was going to do to her. What if he continued to try to get the one who got away? Sandra wouldn't fit the pattern because she was first. She was retaliation for her sister."

"Why not try to go after the sister, too, if she fit the pattern?"

"She did originally. But she was older by the time this happened, even if only by another year and a half. Besides, after what happened, she'd never have gone near him. Someone else wouldn't have known better. By your estimate, his accident was the year after the last girl disappeared. What if that's why no more girls were taken?"

"I don't want to believe that a friend of the family is a serial killer. I mean, I see how it's possible, but it's hardly an open and shut case." He scrubbed at his face with a sigh. "And, no offense, but after what happened with Bruce, who is going to listen to you?"

His question stung, but he wasn't wrong.

"I have to talk to Clayton." I could only hope this meeting would go better than my last one with Bruce.

CHAPTER 44

After a restless night's sleep, I readied myself to go to the hospital. Anxiety bubbled in my gut over facing a potential killer yet again. But I wasn't going alone. Ken was meeting me there, and Sandra was coming too. She hadn't confirmed he'd been the one who killed her, but if anything was going to make her remember, it would be Clayton's confession. If he had done it, of course.

"Are you sure you want to do this?" Ken asked me as he kissed me hello. He hadn't slept well either, and bags hung from his eyes. "You probably looked like these girls when you graduated high school."

"Yeah, I'm sure. And if it makes you feel any better, I'm nearly nine years older than they were. I'm no longer his type."

"And he's fifty years older. What if what's happened to him changed his type? He did attack his therapist, and she's a redhead."

It didn't escape me that Sandra was a redhead too. "I don't think he'll do anything if you're with me."

"I still don't like the idea," Ken said, holding the elevator door open for me. We headed to the fourth floor where the men's inpatient wing was. Normally a hand injury like Clayton's wouldn't have caused him to be admitted, but Ken explained that after the incident, his heart rate had been too elevated, and they kept him for observation. He was due to be released later today.

When we checked in at the nurses' station, I noticed familiar names on the sign-in sheet. Chelsea and David. Why were they here?

"Room 414," the nurse said with a tired smile.

"Thank you." Ken and I walked down the hall. As we and came upon the room, we passed the one where Chelsea and David were, chatting amicably with someone in a bed close to the window.

I followed Ken to the door of Clayton's room, but I couldn't go in. Not just yet. "I need to go talk to Chelsea. I'll be back."

Ken nodded at me quickly, then knocked on Clayton's door.

Three sets of eyes settled upon me as I stopped at the entrance of the room next door and cleared my throat. The third I recognized as belonging to Chelsea's father. I took a step forward, giving them a shy smile.

Chelsea walked toward the bed and then kissed her dad softly on his head. "It was good to see you, Daddy. I'm glad you're okay. We'll be back later."

"Please don't go on my account," I said softly. "What happened?"

Chelsea sighed. "He tripped in the backyard on a garden gnome and hit his head on a tree branch."

"I didn't even know we had a garden gnome," Anthony said. To Chelsea, he added, "Your mom must have put it there."

She shook her head slightly as she looked toward the ceiling. "They were worried about a brain bleed, so here he is. They have several tests to run still, but he should be heading home tomorrow as long as everything is clear. Why are you here?"

"Ken's family has been friends with the man in the next room since his dad was a kid. Clayton also did some volunteer work for Ken looking up grant information here at the hospital."

Chelsea made a face.

I cocked my head to the side. "What was that for?"

"He kinda skeeves me out," she said quietly so no one else could hear. "You should have seen the way he glared at me when we were getting here to see my dad. He was being wheeled out for some tests or something, and I don't know. I just didn't like the look I was getting."

"Your grandma said the same thing about him."

"She did?"

"Yeah. Look, I know I messed up the other day at your barbecue. I shouldn't have confronted Bruce publicly like that."

"About that, it's weird. It's almost like hearing he'd once had feelings for my grandma's cousin deflated the tensions everyone had been having. Things aren't perfect, but it's less. No one has tried to ruin my dress or said nasty things, at least to my face. I haven't cried in two days, and I'd been doing that a lot lately." She shrugged. "So in some roundabout way, it wasn't all bad. Embarrassing, you bet, but you were coming from a good place."

"Is that why I haven't heard anything in the rumor mill about what I did?"

"It's possible, but I think many of us are all too stunned by the true revelations that we're still processing. Or some of the biggest gossipers in the family have learned their lessons from this."

"So are we okay?" I gave her a hopeful smile.

She took my hands. "Yeah, we're okay." Then she pulled me in for a hug.

"Good, because I'm hoping to solve Sandra's case with this visit."

"You mean—"

"I think so."

"Are you sure this time? Surer than you were about Bruce?"

I nodded.

She gave me another squeeze. "Be careful."

"I will. Ken will be there, and I have Sandra as backup."

"Then I will wish you good luck. David and I will be right here in case things go south. Just holler." As I stepped out of her embrace, she turned to her dad. "Looks like you're stuck with us a bit longer."

I gave them a quick wave goodbye, then popped into the next room.

"Joanie, how are you?" Clayton asked. The smile on his face didn't reach his eyes as they followed my movement.

I don't know if it was because I suspected him of being a killer or if his mannerisms were off, but something was putting me on edge. I stuck my hand in my purse and fingered the tiara sitting at the top of everything. It pulsed with energy in a way it hadn't in days. Could Sandra sense something too?

"I'm well. How about yourself?"

"Hand hurts like the dickens, and I'd like to get outta here. I got things to do. Ken said you know the girl visiting in the next room."

"I do. She's a friend of mine," I replied, stopping at the foot of his bed.

"She's pretty." The statement felt loaded. Purposeful. More than a simple observation made to keep the conversation going.

"She is. Do you know her?"

"Should I?"

"She's the granddaughter and great-niece of two of your former neighbors, Nancy and Sandra."

"Is that right?" The corner of one side of his mouth curled upward.

"Do you remember them?"

"I remember Nancy more. She was still around after my accident."

Had he realized he said he remembered Nancy *more*, meaning he remembered Sandra at least a little?

Ken picked up on the wording too. "So you remember Sandra from before your accident?"

Clayton furrowed his brow. "Don't twist around an old man's words, my boy."

"So you don't remember her?" Ken asked.

"Well, I wouldn't say that either." He chuckled. "Bits and pieces come and go."

His memory was coming and going? That sounded a lot like what had been happening to Sandra. Was that it? Were her symptoms not related to her murder but to Clayton's condition? Had my biggest clue also been one of my biggest frustrations?

"Nancy told me a story the other day about something that happened between the two of you before your accident," I began. "Maybe you remember it. She said that you cornered her between your yards."

He looked up as if searching through his brain for the memory. "*Cornered?* Is that the word she used?"

"She also said that Sandra saved her from whatever she felt like was going to happen had her sister not stepped in."

He shifted in his bed, sitting straighter. "And what did she think would happen?"

"She didn't say, but she did tell me she was glad Sandra came along."

"Nancy was the pretty one. Never found another girl quite like her." Was that a veiled reference to the other three girls? "But Sandra, ha! Sandra couldn't mind her own business. Much like you, it seems."

"Clayton"—Ken's voice had taken on a warning tone—"Joanie's my girlfriend. I'd appreciate it if you didn't speak to her like that."

"Eh, she's just like your mother, this one. A busybody who can't leave well enough alone."

Ouch. He certainly knew what buttons of Ken's to press. It didn't help that Ken had said similar things before our breakup a few weeks back.

"Now that's going too far. My mom was a busybody, yes, but she did nothing more than talk about people. Joanie actively tries to help people."

"Yeah? And who's she trying to help by digging around in the past?" Clayton reminded me of Bruce with that telling question.

"Me." Sandra appeared by my side. "Hello, Clayton."

"You?" Clayton yelled, scrambling backward on the bed but not getting far. "I thought I killed you!"

Got him.

Ken pushed his seat back and stood, ready to act if necessary.

Sandra crossed her arms. "You did. Bashed my head with

a rock." She glanced at me. "I remember everything now. He was mad I saved my sister."

Clayton rapidly pressed the call button on his bed. "What is this sorcery? Nurse? Nurse!"

David rushed into the room. "We heard everything. Chelsea is getting help. Do you need me to do anything?"

I shook my head. "Stay there in case he makes a break for it." Truthfully, I doubted he was going anywhere, but it comforted me to have another person in the room.

"Wow, is that?" He pointed at Sandra.

"This is Chelsea's great-aunt."

"I was going to say a ghost," David replied, eyes wide. "How?"

"I'll explain later."

"Right, got it." David rocked side to side on the balls of his feet as if ready to jump into action.

At that moment, Chelsea came running in with a nurse and two security guards behind her. She skidded to a stop, and her mouth dropped as she came face to face with her great-aunt.

"What's going on in here?" the nurse demanded. Her gaze traveled the room before landing on Ken. "Ken?"

"Hey, Sophia. This man confessed to a murder that happened years ago."

"And I'd do it again," Clayton spat.

As the guards closed in, I asked, "Did you kill the other girls too? The ones who looked like Nancy?" I wanted to have closure for them, too, both for their families and in case the girls were still around like Sandra was.

"They weren't as pretty as her. Didn't know until I got them alone." He turned his glare toward Chelsea. "You look a lot like your grandmother."

"That's enough," David warned as he stood in front of Chelsea.

The security guards put straps onto Clayton's wrists, securing him to the bed rails, then did the same with his ankles.

"That sounds like a confession to me," Ken said. He looked to Clayton, a sad expression coming over his face. "Dad and Gramps would be so disappointed to learn this about you."

"Go on and get," Clayton ordered. "And don't come back."

Ken turned away and stuck out his hand for me to grab. I took it, and we left the room, followed by Sandra, David, Chelsea, Sophia, and the security guards.

One of the guards shut the door behind him and stood in front of it.

"I'm going to go call the police," Sophia said. "I can't make you stay, but I'm sure they will have questions for you."

"We can go back into my dad's room," Chelsea offered. "He's gone for another scan, so we won't bother him."

Sophia nodded before returning to the desk at the nurses' station to talk to the nurse who had checked us in. The second security guard followed her.

The rest of us filed into Anthony's room.

"Sandra?" Chelsea asked of her great-aunt as David closed the door to give us privacy.

Sandra nodded.

"But how?"

As we waited for the police to arrive, Sandra and I took turns explaining what had happened in the last few weeks, what had happened between her and Brad, and her and Bruce, my abilities, how she'd been in the tiara all these years except when she tried to save the other girls like she had her sister.

Today hadn't been her first encounter with Clayton since her death.

"I'm the reason he ran off the road that night of his accident. He was off to go take another girl, and I appeared in front of the car. He swerved and hit a stump, causing his car to flip."

"So why did you come back now?"

She tapped her head, where she'd hold it when she couldn't remember. "His memories were coming back thanks to his new therapist and treatment. I feared it was only a matter of time before he'd do something again. Before, I could only make myself appear to him like on the night of the accident. Move a few things around as I tried to help those poor girls. It would have been the same again this time, but then you got Joanie involved. And I'm so glad you did." She sighed. "I can finally move on now."

"Will you stay to see my grandmother?" Chelsea asked, wiping a falling tear from her cheek.

"No. I unfortunately don't have much time remaining for that, but I've never really left her. I don't imagine all of me will now. And I'll be with you too." Sandra leaned into Chelsea and gave her a side hug before Chelsea flung her arms around her great-aunt.

When they'd finished hugging, I took the tiara out of my purse and carefully handed it over to Chelsea. "This is yours."

"I wore it for my prom," Sandra said, "although I'm sure you knew that. I'm so glad you've decided to make it a part of your wedding."

"It means so much more to me now. Thank you."

Sandra hugged Chelsea once more, then reached out her arm toward David. When he took her hand, albeit a bit hesitantly, she pulled him in for a group hug. "Congratulations, you two. I wish you a lifetime of happiness together." She stepped back. "And don't worry about any more of this merrow-selkie can't be together nonsense. They were rules set down years ago by people who should have been more focused on love, and you've got plenty of that to go around."

Chelsea wiped her eyes. "I wish I could have gotten to know you."

Sandra smiled. "There will be time for that. But not for many, many years."

Chelsea nodded, then leaned into David's side.

Sandra approached me next. "Thank you for everything you did. For not giving up on me when I couldn't remember. For not giving up on my family. And for not giving up on this town either. You're doing so much good. I hope you can see it."

"You're welcome."

She hugged me. I'd never fully get over how solid ghosts were when they wanted to be. If I didn't know better and if she wasn't cooler than an average person—although not "as cold as death"—I'd not believe she was a ghost.

"Now if you'll all excuse me," she said as she released me, "I have a few people I'd like to catch up with on the other side." And with that, Sandra faded from sight.

Several minutes later, Nurse Sophia came back, escorting a police officer. They asked us to go to another room so that Anthony could come back in, and Ken offered up his office on the first floor. Chelsea's father waited outside as we filed out. Chelsea gave him a quick hug, telling him she'd explain later but that everything would be okay now.

"Wasn't there someone else with you?" Sophia asked as I exited the room behind everyone else.

Everybody stopped and turned to me as I answered, "Nope. Just us."

"No, there was a redhead with you. I'm sure of it."

"We've all been in here since you left us. You would have seen someone leave the room with your desk right there." I turned to the security guard standing in front of Clayton's room. "You didn't see anyone, right?"

He shook his head. "No one in or out."

"I didn't see anyone leave either, Sophia," a voice said from behind me. When I turned, Bev, Rich's mom, stood near the nurses' station. She smiled and gave me a small wave.

"I must be seeing things," Sophia said. "Can't wait for my nap when I get off my shift."

I smiled at her. After all of this, I was looking forward to a nap too.

CHAPTER 45

The DJ switched to a slow song, and Ken stood, his hand extended out toward me. We walked to the dance floor, then turned toward one another, my arms wrapping behind his neck and his going around my waist.

"I don't think I've danced at a wedding in years," he said as we swayed to the beat.

I laughed. "Stick around for a while, and this will become a regular occurrence."

He threw his head back. "And somehow I think you have a lot to do with that."

I pressed my lips together, and my eyes widened as I looked toward the ceiling in my best trying to look innocent expression. He wasn't wrong, although there'd been several marriages I hadn't been responsible for over my four and a half years in town.

I glanced over at Chelsea and David dancing together as husband and wife. "Her dress is beautiful, don't you think?" Her family had transformed her original dress into something exquisite with added silk ribbon and beading. And atop her head sat Sandra's tiara. She'd been on everyone's minds lately after what had happened at the hospital and in the ensuing two weeks. I momentarily wished Sandra had been able to stick around long enough to be present today, but she was very much a part of the wedding even if she wasn't here. Her picture sat prominently on an *In Memoriam* table along with photos of a few other relatives from both sides of the family.

Clayton ended up being arrested for Sandra's murder as well as those of the three other girls whose lives had been cut short, giving closure to their families. In his confession, he revealed having more and more flashes of his life before the accident, which he retained each time he had them. They had reignited some of those old urges. The old him had already identified his next ideal victim had he ever gotten the opportunity, but the him that he had been for the last fifty years was glad to see it over now that he remembered what he'd done.

It sent Sandra's family reeling with the news that the wrong man had been imprisoned for her death, tearing open some old wounds but stitching them together at the same time. The news had vindicated Marvin Strong's family too, although it didn't bring him back. In the two weeks since the arrest, the police station had issued an apology and was working on some sort of compensation to his family based on state regulations. It wouldn't be enough, but it was more than they ever would have had without the truth coming to light.

"Hey, did you hear me?" Ken asked, drawing my attention away from thoughts of solved murders and all things paranormal.

"Hmm? No, sorry."

"I said you're beautiful."

"Thank you." Heat rose into my cheeks. I'd picked out this aqua-colored dress on my own, no help from Saffy needed. I hadn't wanted to risk cat fur getting on it from her method of choosing.

"I mean it, Joanie." Ken lifted my face until our gazes met. "And not just now but all the time. Seeing you happy and celebrating one of your matches, I get it now. It might not keep me from being worried about you sometimes, but I'm not going to stop you from doing this. It's something you're meant to do."

In my heels, which I daringly wore to give me an extra two inches in height, I didn't have to rise onto my toes to kiss him. But the night was still early, and these shoes would come off eventually. "That means more than you know."

"We make a pretty good team, you and I, you know."

"I agree. I wouldn't have been able to solve this one without you."

At that moment, the DJ got on the microphone. "All right, at this time, we're going to ask everyone to return to their seats so that our bride and groom can cut this amazing cake."

As we sat, Chelsea and David approached the round table that had been wheeled to the center of the floor for everyone to see. Atop it sat a three-tier cake with an ocean theme. Pearls, shells, and starfish adorned the cake in shades of blue and green, all edible. That was the rule with all my cakes. Nothing went on them that couldn't be eaten except for the decorative cake topper, this one a classic bride and groom standing side by side.

"I've been told that the baker of this cake is among the guests today, and David and Chelsea credit her with getting them together," the DJ continued. "Now is that some job security or what?"

Everyone laughed, merrow and selkie alike. After the revelations about Sandra's murder and the real reason behind Bruce's anger, the two groups had formed a truce. No more fighting, no more policing the dating habits of others. Even Bruce had come around. I'd caught him smiling several times tonight . . . just not at me. I doubted he'd ever like me, but I couldn't blame him for that.

Chelsea and David, their hands intertwined, slid their cake slicer into the lower tier. After removing a thin piece of sea-salt caramel cake, they took turns feeding a bite to one another. Then Chelsea dabbed frosting on David's nose. As the guests clapped and cheered, the cake was taken away to be cut. The DJ started the music back up, and people returned to the dance floor. Several minutes later, servers began leaving plates of cake at all the seats. I grabbed my fork and sunk it into my slice.

Maybe it was because I was now embracing who I was, but I could almost taste the something extra everyone claimed my baked goods had. In this case, love, acceptance, and wishes for a long and happy life together.

I'd made dozens of wedding cakes over since coming to Heartwood Hollow. I'd gotten to try several of them as a wedding guest. But this one was my favorite.

I glanced at Ken. He was smiling at me in a way that made my heart flutter. Not a matchmaking tingle, but I'd take it.

I rephrased my last thought. My favorite cake so far.

An anticipated visit brings about unexpected revelations when Joanie's story continues in *Potluck and Powers*, available now.

WHAT'S NEXT?

An anticipated visit brings about unexpected revelations.

And the implications could change Joanie's life forever.

Gram's quick trip promised to teach Joanie how to protect her house from ghosts, a crash course in how to be a witch, and a bit of fun during the full moon. Instead, the two find themselves dealing with more than they bargained for when surprises keep showing up at Joanie's front door.

Now at the center of several mysteries involving all aspects of her paranormal powers, will Joanie be able discover the truth? Or will Gram's antics and embarrassing stories derail her friendships when Joanie needs to trust them the most?

***Potluck and Powers* is now available.**

Grab it today to start uncovering Heartwood Hollow's secrets.

Acknowledgments

I could almost repeat the acknowledgments section from my last two books. Maybe one day I'll do that to see who notices, but today is not that day. Thank you to my family and friends for their continued support of this dream of mine. To Rob, thanks for always being my sounding board no matter the time of day (or night). And to my daughter, Kahlan, who is a fabulous mini-editor. I hope your enthusiasm for my books never end, even after they stop being just printed off chapters on a clipboard for you to steal.

Thank you to Frankie Blooding at Real Indie Author for your continued awesomeness. I am so glad you are loving these books and series as a whole. Thank you to the fabulous cozy mystery community and the author community in general that I have found through social media. I love talking with you all!

My continued thanks go to the website 4thewords.com and the awesome dust warriors I found there. It has been so much fun writing while battling monsters and exploring new locations. I look forward to many more books being written on that platform. If you're reading this and you're a writer, journal, or want to get more motivated writing school papers, definitely check this site out.

And finally, thank you to you for reading this book.

About the Author

Rosie Pease is a native Rhode Islander but has lived in Vermont, New York, and Ohio. She uses the places she's traveled to as inspiration for the settings of her cozy mysteries, pulling the theater from one, the cider mill from another, the river from another to create a fictitious town that feels familiar.

She collects Funko Pops of the Harry Potter, Hunger Games, Doctor Who, DC TV, and Marvel variety, with a few others thrown in for fun. Her desk is a mess, but she can find everything on it, so it works for her as long as things aren't falling onto the keyboard as she writes.

When she's not crafting cozy mysteries, she's playing with her daughter, hanging out with her husband, or being amused by her two crazy cats.

Come find Rosie online:
Website: https://rosiepease.com
Facebook, Instagram, Twitter, and Pinterest:
@WriteRosiePease

The Matchmaking Baker

Coffee and Calicos

Sweets and Santa

Mixing Up Magic

Cookies and Curses

Scones and Spells

Weddings and Witchcraft

Potluck and Powers

Purrfect Travel Companion

Catastrophe on the Road

Catastrophe in the Kitchen